MW01093834

Sanchin

By
Karen van Wyk

J.L. GOLDSWORTHY
P.O. BOX 2546
BRIARCLIFF MANOR, NY 10510

This novel is a work of fiction. The characters and events portrayed are works of the author's imagination. Any resemblance to actual events or persons, either living or dead, is purely coincidental.

ISBN 1 441 46353 4
EAN-13 9781441463531

Copyright ©2009 Karen van Wyk

Karen van Wyk asserts the moral right to be identified as the author of this work.

All rights reserved. No part of this publication may be reproduced, stored in a retrieval system, or transmitted, in any form or by any means, electronic, mechanical, photocopying, recording or otherwise, without prior permission of the author.

For author's contact details please visit
http://www.karenvanwyk.com

Front Cover Image Design ©Lindsay Fulton

Acknowledgements

I'd like to start by thanking my family and friends for putting up with me during the writing and editing of this book. I'm sure there was nothing quite as unnerving as living with the sleep deprived and over-caffeinated crazy person that I had become by the end of the second draft.

Sincere thanks also go to the following people, without whom this book would never have been completed:

To my husband, Tiaan for the inspiration and the encouragement.

To Bett Gresham, Lindsay Fulton, Annemarie Hegeler and Mark van Rensburg for reading the manuscript and pointing out the glaring typos and grammatical horrors that my overworked brain had missed. Any remaining errors are entirely due to my last minute fiddling.

To Tony Gresham for patiently taking dozens of photographs for the cover, and for not killing me when I changed my mind. And to Lindsay Fulton for the design I eventually used.

To Mark van Rensburg for introducing me to National Novel Writing Month (www.nanowrimo.org), where the first draft was born, and for challenging me to enter in the first place. And to all at NaNoWriMo for such a fantastic project.

To everyone who reviewed my work on the Harper Collins Authonomy (www.authonomy.com) and the You Write On.com (www.youwriteon.com) websites. Your support, comments and criticisms were invaluable.

To Gary Armstrong for tolerating my bizarre moods during the times I tore myself away from the book and worked on his websites.

To everyone at the Welgemoed Dojo in Cape Town where I first fell in love with Kyokushin Karate and to everyone I have had the privilege to train with since. OSU!

To Chris Tan from the blog My Kyokushin – The Diary of a Karateka (http://mykyokushin.wordpress.com) for having enough faith to support me, and Sanchin, after reading only the first chapter. And for then going on to read the entire manuscript and allaying my greatest fear – will fellow martial artists relate to my book.

To everyone on the K4L forum (www.kyokushin4life.com). You guys kept me sane during the late nights on the computer and the Workout of the Week motivated me keep training, however little time I had.

To the Palmbooms and everyone at Ansteys Beach Backpackers International (www.ansteysbeach.seventy2dpi-hosting.com) for a wonderful retreat where the idea for this book first began to take shape and for the inspiration for some of the locations.

And to all of you who had the faith in my ability to do this. Thank you for your help and encouragement. You know who you are.

Foreword

Sanchin is a work of fiction and therefore must, to some extent, sacrifice reality for the sake of the story.

It was written with a readership of both martial artists and non-martial artists in mind. I have tried to strike a balance between not boring the former nor overwhelming the latter with martial arts jargon, so I hope you will forgive any stylistically clumsy translations.

No disrespect is intended by the occasional dropping of titles, incorrect forms of address or breaches of dojo etiquette. This is done purely to help the prose flow.

Sanchin is based on full contact karate but I deliberately steered clear of mentioning a style as they vary so greatly, and what may happen in one dojo would be out of the question in another.

As a result of this balancing act, there may be times when something doesn't quite ring true and I know this will be annoying to anybody who is familiar with the subject - please accept that I have used some artistic license simply to keep the drama moving, and enjoy the story for what it is.

Glossary

Dan – Grade, black belt
Dogi – Training suit, uniform
Dojo – Training hall
Dojo Kun – Dojo Oath

Hajime - Begin

Ibuki – A way of breathing used in certain kata, forced tension breathing.
Ichi – One

Jiyu Kumite – Free sparring.

Karateka – Karate practitioner.
Kata – Form, set of pre-determined movements used in training.
Kiai – A forceful yell.
Kiba Dachi – Horseback Stance – a low wide stance.
Kihon – Basic techniques
Kumite – Sparring
Kyu – Grade below black belt

Mae Keage – High front kick
Mawashi Geri – Roundhouse kick

Ni – Two
Nidan – Second Dan, second degree black belt

Obi – Belt
Osu - A respectful way to reply to a senior

San – Three
Sanchin – A kata practised in many martial arts
Sandan – Third Dan, third degree black belt
Seiza - Kneel
Sempai (also Senpai) - Senior, also title given to first and second

degree black belts.

Sensei – Teacher, also title given to third and forth degree black belts.

Shihan – Master, also title given to grades of fifth degree black belt and above.

Shime - a series of blows aimed at various parts of the body, is used to assess the practitioner's posture, stability and level of focus during the performance of certain kata. It also serves as excellent conditioning training, preparing the student for the inevitable blows received during a fight.

Shitsurei shimasu – Excuse me.

Shodan – Literally beginner grade, first degree black belt.

Taikyoku Sono Ichi – The first kata

Tameshiwari – Breaking techniques

Yame – Stop

Yantsu – A kata

Yasume – Relax, rest

Yudansha – Black belt, holder of a dan grade

Sanchin is a kata, or form, practised in many styles of martial arts. The name, translating as three battles or three conflicts, is often interpreted to mean the battle for unity of mind, body and spirit.

For Tiaan
My inspiration

Chapter One

Greenside Bushido Kai Dojo,
January 1995

Tristan Steyn's mouth was dry, his throat tight. He gritted his teeth as the young girl took a second heavy blow to the stomach. She staggered backwards, leaning to her left, her elbow tucked firmly against her hip. Her attacker advanced again and still she made no effort to raise her arms and defend herself.

The knot in his stomach tightened and he resisted the urge to run his moist hands down the front of his jacket.

"*Yame!*" Stop, he called, the sound surprising even him.

The fighters on the mats stopped, scanning the room for the source of the command.

"Sempai!" Shihan Dean Stander's voice cut the silence. He seemed, from across the mats, to have grown taller than his six foot six. "I trust you have a very good reason for stopping *kumite* in the middle of a grading?"

Tristan swallowed, suddenly not so sure he did. "Shihan, I'm so sorry," he said, his voice low. "But I desperately need to use the bathroom."

A gasp circled the room. The Shihan's mouth came open slightly. Tristan felt a heavy chill slide from the top of his head and settle in the pit of his stomach.

"Go!" snapped the Shihan, inclining his head towards the changing rooms.

"Thank you," Tristan managed.

As he stepped around the mat he made eye contact with the girl. Slipping a thumb up under his belt, he jerked the waistband of his dogi pants. The relief in her eyes told him she understood.

Painfully aware that every eye in the dojo was on him, he ducked into the changing room. He closed the door, leaning, for a moment, against its cool surface.

* * *

Self control was important to Dean Stander. But, right now, it was only 30 years of diligent practice that stopped him losing sight of the fact. He paced to the window.

"What on earth were you thinking?" he bellowed, resting white-knuckled fists on the windowsill. "Sempai, you know how important focus is in sparring. You could have ruined the grading for everyone!" He turned to face Tristan, small beads of perspiration breaking out on his shaven head. "And all because you can't control your bodily functions!"

Tristan looked up, his face flushed but expressionless. "I'm sorry, Shihan," he said.

Dean sighed. Despite early evening weakening the harsh South African sun, it was hot in the small office. It had been a long, hard day and he was booked to fly to Japan tomorrow; more long, hard days.

He wanted to put his feet up and relax. He didn't want to deal with this, not now. "Go!" he said, waving a hand at the door. "Just go."

Dean's most senior instructor and right hand man, Sensei Gavin Richardson, closed the door behind Tristan. "Fancy a beer?" he asked.

"You read my mind," said Dean. "Let's get out of these and grab a bite to eat and a cold one," he said, tugging at the jacket of his dogi. "I'd like to put this day behind me."

Dean and Gavin sat on the terrace of the Blue Porpoise waiting for their seafood baskets. They sat in silence gazing out over the Indian Ocean. Dean lifted his glass and drained it. "Ah," he sighed. "That's better."

Gavin picked up his own and tilted it towards Dean. "Another?" he asked, downing the dregs.

"My round," said Dean coming up out of his chair and gathering the glasses in his large hands.

Dean may have been Gavin's senior in the dojo but, with the dogi off, they were just a couple of good friends. Dean returned from the bar, placing two foaming beers on the table.

"Thanks," said Gavin, leaning forward and catching the foam before it slid down the side of the glass.

Dean sat and stretched his long legs out in front of him. "So," he said. "The obvious hiccup aside, what did you think of the standard today?"

Gavin leaned back in his chair and ran a finger round the rim of his glass. "You underestimate him, you know," he said. He looked up. "I know he's young and..."

"He's too young," interrupted Dean. "It was a mistake to give him so much responsibility. And I still think it was a mistake to grade him to *shodan* when we did."

They had graded Tristan to first degree black belt almost two years ago. In terms of ability he had been ready much earlier, but the school's tough style of karate demanded all candidates be at least fourteen years of age to grade. Prior to Tristan, Dean had never graded anyone under the age of eighteen to black belt.

To Dean's chagrin, Tristan's birthday had fallen just before that year's winter grading camp. With pressure from his Sensei and no reason, other than a gut feeling, not to grade him, Dean had felt he had no choice.

Despite a tough exam Tristan had qualified for his first dan only eleven days after turning fourteen, the youngest shodan in the history of the club. Dean knew that Tristan was hoping to do the same with his next grade, nidan, when he turned eighteen.

He sensed Gavin's disapproval and felt a prickle of annoyance. He had heard it all before. He was well aware that in terms of physical fitness, technique and determination, Tristan Steyn was more than worthy of his grade. But it wasn't the boy's physical ability that concerned him.

"I know how you feel about him, Gavin," he said. "Yes, he knows his stuff, he's committed, he's got guts, on the surface he's good. But damn it," He leaned forward and jabbed a finger on the table. "He just doesn't have the right attitude. He's still a kid, Gav. Look what happened today, no insight whatsoever. He doesn't have the mindset for his level of training. And that makes him dangerous."

Gavin shook his head. "Look, Dean," he said. "I'm not going to push the point, but I think you're wrong. You missed something out there today."

Chapter Two

Tristan felt the stretch pull strongly behind his knees. He released his grip on his wrists and brought his arms round from behind his ankles. He came slowly upright.

They hadn't trained since the grading last weekend and he was feeling it in his flexibility. He was finding it hard to concentrate.

There was a new girl in the class. She was standing alone, stretching by the mirrors. He started towards her. He had heard that she was from Cape Town but he didn't know her name.

As he came closer he recognised her from the grading and had second thoughts about approaching. But she had seen him and was coming towards him.

He guessed she was about his age. Her long brown hair was caught back in a neat ponytail. Her crisp white dogi was immaculate and, were it not for the yellow belt around her middle, he would have taken her for a beginner.

"Hi," said Tristan. "Welcome aboard."

"Osu!" said the girl, acknowledging his senior grade. "I'm Megan Taylor."

"Tristan Steyn," he said, hoping he sounded more relaxed than he felt.

"I know who you are," she said, with a smile. "You saved my neck last weekend." Her eyes left his. "I hope your Shihan didn't give you too much grief."

"It was more embarrassing than painful," said Tristan.

"Did you tell him?"

He shook his head.

"So I guess I owe this to you then," she said, catching the end of her belt and flicking at the brand new green tag.

"Nope," said Tristan. "You did really well in your grading. But next time, make sure you tie your pants up properly before you start a bout."

Sensei Gavin called them into the dojo. Tristan struggled through the first fifteen minutes and by the time the warm up was over he was sore and moody.

"Okay," called Gavin. "I know it's tough getting back into the swing of things when you've had a break, but I've got my nice hat on today so we'll take it easy. I'm going to teach the white belts *Taikyoku Sono Ichi.*" He turned to the white belts. "That's the first kata you need to learn. The rest of you, in groups with a senior for some *kumite,* sparring," he said. "Seniors, vigilance please. I don't want any accidents!"

Tristan got the orange and blue belts. He enjoyed working with the juniors, most of them were young and his own youth helped him to relate. His endless patience and almost naïve lack of judgement made him a hit with them too.

He paired up his group and got them sparring on the mats, watching them closely.

"Okay guys, pull up a sec, will you?" he said, waving them towards him.

More than once he'd seen orange belts partnered with blues losing concentration and glancing at their opponent's middle. "Two things." He held up a finger. "First, this is your opponent." He patted Paul Hendry on the head. "Not this," he said, catching Paul's blue belt and giving it a yank. "Don't be frightened of the belt."

He pointed two fingers to his eyes. "Watch what your opponent is doing, not what he's wearing. You need to know where his hands and feet are going, you already know the colour of his belt."

He waved the end of his own belt at them. "Forget this. Golden rule!" he said. "Keep your focus on your opponent at all times!" He stuck up two fingers. "And the second thing," he said. "It helps to know how long your arms and legs are."

He waved to a young orange belt to come forward. "Okay, Michelle," he said. "I want you to go for it. I'm just going to move around and I want you to punch and kick as hard as you can."

Tristan stepped closer. "We're not sparring," he said. "It's just you going for me to get a feel for a moving target. I want you to practice judging distance."

Michelle Turner nodded and landed a couple of soft punches. She was a stocky girl, and tall for her age. She had the potential to pack some real force into her techniques but was afraid of hurting her opponents. Tristan knew this.

"Come on, Michelle," he encouraged. "Put some power into it. You won't hurt me, I won't let you."

It took Michelle a few moments to warm to the idea but when she did, he found himself having to block her punches and kicks to avoid the sting.

"Now, you're getting it," he said. "Right, let's have a go at some free sparring, *jiyu kumite,*" he said, reminding them of the Japanese term. "Okay, remember. Focus."

Tristan and Michelle took their positions and bowed to each other before beginning. Michelle was more confident now and was coming at him as hard and as fast as she could. Her focus was good and her strikes had some decent power. She seemed to be enjoying the fight.

Tristan was not. He was tired and hungry and he didn't like kumite at the best of times. He broke his own golden rule and let his mind play with blissful thoughts of a hot shower and a peanut butter sandwich in bed. He didn't even see it coming.

Michelle's instep thumped into his lower abdomen lifting him clear off his feet. Totally unprepared, there was no muscle tension. He was too relaxed to take the kick and still get up.

"Urgh!" his breath exploded from his lungs. He hit the floor and doubled up, pushing both arms into his aching gut. He struggled in vain to draw air into his deflated chest.

Sensei Gavin was beside him in an instant. He rolled him on to his back and looked into his watering eyes. "Okay, Sempai, let's get some air into those lungs."

Gavin eased Tristan's knees away from his chest and slipped a hand up under his arms. "Come on," he said. "A couple of nice deep breaths will do the trick." Gavin worked a hand over

Tristan's abdomen, gently prodding and pressing. "No harm done," he said. "Up you get."

Tristan groaned and looked up into Michelle's shocked and frightened face, peering from behind Gavin.

"I'm so sorry," she said, close to tears. "I didn't mean to hurt you."

Tristan shook his head and held up a hand. "No," he groaned, coming up onto one elbow. "My fault, not yours."

Gavin turned to the girl. "Are you hurt?" he asked.

She shook her head. "I'm so sorry," she said again.

"Uh uh, Michelle," said Gavin. "In this dojo you never apologise for hurting a senior grade. If they don't have enough about them to avoid a good whack then they deserve the wake up call." He aimed the last part of the sentence firmly in Tristan's direction.

Tristan rolled onto his side and came to his knees. The nausea hit as hard as the kick had, and for the first time that day he was glad he'd eaten nothing since breakfast.

He felt a surge of hot liquid gush into his mouth. Bending forward, he vomited onto the dojo floor.

"Okay," yelled Gavin. "Everyone to the mat room please. And, Sempai, get that mess cleaned up then join us on the mats."

Tristan wandered into the mat room still holding his stomach. A dull, empty feeling had replaced the pain but he still felt sick. He smelled of vomit and disinfectant.

Gavin came over. "Sempai, you stink, and you look like week old laundry," he said. "Go and change your dogi and then I want you to do self defence with the juniors."

"Yes, Sensei," said Tristan. "Okay juniors, back in the dojo with me. I won't be a minute," he called. He excused himself and went to change, before hurrying back to the dojo.

"Jamie," Tristan stood in the doorway and watched the young boy try in vain to land a roundhouse kick. The bag was hung much too high for him. "What are you doing?"

"Practising my mawashing geri," Jamie replied with pride.

"*Mawashi geri*," corrected Tristan mildly, pulling the bag out of the way. "I admire your ambition," he said. "But we're doing self defence now. Remember what I told you about feet last time?"

"Yes," said Jamie. "In self defence you use your feet to run away!"

"That's right," said Tristan. "So if one of yours is higher than your head then something is not quite right, hey? Okay, come," he said. "Who can tell me what the first line of defence for a kid is?

"Noise!" came the united cry.

After class Tristan helped to stack the mats at the end of the dojo. Finishing up, he walked over to where Michelle was waiting for her lift home.

"Nice going, Michelle," he said.

She flushed. "I think it was just luck really. I didn't think you were concentrating."

He nodded. "I wasn't. And you took advantage, that's good."

"Yes," said Gavin, joining them. "Sparring's not just about landing your strikes. It's about knowing your partner, getting inside his or her mind and capitalising on their weaknesses.

Gavin was warming to his topic and more students gathered round to listen.

He addressed them all. "A senior grade," he said. "Is simply more experienced than you are. And, as you saw today, that experience counts for nothing without concentration and focus. There are always opportunities to get the better of a more experienced fighter. Focus and technique can often win over seniority, especially if that senior is slacking."

Tristan turned away from the little gathering and stood by the door for some fresh air. Megan joined him.

"Well, I'm glad that's over," he said. "Nothing like a nice bit of public humiliation to end the day."

"Oh well," She grinned at him. "Two down, one to go. My grandma always says these things happen in threes."

Chapter Three

Mr de Lange brought the morning assembly to an end and dismissed the boys. Tristan yawned, although the long summer holiday had ended two weeks ago, he hadn't quite adjusted to the early starts.

"Miss Price was on top form today," said Rico as they filed out of the assembly hall. "Did you see her flash her knickers to the whole school?"

Tristan frowned. "She did not!" he said, rubbing his abdomen. Despite spending most of Sunday lounging on the sofa, he was still sore and a little queasy and was in no mood to hear what his chemistry teacher had up her skirt.

"What, you mean you missed it? Geez, Tristan, don't you have eyes?" Rico Martins stopped and pulled Tristan out of the throng of boys leaving the hall. "Okay, bru," he said. "Genuine, next time she's wearing one of those short skirts you have to watch her. When she gets up to go to the piano she..."

"Well, well, well, if it isn't the high and mighty black belt." A tall, sandy haired boy sauntered out of the crowd, stepping between Tristan and Rico.

He grinned at Tristan, his sharp blue eyes mocking. "I hear you had a good weekend, Steyn," he said.

Andre Turner towered over him but he stood his ground, refusing to be intimidated. Tristan had inherited his father's fair looks but his mother's dark temper. He bristled. "Piss off, Turner!"

He turned away, pressing his fingers into the palms of his hands and biting down on the inside of his cheek. Ever since he had received his first taste of the head's paddle, courtesy of Andre Turner, there had been tension between the two of them.

"Or what?" asked Andre. "You'll beat me up? Oh no, I forgot. My little sister kicked your lunch right out of your guts."

Tristan turned back to face Andre.

"Pull your horns in, Tris, he's not worth it," said Rico, catching his arm and walking him away.

Andre followed alongside. "You're never going to live this one down, Steyn," he said. "By first break the whole school will know that you got your arse kicked by a twelve year old orange belt."

Tristan spun around.

"Back off, Turner!" said Rico, moving between the two of them.

"*En 'n meisiekind, nogal.*" And a girl, no less, added Andre.

Tristan's mother was Afrikaans, and Andre had nicknamed him the Diminutive Dutchman. He hated it. Andre's use of the language needled him and he took the bait.

He lunged around Rico and caught Andre by the shirt, sending two white buttons spinning in the sunlight. Ramming his tormentor backwards into the side of the hall, he drew back his fist.

He knew it was dangerous, he knew it was wrong, he saw Andre's terror, but still he let fly. At the last instant some sense prevailed. He opened his hand, slamming his palm into the side of Andre's face. Andre shrieked.

Rico stepped in, elbowing Tristan aside and pulling Andre out of his grip. Yanking Andre's arm brutally up behind his back, he marched him away.

Rico's red hair and pale complexion had once made him one of Andre's prime targets. But in the past year he had shot up and filled out and he now surpassed Andre in size.

Tristan shoved Rico aside and caught Andre round the neck.

"Tristan, don't," yelled Rico.

"That is enough!" a voice behind them boomed. The three of them stopped dead.

"Steyn, let him go. Now!" Tristan shoved Andre roughly away. He stumbled forward, Rico catching him before he hit the ground, and helping him to find his balance. Once he was steady, Rico let him go.

"My office, now. All three of you."

They walked in silence, the headmaster behind them. Mr de Lange marched his miscreants through the door to the wood panelled office. The three of them stood before the large teak desk, hands behind their backs facing the headmaster.

Still seething, Tristan fixed his gaze on the head's paisley tie, refusing to make eye contact.

"Turner, since you appear to be the victim here, perhaps you would enlighten me as to what started that little display of savagery?"

"I'm not sure, sir," said Andre, rubbing his reddened cheek.

Rico shot him a warning look. A ghost of smirk pulled at the corner of Andre's mouth. "I just asked Steyn if he had a good weekend." He looked down at Tristan. "Apparently he didn't, sir."

"Sir, Tristan was just..."

"Save your breath, Martins," said the head. "I saw what happened. I don't need a blow by blow account." He turned to Tristan. "And neither do I need an action replay, Steyn!" he bellowed, catching Tristan's elbow jab to Andre's ribs. "Turner, you may go to class. And I don't want to see you involved in anything like this again, understood?"

"Yes, sir, thank you, sir," said Andre. Grinning, he made his way quickly to the door.

"You two sit down," said the head with a sigh, taking his own seat. Rico pulled out a chair and sat, Tristan remained defiantly standing.

"That was not an invitation, Steyn," said the head. "It was an order. One I suggest you obey while you still can!"

Tristan looked at him for the first time. "Sorry, sir," he said, his temper cooling enough to register his predicament. He sat down and trapped his hands between his knees, suppressing the urge to fidget.

"I'll come straight to the point," the head said. "The behaviour I witnessed from you two this morning will not be tolerated. You can consider yourselves lucky that I'm prepared to deal with it rather than getting your parents involved and having you both suspended."

"Sir," said Tristan. "It wasn't Rico's fault. He was just trying to stop me from..."

"I know that, Steyn and I will take it into account. However, he did use force on a fellow pupil and it won't go unpunished."

The head stood and lifted a heavy wooden paddle from a hook set into the edge of his desk. He moved to the centre of the room and stood beside a small square of red carpet. Tristan hated that carpet. It served no purpose; other than to appeal to the head's sense of ritual, perhaps.

The two boys remained silently seated.

"Martins, if you would please."

Rico got up and walked over to the headmaster's side.

"You know the drill," said the head. "You'll take two."

Rico stepped onto the mat and leaned forward, grasping his shins.

Tristan stared out of the window wishing he was anywhere but where he was. He heard the paddle thump twice in rapid succession. He heard Rico's low moan as he came upright and stepped off the mat.

"Wait by the door please, Martins," said the head. "Steyn, over here please."

Tristan rose and went to stand on the small red mat.

"I expect better than that from you, Steyn," said the head. "And I'm going to see that there is never a repeat of that behaviour from you as long as you are in my school."

The head placed the paddle on the desk and walked over to a tall, double-doored cupboard. He reached inside and brought down a long flexible cane. On route back to the mat, he bent it fully in half and sliced the air with it a couple of times. "You'll take four," he said.

Tristan felt a cold fear flip like a dying salmon in his gut. He realised, with dismay, that Andre Turner had just earned him his first encounter with the cane. "But, sir, I..."

"Steyn!" roared the head. "You have a choice. Either you can take four now or you can try my patience and earn yourself an invitation back to my office every day for the rest of this week. I strongly recommend the former!"

"Yes, sir," said Tristan, biting his tongue. *Stupid, stupid, stupid*, he thought as he turned to face the wall.

"Bend," said the head. Tristan obeyed, reaching down and resting his hands on his knees. The head gave him a gentle shove between the shoulder blades, forcing him a little lower. Tristan felt the fabric of his trousers pull tight across his buttocks. He closed his eyes and waited.

The head swung the cane back and brought it down, hard and fast. It cut the air with a hiss, landing with a wicked crack. Tristan gasped, the impact slamming him forward, forcing him to reposition his feet. He recovered his composure just as the stroke took effect.

Wholly unprepared for the intensity of the pain, Tristan sucked in a lungful of air and held it. The vicious sting continued to build until, just as he thought he could stand it no more, it began to ease. He let out a long slow breath.

"One," said the head. Tristan bit his lower lip hard and curled his toes inside his shoes.

Again the hiss and crack. He couldn't help himself. He let out a pitiful yelp and shot upright. The second stroke rekindled the fire of the first and added a searing burn of its own. The pain was worse than he could ever have imagined.

Struggling for control he walked to the wall and rested his forehead against it. He pushed himself away with a clenched fist and rocked back on his heels. For the second time the pain began to subside and he could breathe again.

Mr de Lange stood with the cane at his side. Tristan turned to face him. Head bowed, he pressed a fist to his mouth, one arm hugged across his body, his hand clutching his elbow. He shifted his weight from one foot to the other.

"That," said the head. "Has to be the most appalling lack of self control I have ever witnessed!"

Tristan was mortified. "I know, sir." He held up his hands in a gesture of submission. "I am so sorry."

The head regarded him a moment longer. "I'm going to pretend it never happened," he said. "But if you so much as twitch before I'm done I'll have you restrained and I'll start the count at one. Is that clear."

"Yes, sir, thank you," Tristan mumbled.

"Now, no more of that skittish behaviour. I don't want you getting hurt."

I don't want you getting hurt? Tristan almost laughed out loud.

"Take your place," the head said, pointing with the cane.

His hands shook as he bent forward and rested them on his shins. His heart hammered so hard he feared it would burst. He gripped the thin fabric of his school trousers and prayed for the fortitude to stay down.

For the third time the cane lashed his backside. And then, before he had time to react, the fourth stroke cut diagonally across the already raised welts. Tristan howled and pulled away from the cane. He turned and backed away.

"Please," he wailed, terrified the head would carry out his threat to start over. "I'm sorry. I can't."

Choking back tears, he reversed until he felt the cold, hard wall behind him.

"*Ruk jou reg*, Steyn!" Pull yourself together, snapped the head. "Now get to class, both of you."

"Oh my God," moaned Tristan, pulling the office door closed behind him. "I cannot believe I just did that!"

"I can't believe you got away with it," said Rico. He began to laugh.

Tristan was stung. "What?"

"God, Tris, I'm sorry but you were so funny in there."

"Funny?"

"It's just that I've never seen you kick up a fuss like that before," Rico said.

"Well nothing has ever hurt like that before!"

Rico snorted with laughter.

"Oh, forgive me," said Tristan. "If I'd known you found my extreme pain and utter humiliation so entertaining, I would have ramped up the performance for you. I could go off you, Rico Martins!" He stalked off.

"I'm sorry," giggled Rico, tripping after him. "That was a bit harsh! Are you okay?"

Tristan stopped and gaped at his friend. "Hell, Rico, no!" he said "I am not okay. It feels like someone just blow torched my arse!"

By the time they had crossed the school to the science block the vicious sting had eased to a warm glow and he was feeling much better.

"Crap," said Rico. "We forgot to get a hall pass." They stood outside the classroom. "Should I go back and get one?"

"Well one of us better," said Tristan. "I'm not taking another whack for being late."

"Oh, go on," said Rico. "Give us a show. It would be worth at least five bucks a ticket." Rico started back towards the office, "Ten from Turner," he called over his shoulder.

Tristan flicked a finger at his retreating mate just as the classroom door came open.

"Rico Martins! Come back here," called Mr Pietersen, peering around the door frame.

Rico shot round and marched back. "Sorry, sir," he said. "I forgot our hall pass from Mr de Lange. I was going back to get it." He pointed back over his shoulder.

"Just get inside," said the teacher. "Never mind the pass."

The boys filed into the classroom. Mr Pietersen's chalky hand landed Tristan a half hearted slap on the back of the head as he walked past. "And less of the sign language from you," he said. "Or you'll need more than a hall pass."

"Sorry, sir," said Tristan. He made a point of ignoring Andre Turner as he shuffled to the back of the room and slipped into the seat next to Rico.

He winced as he settled onto the hard wooden chair.

"Hey," hissed Rico. "No more of that skittish behaviour. I don't want you getting hurt."

Both boys ducked under their desk lids to retrieve their text books, and to hide their giggles.

Chapter Four

Irritated by the sudden loud knock, Gavin opened the office door. He frowned at Michelle Turner standing in the doorway.

"Osu!" she said, her face flushed and her chest moving rapidly in time to her heavy breathing. "Sorry, Sensei," she said. "But my mom is in the mat room. She wants to speak to you and she's a bit cross, Sensei."

"Right," said Gavin, taken aback. He had been about to reprimand her for not wearing her dogi but, sensing her urgency, he moved quickly into the mat room.

Kathryn Turner, arms akimbo, was standing on the mats in her high heeled shoes. Gavin cringed but said nothing. Shihan would have a fit. He would have insisted she either remove her shoes or step off the mats but Gavin didn't fancy his chances of getting her to do either. The woman was clearly furious.

"Who is in charge here?" she snapped.

"Mrs Turner, I'm Gavin Richardson and I'm the senior instructor here tonight. What can I do for you?"

"You can start," she said. "By getting Tristan Steyn out here."

Gavin looked around. His sweep of the room was met by dozens of wide eyes, but Tristan was not among them.

"I'm afraid he isn't here yet. May I ask why you want to speak to him?"

"Do you have any idea what kind of savages you're breeding here, Mr Richardson?"

Gavin shifted uncomfortably towards the woman. "Mrs Turner," he said quietly, leaning in. "Perhaps we could discuss this in the office?"

Gavin was acutely aware that most of the class had stopped stretching and were following the woman's ranting with interest.

"No, Mr Richardson, we cannot discuss this in the office. These people..." she said, waving a hand towards Gavin's students. "These people, need to know that that boy is an out of control little hooligan and that my son is lucky not to be in the hospital because of him!"

Gavin cast a glance at the stricken Michelle, her face scarlet and her lower lip trembling. "I think that maybe there's been a mistake," he said.

"There's no mistake, Mr Richardson," Kathryn said. "And if you would like confirmation then you may contact Paul de Lange at Ridgewood Boys' High." She went on. "That boy attacked my son at school this morning. He's black and blue. The little thug should be made an example of. He should... He should be horsewhipped right here!"

"Mrs Turner, we don't horsewhip our students," said Gavin, his temper flaring. "But I will speak to him and, if it's true, I will personally see that he is appropriately punished."

"You'd better," said Kathryn. "And if I'm not satisfied with your punishment I will be taking the matter further." She spun round, digging her high heel into the mat. "Come on, Michelle," she snapped, snatching at the poor girl's shoulder. "You're not staying here with these people!"

For the first time ever Tristan was late for training. That afternoon he had taken a couple of paracetamol and fallen asleep on the sofa. If Rico hadn't phoned he would still be there.

The session was already under way when he arrived. He bowed at the door and entered. He knelt respectfully, facing away from the class. Head bowed, eyes closed he waited to be acknowledged.

With the formalities over, Sensei Gavin called to him. "You may join the class, Sempai," he said.

Tristan bowed forward. "*Shitsurei shimasu*," he said, excusing himself for disturbing the class. Tristan came to his feet and turned to the front of the dojo. He bowed to his instructor. "Osu!" he said, and started towards the back of the room.

"Sempai," called Gavin. "Come to the front please."

Tristan felt a twitch of nervousness. Dojo etiquette dictated that latecomers join at the back of the class, regardless of rank. He stepped up to Sensei Gavin and waited for further instructions.

He pushed his hair behind his ear. Thick and unruly, it didn't matter how often he combed it, his hair always seemed out of control. Short of his mother's suggestion of a brush cut, which he refused to even contemplate, he was always going to look like a scarecrow. He kept his hair just short enough to avoid the wrath of the prefects who regularly checked that everyone conformed to school rules.

"Sempai," said Gavin. "What is the fourth line of the *Dojo Kun*?" The dojo oath.

Tristan moistened his lips. "We will observe the rules of courtesy, respect our superiors, and refrain from violence," he said.

"Repeat the last four words please, Sempai."

Tristan had a good idea where this was going and he didn't like it. He swallowed hard. *How could Sensei possibly know?* "And refrain from violence," he repeated, his eyes fixed on the four gold bars on the end of Gavin's belt.

"Right," said Gavin. "And do you understand what that means, Sempai?"

"Yes, Sensei," said Tristan.

"Good," said Gavin. "Now tell me, did you use violence against Michelle Turner's brother this morning?"

Of course, Michelle. Tristan closed his eyes and inhaled deeply. He saw no point in arguing a case he didn't have. There were no excuses for what he had done, and he knew it. "Yes, Sensei," he said.

"Go to the mat room and warm up please. Then you may go to the back of the class and perform Taikyoku Sono Ichi until the end of the session."

"Yes, Sensei," said Tristan.

He pushed himself hard during his warm ups and made an effort to perform the kata well every time. By the end of the session he had lost count of the times he'd performed it. The soles of his feet were sore and blistered from the repetitive turns on the wooden floor.

He took a place in the back row with the white belts when Gavin lined the class up. He knelt stiffly at the call of "*Seiza!*"

After the Dojo Kun had been recited and Gavin had dismissed the group, he came over to Tristan and handed him a broom.

"Sweep the dojo floor, please," he said. "And when everyone has left, come and see me in the office."

"Yes, Sensei," he said, taking the broom. He swept the dojo from one side to the other and then began again as there were still some students waiting for lifts.

Gavin sat behind the desk in the small office dreading Tristan's knock. He looked at the framed photo of Shihan Dean with the group he took to Japan last year. The image seemed to scream, *I told you so!*

Damn it! All the times I defended you to Shihan, all the times I fought your corner, and you do this. He laid the photo face down.

The knock came. He went to the door and opened it, ushering Tristan in. "Sit," he said.

Tristan obeyed.

Gavin rounded the desk and took his own seat. He rested his elbows on the desk and put his head in his hands. Sliding his hands from his face he regarded Tristan over steepled fingers.

"I'll make this short because I don't want to say something I'll end up regretting," he said. "What you did this morning was stupid beyond belief. You know how dangerous it is to strike someone outside the dojo with your level of training!" He slammed his palm on the desk. "Is there anything at all that you can say that will at least help me understand your motivation?"

"No, Sensei," mumbled Tristan.

"Well then, I'm really disappointed in you," Gavin said. "And you've left me with a big problem."

"I'm sorry, Sensei."

"That's not good enough, Sempai. We, as a school, have a reputation to uphold. We teach a creed of non violence and the people out there need to be able to trust that." He jabbed a finger towards the door. "Now, thanks to you, Mrs Turner thinks we are training a bunch of thugs in here and she's pulled Michelle out of classes! Damn it, Sempai!" he said, leaping to his feet and leaning over the desk. "I don't know what to do with you. Just over a week ago I saw you risk everything to help out a young girl that you didn't even know. Shihan could have had your belt for that. He still has no idea why you really stopped that fight. And now you go and do something I would expect from a five year old white belt!"

Tristan pushed his hair behind his ear. "I'm really sorry," he said. "It won't happen again."

"You're damn right it won't," said Gavin. "And I told Mrs Turner you would be appropriately punished. She came storming in here demanding you be horsewhipped, for heaven's sake."

Tristan chewed on his lower lip and looked up at Gavin. "What are you going to do, Sensei?" he asked.

"I don't know, Tristan. This is too serious for hasty decisions. Besides, Shihan needs to be involved. But you can start with an apology to the boy in question. And I will be checking up on that!"

"But, Sensei..."

"Don't!" snapped Gavin. He continued. "And then you will come in early and sweep the dojo before every training session and you'll do it again before you leave. You will also do everything that's asked of you in training and you will give it 100% effort, no matter what it is. As for the trials for the national team, I'm leaving that decision to Shihan. He'll be back from Japan on Saturday so you'll just have to wait until then. But I wouldn't hold my breath if I were you."

Gavin got up and walked to the door. "Now," he said. "Go home and get a good night's rest because by the time this week's over you're going to wish I'd opted for the horsewhip."

Tristan already did. He was desperate to represent South Africa but, with Shihan probably still angry with him over the grading, his chances of even trying to make the team were slim indeed.

Waiting until Saturday to find out would be torture.

Chapter Five

A ndre Turner was not in class the next day and Tristan was relieved. But when, by Thursday, he was still not back, he began to worry. "What if I really hurt him, Rico?" he said.

"What if you did?" said Rico. "He's a bully, he deserved it. Stop freaking out about it."

That night at training Tristan asked to see the register.

"What do you want that for?" asked Gavin.

He looked down at his feet. "Sensei, Andre Turner hasn't been at school since Monday. I just wanted to check Michelle's record for their address," he said. "So I can go round to apologise and see if he's okay," he added quickly.

He shifted uncomfortably under Gavin's scrutiny. Nothing had been said about the incident since that night in the office and he feared Gavin would be angry all over again.

Gavin gathered a pile of papers from the desk. "You know I can't give out students' addresses, Sempai. I appreciate your intention though." He tapped the papers on the desk and handed them to Tristan. "File these in the blue box file in the top of that cabinet, please." He rooted in the desk drawer for a bunch of keys. "When you're done, put the keys back in here, then you can go home. Forget the dojo floor tonight."

Gavin left the office and Tristan opened the filing cabinet drawer. He laid the box file on the desk and opened it. Inside was the attendance register.

After school, Tristan walked up Marine Park Road, checking the numbers on the houses as he passed. At 242 he studied the wall and gate for a beware of the dog notice and looked for signs of animals on the loose in the garden. There were none so he opened the gate and trudged up to the door.

His mouth was dry and his hand shook as he reached for the doorbell. *Oh, come on,* he thought. He pushed the bell and waited.

He noticed the curtains were closed and began to think there was no one home. He was just about to leave when the door came open.

He stepped back in surprise and looked quickly at the number on the wall, sure he had made a mistake.

"Um, I'm sorry," he said. "I didn't mean to disturb you, I..."

The man leaned one hand on the door frame, squinting myopically at him. He wore only a vest with no shirt, the belt and button on his trousers were undone, his hair unkempt. He raised his eyebrows.

"I... I just wondered if I could speak to Andre but..."

The man stood aside and inclined his head to the entrance hall. "Andre!" he yelled. "Get out here. There's someone to see you."

The man disappeared through a door to his left, leaving Tristan still standing on the step. He went inside but left the door open.

Andre appeared at the end of the hall. He saw Tristan and immediately backed away.

Tristan stepped forward, his mouth dropping open. "Andre, I..." he stared in disbelief. "My God, I'm so sorry. Did I do that? I..."

Andre's left eye was swollen shut and his lip was puffy and lopsided. "Piss off, Steyn!" he said. "You had no right to come round here. Just get out."

"But I..." began Tristan. The man re entered the hall behind him. He turned. "I'm sorry, sir," he said, edging past to the door. He rushed down the steps and onto the lawn as the door slammed shut behind him.

He blinked in the light, a sharp contrast to the muted interior. Despite the sun's warmth, he felt a cold shiver as he breathed in the fresh scent of the summer afternoon. A grasshopper buzzed past his head, startling him.

He looked back at the door, not sure what to do. He heard someone start to shout inside and walked away.

Michelle rounded the wall and stopped dead in the gateway. Her eyes, as they locked on to his, revealed a fury that no child should know.

"Michelle, wait I..." She shot past him, fled up the steps and disappeared into the house.

Tristan poked at the pile of spinach with his fork. He couldn't get the image of Andre's battered face out of his mind. He was sure he hadn't hit him that hard. He went over the afternoon again and again.

The dishevelled man. Andre's horror at seeing him standing there. The shouting. Michelle.

"What's wrong, Tris?" asked his mother.

I should have gone back, he thought. *I should have done something*. He pushed his plate to one side.

"Are you just not hungry, or are you not feeling well?"

He looked up. "I'm sorry," he said. "What did you say?"

Elize Steyn frowned and repeated the question.

"Sorry, Ma. I'm just not hungry. I'll maybe nuke it and eat after training."

Tristan didn't eat after training. He came in, showered and went to his room.

Elize scooped the meal into the bin. "I'm worried about him, Brett," she said. "Don't you want to talk to him?"

Tristan's father reached up and took a third mug out of the cupboard. "I'll take him a drink and have a word," he said.

He took two mugs of tea to Tristan's room and tapped on the door. "Tris?" he called quietly. "May I come in?"

"Okay," said Tristan.

He pushed the door open. Tristan was lying the on the bed with his feet up the wall, reading Gichin Funakoshi's *Karate-Do: My Way of Life*.

"I've brought you a cup of tea," said Brett. "Rooibos with lemon and honey."

Tristan swung his feet off the wall and sat up. "Thanks," he said, laying the book on his pillow and taking the proffered mug.

Brett sat on the bed next to him. "Your mother's worried about you," he said.

Tristan frowned. "Why?" he asked, blowing onto the steaming liquid and taking a sip.

"Oh, I don't know," said Brett. "Just being a mother, I suppose. You know what they're like." He sipped from his mug too. "Are you okay?" he asked. "You do look a bit washed out, and it's not like you to refuse food."

"No, I'm fine," said Tristan. "Training's a bit tough and...ag, it's nothing," he said.

Brett raised an eyebrow. "Are you sure?"

Tristan fiddled with the the corner of the duvet. "Sensei Gavin is hacked off at me," he said. "And Shihan is back tomorrow and he's probably going to kick me off the team for the try outs for national selections."

"Oh, is that all?" asked Brett, reaching over and placing his tea on the bedside table. "And may I ask what you did to prompt that?"

Tristan's soft hazel eyes regarded him over the rim of the mug. "On one condition," he said, lowering the tea.

"Which is?"

"Amnesty. No punishment for something I've already been punished for."

"Sounds fair enough," said Brett. "But I want a get out clause. If it's something horribly illegal, I reserve the right to kill you."

"Deal," said Tristan. "I smacked Andre Turner at school on Monday and..."

"Ah," said Brett. "From the horse's mouth at last. You always used to tell me when you got into trouble at school."

"You knew?"

"Yes," said Brett. "I got a call from the school about it."

"Ouch," said Tristan. "Sorry, I would have told you but... Oh help, is mom really mad at me?" He looked up, wide eyed.

Brett grinned. "You would have known about it by now if she was," he said. "I didn't tell her."

"Thanks, Dad."

Brett gave Tristan's shoulder an affectionate squeeze. "Do you want to tell me about it?"

"Not really." Tristan lowered his eyes and flicked at the rug with his big toe. "I was really upset that Shihan might drop me from the team," he said. "But something happened today and..." He paused, pulling his feet up onto the bed. "I just feel really crappy about doing it, Dad," he said. "I think I deserve to be dropped from the team."

Brett frowned. "Tris, we all do things we regret but we have to move on. Feeling crappy about it isn't going to help you or Andre, is it? And if Shihan Dean does give you a chance on the team I don't think you should throw it away because you feel bad. Competing for South Africa is a big thing, Tris."

Tristan plucked at a blister and ripped the skin from his foot. He rolled it between his fingers before flicking it at the bin and missing. "I guess," he said.

"Tristan!" said Brett. "That's disgusting."

"Sorry." He got off the bed and retrieved the offending body part. This time he dropped it carefully into the bin and wiped his hands down the front of his pyjama top.

Brett sighed and shook his head. "Okay," he said. "So you've got a few issues at the moment, but otherwise you're all right, yes?"

Tristan nodded. "Ja, I'm fine. Thanks."

"I'll leave you to it then." Brett stood up and collected the mugs. He was half way out of the door when Tristan spoke again.

"Dad." he said. "Can I ask you a sort of legal type question?"

Brett's mind snagged somewhere between father and lawyer. "Go on," he said.

Tristan hesitated, worrying the dog-eared cover of *Karate-Do*. Brett returned to the bed and sat down. Placing the mugs at his feet, he turned to face his son. "You're not in any kind of trouble are you, Tris?"

Tristan looked up. "No," he said. "But if something bad was

happening, as in illegal type bad. And you knew if you said something you might be able to help someone, but that if you were wrong, or if no one believed you, then the paw paw would hit the fan and the person you wanted to help would be in even bigger trouble, what would you do?"

Brett thought a minute running the clumsy question through his mind to be sure he understood. "It would depend on the something," he said. "Can you be a bit more specific?"

Tristan frowned. "Not really," he said. "It was just a what if kind of question."

"Tristan," said Brett, "It sounds like a pretty serious what if kind of question. You know if you need to talk I'm always here for you, don't you?"

"Yes, Dad, I know," he said. "Thank you. But really, it's nothing."

But it wasn't nothing. Tristan knew something was wrong, and he had to find out what.

Chapter Six

Since Sensei Gavin's reprimand, Tristan had worked harder than he had ever worked before. He had pushed himself to the limits of his endurance and put heart and soul into everything his seniors had asked of him. At the end of every session he had been sweat-soaked and hurting. Tristan was exhausted and his aching body protested as he rolled out of bed.

Still in his pyjamas, he wandered into the kitchen and opened the fridge door. He stood in the curl of cool air, taking in the contents before retreating with a carton of Berry Blaze.

Elize was sitting at the kitchen table reading the morning news. She regarded him over the top of the paper. "I hope you're planning to use a glass," she said.

"Ja, Ma," said Tristan, taking a sunflower-yellow coffee mug from the drainer and filling it with the deep red fluid.

Elize sighed and returned to her daily reality check. She looked up again as he reached into the cupboard for the cereal and began munching cornflakes straight from the box. Laying the paper down, she watched him pick up a bowl and his mug and shuffle to the table with the cereal box under his arm.

He eased himself into the chair opposite her.

"Are you sore, my boy?" she asked.

"Bit stiff from training," he replied, upending the box and depositing a heap of cornflakes into the dish.

"You must be careful. You're too young to be training so hard. You're still growing. You might do yourself some damage."

"I'm fine, Ma. Stop fussing." He scooped up a handful of dry cornflakes, tipped his head back, and poured them into his mouth.

"Ag nee, Tristan. No!" said Elize. "Can't you put milk on that and eat a like person instead of a savage?" she snapped. "At least use a spoon."

Tristan sometimes wondered if he and his mother shared the same planet, let alone the same house. He hadn't touched dairy since his standard three teacher, Mrs Botha, had brought to his attention that milk was the mammary secretion of another species. But then it had taken her years to accept that he didn't eat meat.

"Don't be ridiculous," she'd said. "Of course you eat meat!"

Tristan didn't eat meat. He hadn't eaten meat since that day on the farm when he'd skirted the barn and witnessed his grandmother hacking the head off a chicken. He had stood, repugnance lending him roots, as the headless body flapped past his feet, a jet of liquid scarlet spattering his bare legs and khaki shorts.

His grandmother's suppertime announcement, that the chicken was fresh that day, had brought a wave of nausea that sent him running for the bathroom. It was the first time he had associated the meat on his plate with the living, breathing, trusting creatures on the farm.

He had refused it ever since. His mother only noticing when a neighbour left the gate open depriving him of his means of disposal when, thanks to a careless driver, the family dog was later found dead in a storm drain.

He wondered whether his mother would notice if he paraded through the kitchen wearing nothing but her high heels and make up. The mental image made him shudder.

He looked, with disgust, at the mug of juice and pushed his breakfast aside. He was too nervous to eat anyway. Shihan was back from Japan today and had the potential to shatter his dreams.

Training began at two o'clock. At one thirty Tristan knocked on Shihan's office door.

"Come in," he called.

He opened the door and closed it quietly behind him, waiting for Shihan Dean to acknowledge him.

"Sit please, Sempai," said Dean, not looking up from the form he was filling in. He did as he was told.

Dean eventually put the pen down and looked up. "Sempai," he said. "Sensei Gavin has filled me in on your behaviour while I was away. And while I'm not at all happy about it, I know you've worked hard this week to make amends. Plus, I've had some time to cool off." Dean shifted in his chair. "So," he said, resting his arms on the desk and leaning forward. "Here's what I'm going to do. I'm not going to bar you from team selection, but you're not going to be an automatic choice either. You are going to have to prove to me that you deserve a place on that team. And I'm not going to be basing my assessment on your ability. That's not in question here, it's your attitude and your self control I'm concerned about. Now, you've got three weeks until try outs so you'd better get working on it."

Dean studied Tristan through narrowed eyes. "Show me you deserve a place on that team and you'll get it, but one more performance like that and you're out of this dojo for good. Got it?"

"Yes, Shihan. Thank you," said Tristan, breathing a sigh of relief.

"There's one other thing," said Dean. He leaned back in his chair and picked up the pen. Fiddling with it, he tapped the end on the form in front of him then looked directly at Tristan. "This is not a decision I made lightly," he said. "Despite what you may think."

Tristan's throat tightened.

Dean put the pen down on the table and leaned forward. "Tristan, I'm not going to let you grade to nidan when you turn eighteen. I want at least another four years out of you at shodan."

Tristan couldn't have been more stunned if Dean had leapt over the table and slapped him in the face.

"I know it seems harsh now," he said. "But you will understand one day."

Tristan opened his mouth to speak but didn't trust his voice.

"Those gold bars on your belt represent more than just physical ability, Sempai. A certain level of emotional maturity is required too, that's why we set age limits. You're just not there yet." said Dean. "I don't even think you were ready for the one you have, I'm not letting you go for a second until I'm 100% convinced."

Dean held up a hand to still Tristan's protest. "Tristan, getting that first dan is all about your technique and ability. It's about your courage and strength and fitness. You have all of that by the bucket load, we know that. But once you have that first dan, it's like starting all over again, only this time you're working on a whole new level. This time it's about the inner journey. It's about the understanding. It takes time, but it will come to you. You should be enjoying the journey, Sempai, not trying to kick the door down. It will pay you to remember that."

"But I don't turn eighteen for over two years," cried Tristan. "How do you know I won't be ready by then?" If I am will you change your mind?"

"No, it's not negotiable!"

"But how do you know I won't be ready by then?"

"Sempai!" said Dean, sharply. "The very fact that you don't get it just proves my point. Now, if you are ready by then you'll look back on this conversation and you will understand exactly why I'm doing this. And if not, well then we'll both know that I made the right decision today."

"But that's not fair," Tristan wailed. "You can't possibly know..."

"Sempai," hissed Dean. "That is enough! Now get out in that dojo and get ready to train. You've pushed me too far this time."

Tristan left the office shaking with fury. He bolted to the changing room and locked himself in a toilet cubicle. At one minute to two he took his place in the dojo, still angry and hurt.

Shihan Dean led the class. After the warm up he called Tristan out of line to the front of the group.

"Sempai," he said. "Step forward please." Tristan did.

"Hand me your *obi*, Sempai."

He hesitated, then loosened the knot at his waist and handed the belt to his Shihan.

"Thank you," said Dean. "Wearing a black belt, any belt, in this dojo is a privilege you earn. It is not a right." Dean looped the belt and slipped it though his own. He reached behind him and pulled out another which had been looped behind his back.

He held it out to Tristan. "When you remember the standard of behaviour expected of your grade, you may have your belt back. Until then, you will wear this one."

Tristan sucked in his lower lip and regarded the proffered white belt. He looked up at his Shihan and then extended his hand and took it. He dropped to his right knee and tied the belt around his waist before rising, bowing to Dean and saying simply, "Osu! Thank you, Shihan."

"Take a place at the back of the class please," said Dean.

He turned and walked the length of the dojo, falling in as the most junior ranked karateka. When training was over, he fled the dojo.

Gavin was seething. As soon as the last of the students had left, he barged into the office.

"Sensei," said Dean, laying down *The Independent on Saturday*. "Since when do you not knock?"

"That was too much, Dean," snapped Gavin, ignoring the question and brushing aside all formalities associated with the uniforms they were both still wearing.

"Sensei!" Dean paused. "You were not in this office. You did not hear what went on."

"My point exactly!" snapped Gavin. "I wasn't, and neither was anyone else! You had no right to humiliate him in front of the whole class because he pissed you off behind closed doors. You should have punished him behind closed doors too."

Dean pushed his chair back and came upright.

"I see," he said. "And you making him sweep the dojo floor in front of the whole class was not humiliating?"

"That was different," said Gavin. "That bloody woman came in here shouting her mouth of in front of everybody. He might as well have teed off on a junior in the middle of the dojo. The whole class knew what had happened anyway." Gavin ran his hands through his thick dark hair. "You are wrong about that boy, Dean.

You are so wrong!"

Dean folded his arms and inclined his head. "Are you suggesting I'm not doing my job properly, Sensei?" he asked. "Are you saying I don't know what's going on in my own dojo?"

Gavin sighed. He removed his belt and tossed it on the desk.

"Can we please discuss this as friends? I'm not suggesting you're not doing your job properly, but be fair, Dean. How can you possibly know enough about these guys when your job takes you out of the dojo so often? I'm with them all the time."

Dean conceded and removed his belt too. The two of them sat down and regarded each other over the desk.

"Dean, please," said Gavin. "You only have to look at the way he handled himself today. If he was as immature as you say he is, do you really think he would have taken that belt and fallen in at the back of the class the way he did?"

Dean leaned back in the chair and steepled his fingers. He lifted a foot onto the desk and swung the swivel chair in time to the ticking of the clock. "He won't be back, you know."

"Bullshit!" exploded Gavin. "He came into this dojo as a snotty nosed five year old and he's dedicated the last ten and a half years of his life to working his guts out to get where he is today." Gavin leapt up. "There's no way that kid will throw that away. He'll be back in here on Monday and he will work as hard as you can push him for as long as you can push him." Gavin stabbed his finger on the desk. "Even if you make him work though every *kyu* grade again to earn that shodan, he'll do it. You'll see."

Dean nodded. "Fair enough," he said. "I'll give him the benefit of the doubt. If he walks into this dojo on Monday and trains in that white belt, I'll personally tie this one back around his waist, in front of the entire class." He waved Tristan's belt at Gavin.

"Right," said Gavin. "And if he doesn't I'll buy your beers for the next three months."

Tristan slammed his bedroom door. He tossed his training bag onto the floor, kicked it violently into the corner then flung himself face down on the bed. A moment later there was a gentle knock on the door and it came open a crack.

"Tris? Are you okay?" He didn't respond.

His mother came into the room and sat on the bed. "Bad day?" she asked.

"Not good," he said into the pillow. "And I don't want to talk about it."

"All right," she said. "I'll call you when supper's ready."

"I'm not hungry."

"You will be by the time it's ready. See you later then," she stood up.

He waited for the door to close, then screamed out his frustration into the pillow before turning onto his side and flinging it against the door.

Elize was worried. Tristan hadn't touched his food. "Come on," she said. "I don't cook for the fun of it, you know. Eat up."

He picked up his fork and prodded at a pea. "I'm not hungry," he said, tracing round a bright sunflower on the tablecloth with the back of his fork.

Brett looked up from his own meal. "Are you not well?" he asked.

"I'm just not hungry," snapped Tristan.

"Don't speak to your father like that! Where are your manners?"

Tristan pushed his chair back violently, scattering peas across the table and sending cutlery clattering to the floor. "Why can't you just leave me alone?" he yelled and fled the room, slamming the door behind him.

Elize leapt up from the table.

"Leave him, Elize," said Brett mildly. "Finish your meal and I'll go and talk to him later."

"Huh, talk to him!" she snorted. "Honestly Brett, you're too soft with that boy. He came home in a filthy mood and he's been shut up in his room all evening and now he acts like a savage at the supper table and you'll *talk* to him!"

Brett poured two glasses of *Kanonkop Paul Sauer* and handed one to the fuming Elize. "I'll sort it out after supper," he said. "Now, just calm down and enjoy your food."

Elize took a large swallow of the wine and felt it ease her temper. Her strict Afrikaans upbringing was a frequent cause of tension between her and her mild mannered husband when it came to the disciplining of their son. She stood up from the table and began to clear the plates.

"Leave that," said Brett. "Tris made the mess, he'll clean it up."

She sighed. "I don't know why you don't give him a good hiding and get it over with."

"I would if I thought he deserved it," said Brett. "Come on Elize, he's a teenage boy, and he's got a lot going on at the moment. Kids are under pressure these days and he just hasn't learned to handle his emotions yet. Besides, he's too old for a hiding."

"Nonsense," snorted Elize. "My brother was 19 the last time pa took the *sjambok* to him."

Brett raised his eyebrows and opened his mouth but Elize was on a roll.

"You spoil that boy and now he's turning into a... a *skollie*. A hoodlum!" she said.

"He's not turning into a hoodlum, love," said Brett. "He's just pushing the boundaries a bit. He'll come round."

As if on cue, Tristan pushed the dining room door open and came in. "I'm sorry, Dad," he said.

Despite the warm and humid sub-tropical evening he was wearing a jersey. He pulled it tightly around him and turned to his mother. "*Ek's jammer, Ma.*" I'm sorry. "I'll clean the dining room and the kitchen," he said, pushing his hair behind his ear.

"Yes, you will!"

Brett picked up the wine bottle and ushered Elize out of the room. "I rest my case," he said as they settled in front of the television.

It was after eleven thirty when Tristan finally got into bed. He was about to turn off the light when there was a knock on the door.

"May I have a minute?" his father asked.

"Okay," he replied.

Brett came in and sat on the bed. "Is everything okay with you?" he asked. "That was a rather dramatic way of excusing yourself from the table tonight."

Tristan groaned and pulled the duvet over his head. "I'm sorry," he mumbled. "I had a crap day. I was just upset."

"Anything you want to talk about?"

"No!" he said, turning the quilt back down. "I just want to go to sleep."

He wanted to forget the day had ever happened, and he needed to figure out a way to get back on the right side of Dean.

Chapter Seven

Sunday dawned bright and warm. Tristan hadn't slept well and was glad of a day without training.

"Tristan, don't you have something to do?" asked Elize. "I can't put up with that television on all day." She set a dewy glass of milky iced coffee on a coaster at his elbow.

Tristan looked at it with disdain. He flicked the television off with the remote and hauled himself out of the chair.

"Why don't you drink your coffee then call Rico and go to the beach for the day?"

"Not in the mood," said Tristan.

"Why not?" she asked. "It's lovely out there."

"I'm tired and I don't feel like doing anything,"

"Tristan, sit down," said Elize.

He dropped back into the enormous leather chair.

"Just what's going on with you these days?" she asked, sitting on the wide chair arm and resting a hand on his shoulder. He shrugged it off and picked up the remote again, flicking at the on button with his thumb. The TV blared.

Elize snatched the remote from his hand, turning it off and tossing it onto the sofa. "Well?" she asked.

"Nothing!" he snapped.

"Tristan, I'm your mother. I know when there's something wrong."

"No, you don't. You don't care!" he yelled. He shot out of the chair sending a scatter cushion spinning, like a burnt orange Catherine wheel.

The iced coffee teetered and fell. The creamy liquid danced with the shattered glass on the slasto floor.

Tristan turned on his mother. "You have no idea what's going on in my life. You don't give a shit," he snarled. "You don't even know that I don't drink milk. You didn't even notice that I stopped eating meat when I was seven!"

Elize remained seated. Her face pale, her fingernails bleaching white as she gripped her knees with her hands. "Tristan, you were nine," she said. "And of course I noticed. I thought it was just a phase. I thought you'd grow out of it if I didn't make a fuss."

Elize locked her eyes onto his. "And," she said. "That iced coffee was made specially with very expensive rice milk! Now, are you going to tell me what's bothering you or am I going to have to get your father involved?"

"No," Tristan said, storming out of the room to avoid further interrogation.

He went outside. His mother would wait for his father to come in rather than go looking for him but he still felt a pang of concern. He knew he could only push Brett so far, and he knew the last couple of days had brought him close to the line. Today he may well have stepped into touch.

The soothing scent of warm earth and frangipani eased his mood. He decided to get to his father before his mother did.

He found him in the garage tinkering with the car. Tristan worried when Brett did that. He'd had little faith in his father's ability as a mechanic since the day the car had stopped dead on Breville Drive, spewing steam from under the bonnet in the middle of rush hour. He walked round the garage picking up tools, examining them and putting them down again.

Brett's voice called out from somewhere in the engine. "Tris? Pass me that lead light please," he said, holding out his hand.

Tristan picked up the light and shoved it in his father's hand. He went to the wall and flicked it on at the socket. "Dad," he said, intending to bring up the incident with his mother. His nerve failed him. "Can I borrow a board, please?" he asked, instead. "I think I want to try surfing again."

Brett put the light down and emerged from the innards of the ancient Mercedes. He walked over to the rack of surfboards on the back wall of the garage. "Well, that's good to hear," he said. "Take one off the beginners' rack."

As well as professional lawyer and amateur mechanic, Brett was a keen surfer. But for a serious knee injury in his teens, he could have gone pro. He still taught surfing on occasion and had a good selection of starter boards.

"Don't take a shortboard, you'll kill yourself." Brett had tried, in vain, to teach Tristan to surf. He had the sense of balance and the feel for the board, but the interest just wasn't there. "And don't even look at Tallulah! Or I'll kick you from here to Cape Town."

Tallulah. Brett's pride and joy, shaped by the late Darren "Dingo" Uys, one of South Africa's top shapers. Tallulah was the board Brett had won his last competition on and he'd never ridden her since.

Tristan resented his father's insinuation that he wasn't capable of riding a decent board. He studied the rack on the wall.

"And, Tris," said Brett, wiping his hands on an oily old rag. "Stay this side of the Rock, okay? I want the lifeguards to be able to see you."

That did it. "Yeah, okay," he said. He watched his father retreat into the house and then grabbed the top board off the shortboard rack and trotted down the driveway.

There was a reasonable swell for the time of year and there were quite a few surfers out in the line up. Tristan looked down the beach towards Shark Rock. It wasn't so crowded that side and, ignoring his father's request, he headed along the shore.

Tristan removed his T shirt and tossed it onto the beach. He kicked a heap of sand over it to prevent the stiff offshore taking it out to sea.

The water was cooler than he was expecting and balancing on the board was more difficult than he remembered. He paddled out, giving the other surfers a reasonably wide berth. He didn't surf often, but he knew that localism was rife on a break like Shark Rock and he didn't want an altercation.

He saw the other surfers watching him. They seemed to be holding back, waiting to see what the new kid would do with a wave. A new set came rolling in and he took a chance.

Karen van Wyk

He paddled hard and, as he felt the board begin to lift, he popped quickly to his feet.

Shit, wax! As his foot slipped Tristan remembered he'd forgotten to wax the board. With his weight too far forward, the nose pearled downwards dipping below the surface. The swell behind him tipped the board and pitched him head first into the trough of the wave.

The full weight of the water crashed down on top of him, holding him under. His shoulder hit the reef, jarring precious air from his burning lungs. Pain shot down his arm leaving it hanging uselessly in the churning water.

He opened his eyes and tried to see the surface. He could feel that his leash was still attached to his surfboard as it dragged him along the seabed.

Bouncing along the sand, he hit the reef again and felt the skin tear from his exposed back. His consciousness began to slip as he tumbled again and again in the dark underbelly of the wave.

Tristan came to on the sand. An angry surfer, with green hair, was kneeling beside him.

"What the hell did you think you were doing?" the surfer yelled. Tristan blinked up at him. He was dizzy and it took him a moment to realise that the rushing sound in his ears was the sound of the ocean breaking next to him.

He struggled to sit up. His chest heaved and he coughed up a mouthful of foul tasting liquid. He spat it onto the sand and looked at the surfer.

"Prick," said green hair. "You could have killed yourself. Have you ever even been on a surfboard before?" He glared at Tristan. "Do you have any idea how close to the reef you are when you come down the face of a wave out there?"

"I do now," said Tristan, gingerly poking at the raw, fiery graze around his ribs.

"Here, let me see," said the surfer, roughly pulling him forward. "Jesus Christ, man," he said. "That's got to sting like hell. This yours?" He pulled Tristan's T shirt from the sand.

He nodded. The surfer got up and waded into the white water. He soaked the shirt and brought it, dripping, back to Tristan. He squeezed the water out down his back.

"Ow, don't," he yelped, the salt water burning like a jellyfish. "That really hurts."

"Here," said green hair, tossing the wet shirt into his hand. "That's got most of the sand out. Now, go home to mommy and let her get you cleaned up properly." He yanked his surfboard out of the sand and started back to the water.

He bent down and picked something out of the foam. "Yours, I believe," he said, sending the broken nose of Tristan's surfboard spinning like a frisbee, to land at his side.

Tristan knew Jonno would be at the workshop. He usually worked Sundays, preferring to take his time off when everyone else was at work. He pushed the door open, feeling the creak rather than hearing it, the sound masked by a blast of noise from within.

A shaft of faded sunlight struggled through a single, salt-coated, window high to his left. It cut a diagonal across the room, spotlighting a dancing column of dust.

He closed the door and stood, waiting for his eyes to adjust. He crossed the small makeshift office and laid the broken board on the counter. Reaching over, he yanked the stereo's power plug from the wall, instantly silencing *Credence Clearwater Revival*. The tinny shriek of a power tool, suddenly audible from behind a heavy, dust-laden curtain, stopped too.

"You'd better be from the Noise Action Task Group or have a death wish!" called a voice.

The curtain twitched and Jonno Steyn ducked into the room, extracting a pair of bright orange ear protectors from a long blond dreadlock.

"Tris, howzit?" he said, genuine delight lifting his voice. "What brings you here?"

"Just wanted to see my favourite uncle," said Tristan, brushing the counter's dust from the front of his still damp shirt. "Oh yeah, and that." He pointed to the surfboard.

Jonno picked up the broken nose. "Christ in a tree!" he exclaimed. "Tris, is this Tallulah?"

He nodded.

"Please tell me it wasn't you? He's going to have your balls in a vice!"

"Uh huh," he said. "Can you fix it?"

"Short answer," said Jonno. "Not a snowball's." He flicked at the jagged fibreglass with a thumbnail.

"And the long answer?" asked Tristan, not quite ready to give up hope.

Jonno put the nose down and leaned on the counter. "Not a snowball's chance in the Sahara," he said, resting his chin in his hands. "All I can do is shape him a new one, but it won't be the same. He's going kill you." He nodded to the back room. "Come on, let's go in here and see if we can make a plan."

Jonno wiped the dust off a couple of high stools and placed them at his work bench. He ran a forearm over the bench clearing the thickest from there too.

"You're going to die from this stuff one day," said Tristan, drawing circles in the remaining dust.

"We're all going to die from something, Tris. Might as well be something you love as something you hate that takes you out."

Jonno reached under the bench and pulled a cold can of Windhoek and a foot-long *boerewors* roll from a small bar fridge.

"You hungry?" he asked, pointing to the hotdog.

Tristan grimaced. "No thanks, that stuff's made of sheep's nostrils and sawdust," he said.

"Uh uh," grunted Jonno, taking a bite. "This one's cows' o-rings." He munched contentedly. "There's some Coke in here somewhere," he said, scanning the room. "It's not cold though."

"Hmm," grunted Tristan. "God forbid it should take up any of your beer space in the fridge. Anyway, I just swallowed a couple of litres of Indian Ocean. I'm good fluid wise."

Jonno pulled the tab on the beer and took a long draught. He prized his hotdog open, examining the inside. "They never put enough ketchup on these things," he said, removing the sausage and tossing the bread into the bin. "I'll bloody starve now."

"Why don't you come over for supper tonight?" asked Tristan, brightening a little. "Then you can tell dad you'll make him a better board."

"Not likely."

"But why? You haven't been round for ages."

"Because your mother hates me, is why."

"She's not my biggest fan either," said Tristan. "But she still feeds me. Anyway, she doesn't hate you, she just thinks you're a bad influence."

"Hey!" snapped Jonno. "Apparently she's right."

Tristan swallowed the mouthful of lager with a grimace.

"How old are you?"

"Almost sixteen," he said, taking another gulp.

"Give me that!" said Jonno, yanking the can from his hand, slopping lager over the front of his shirt and down his arm. "What happened to the whole, 'my body's a temple and I don't eat dead stuff and junk' thing?"

Tristan wiped his mouth with the back of his hand. "I never said anything about my body being a temple, I just prefer it if my food never had a face." He added eyes and a down turned mouth to one of his circles.

"You know," said Jonno, waving the sausage at him. "At least you're sure meat is dead. Think about it," he went on, studying it closely. "How do you know when you're peeling a carrot that you're not skinning it alive?" He launched the empty beer can onto a pile in the corner, sending several more skimming across the floor.

Tristan pulled a face and shook his head. "How much of that pile did you build today?"

Jonno didn't respond. He took another two beers out of the fridge and opened one, pushing the other over to Tristan.

He plucked at the ring-pull but didn't open it.

"If you really want to try that stuff," said Jonno, pointing at the can. "Do it now where I can keep an eye on you. I don't want you passing out under a bloody tree somewhere with your mates."

Tristan pushed it back. "No thanks," he said. "I'm in enough *kak* as it is without adding drunk and disorderly to the list."

Jonno ruffled Tristan's hair. "Cheer up," he said. "Brett never rides this thing anyway. Let's have a look." He picked up Tallulah's nose. "Maybe I can smooth the edges a bit and do a patch job and a re glass."

Jonno caught his dreadlocks and tied them in a knot behind his head. He slipped the ear protectors round his neck and picked up his power sander.

"You're supposed to wear those on your ears," said Tristan. "You'll be deaf by the time you're thirty."

"According to you, little lord doom and gloom, I'll be *dead* before I'm thirty. So what's your problem?"

Tristan sighed. "I'll be lucky to make sixteen when dad sees his board."

Jonno pulled the ageing Beetle onto the driveway and eased up the handbrake. The engine died as soon as he removed his foot from the accelerator.

"Well, go on," he said. "You've done nothing but moan about her since you got in, so now get out."

Tristan unfastened his safety belt and reached for the door handle.

"Hang on," said Jonno, leaning over him. "I'll get that. If you don't do it just right the window falls out of the bottom of the door."

Tristan shook his head. "You're a menace on the roads, you know that?" he said. "This thing should be melted down and turned into a fridge."

"Excuse me," said Jonno. "Meryl is sensitive. Don't talk about her like that."

Jonno had named the Beetle after Meryl Streep because he liked '*her lines'*. Tristan was never quite sure whether he meant the car's lines, the actress's, or both. Or, for that matter, what he even meant by lines.

"*Kom, roer jou gat*!" Shift your arse, said Jonno. "Go warn your mother I'm here and I'll try and talk your old man round before you show him this."

Jonno took Tallulah's nose from the back seat and planted it in Tristan's hand. He had smoothed the jagged edges but the wet foam would have to dry out before it could be patched.

Tristan was dreading facing his father.

Chapter Eight

Elize screamed, throwing herself between her husband and her son. "Brett no!"

Caught completely off guard, Tristan let out a surprised yelp and stumbled against the sofa. Losing his balance, he fell onto the small coffee table then landed hard on his side on the floor. He instinctively curled up to present a smaller target.

Jonno's attempt to talk Brett round had only added fuel to the fire. He lunged at Brett pinning his arms to his sides.

"Jesus Christ, Brett," he said. "There was no need for that."

Brett yanked himself free from Jonno's grip and stood, rubbing his knuckles.

"Get him out of here," he hissed at the sobbing Elize.

Jonno and Elize helped Tristan to his feet. He held his filthy T shirt to his face to stem the flow of blood.

"I'll talk to him," said Jonno, quietly to Elize. "You sort Tris out. And don't worry, I'll stay until he's cooled off."

Elize led Tristan out of the room.

"Hell's teeth, Brett!" said Jonno. "Have you lost it completely? It was only a bloody surfboard!"

Brett crossed the lounge to the bar and poured himself a glass of single malt.

"Is that a good idea?" asked Jonno, righting the coffee table. "You know that stuff makes you aggressive. And you did just wallop your son in the face."

Brett turned to face him. He pointed the glass at Jonno. "He's lucky that's all he got," he said.

"Brett be cool, *boet*," said Jonno. "He didn't do it on purpose."

"J, don't even go there! The last thing I said to him before he went out this morning was that he was to take one of the novice boards. I warned him not to take a shortboard and I specifically told him not to touch this one." He snatched Tallulah's broken nose from the chair arm and tossed it aside.

"It's not just about him breaking the bloody board. It's about him blatantly disobeying me and about him putting himself in serious danger. For God's sake, sometimes I think that boy has a vacuum in his head." He sat on the sofa.

Jonno helped himself to a beer and sat in an armchair, his legs stretched out in front of him.

"You know," said Brett. "He's been a bloody brat for the past week. In trouble at school, in trouble at the dojo, went off on his mother this morning. I just don't know what to do with him. I've tried to be tolerant. Damn it, I even defended him when his mother lost her cool and..."

"You feel like shit, don't you?" needled Jonno.

"Yes," said Brett. "I feel worse than shit."

"Well, you wanted a kid. I would have thought a vile little brother like me would have put you off."

Brett swallowed the contents of his glass. "Ah, but what you forget," he said. "Is that I'd already left home by the time you were six. You were still cute then."

"Hmm," said Jonno. "And Tristan's just about the age I was when I turned into a little Hitler. Oh, the joys of parenthood," he said, shaking his head.

Tristan sat up in bed. His face felt heavy and hot. His cheekbone hurt and his nose was blocked. He had to breathe through his mouth. His head and neck ached.

He was numb with shock. Brett had only raised a hand to him twice before, and no one had ever hit him in the face. Not even in the dojo.

He pressed a finger to his tender cheekbone. He was beyond tired but couldn't bring himself to rest. There was the pain. There was the shock. There was the anger. But, most of all, there was the overwhelming feeling of misery.

Tristan couldn't get Andre out of his mind. Was this how he felt? Was this why he picked on other kids? Was bullying and causing trouble for others the only way he could feel any sense of power?

He laid down, switched off the light and closed his eyes. Hot tears slid from under his eyelids and ran down his face He sobbed bitterly.

He cried for the mess he'd made in training and for breaking Tallulah. He cried for pushing his father to the point of violence and for misjudging his mother.

But most of all, he cried for a boy he really didn't know at all.

Chapter Nine

Tristan left the house early. He didn't want to run into his father. By the end of the third period he was feeling awful. He hadn't slept, he'd eaten nothing but a banana and two packets of Mint Imperials since Friday lunch time and Andre Turner was not in chemistry class.

He caught up with Rico at first break. "Hey, Ric," he said dropping down onto the grass in the shade of a Jacaranda tree.

"Howzit," said Rico, looking up from the latest copy of his surf mag, *ZigZag*. "Did you do... Geez, Tris, what happened to you? Not another orange belt, I hope."

Tristan reached over and took Rico's apple from his hand. He touched his swollen face. "No," he said, biting into the apple. "Not even graded. But, to be fair, he was bigger than me."

Rico's mouth dropped open.

"No, seriously," said Tristan. "It's nothing, just a bit of a knock. Shit happens sometimes." He swallowed the apple and took another bite.

Rico nodded. "Just don't let bully boy Turner see it or he'll have a field day."

Tristan frowned and turned the apple in his hand.

"Um, excuse me," said Rico. "My breakfast, please?" He held out his hand.

"Sorry," said Tristan, handing it back. "I'm starving."

Rico took a bite and gave the apple back to him.
"Was Andre in your history class this morning?" asked Tristan, around a mouthful of apple.

Rico shook his head. "No," he said. "Probably too scared to come back in case you rip into him again."

"Stop it," snapped Tristan. "Rico, leave him alone. We don't know anything about him! He..."

Rico looked up sharply.

"What's biting you?" he asked. "Since when do you defend the school's biggest creep?"

Tristan tossed the apple against the trunk of the tree and got to his feet. "Just drop it, Rico," he snapped and stalked off.

He got through the rest of the day on a cocktail of paracetamol, sugar and caffeine. He washed the tablets down with cola every three hours instead of four, but still the headache wouldn't shift.

He avoided Rico at lunch break and as soon as the final bell rang he rushed out of the school grounds and headed for Marine Park Road.

This time he was going to find out what was going on. This time he was going to do something.

Tristan pushed the doorbell for the fourth time and knocked as well. The curtains were still closed and nobody came to the door.

He dragged his feet as he went back to the gate, looking over his shoulder every few steps. He closed the gate behind him and walked back down the street.

As he neared the end of the block he saw Andre round the corner in front of him. He was carrying two plastic shopping bags. They looked heavy. "Andre," he called, breaking into a trot.

Andre looked up, startled. He turned and walked quickly in the opposite direction.

"Andre, please wait," called Tristan, pulling up alongside him.

Andre spun to face him. His face was no longer swollen and his pale skin had taken on the sickly yellows and greens of old bruises, his lip was darkly scabbed. He backed up. "Piss off, Steyn," he said. "You're not welcome around here."

"I want to help you, Andre," said Tristan. "I..."

"Help!" spat Andre. "Help with what exactly? Just bugger off home and stop harassing me."

"But, Andre..."

Andre swung round and, as he did, the bag in his left hand split. Two sachets of milk and a bottle of vodka hit the ground at his feet. One of the sachets burst open, spraying his shoes with flecks of white liquid. Andre descended on the vodka bottle and the intact litre of milk.

"God Steyn, you idiot," he erupted. "Now look what you've made me do." His face had turned as white as the spilt milk and the fading bruises stood out like rotting vegetation.

Tristan felt terrible. He had wanted so desperately to help but had only made matters worse. He reached into his pocket and pulled out two R5 coins. "Here." He held out the money. "It's all I have but it will get some more milk."

Andre knocked the coins from his hand. "You really don't get it, do you Steyn. I don't want your bloody charity. Just piss off home and leave me alone."

Tristan was hurt and suddenly angry. "Fine!" he yelled. "I only wanted to help but Rico was right. You are just a creep. No wonder you don't have any friends!"

Tristan turned and ran - straight into the road.

He didn't see the car. But he heard Andre scream his name, he heard the screech of rubber on tarmac, he heard the thud as the car mounted the pavement and, as he turned, he saw Andre flung high into the air.

Still clinging to one of the plastic bags, Andre somersaulted, seemingly boneless, and landed with a sickening thump on the roof of the car. His body bounced. The bag, ripped from his hand by the impact, caught Tristan hard on the shoulder knocking him off balance.

A packet of sugar burst sending a sparkling cascade of tiny crystals arcing in the sunlight. Tristan tasted their sweetness as he fell. He hit the ground only seconds before Andre did.

"Andre, noooooo!" He heard himself scream as Andre slammed to earth and skidded across the dry grass verge coming to a sudden halt against his chest. "Nooooo," he screamed again. "No, please!" Tristan was on his knees holding Andre's head in his hands. "Please," he sobbed. "I'm so sorry."

He saw Andre's eyes roll back into his head and his body begin to convulse before he felt a firm pair of hands lift him away.

"Well Sensei," said Dean. "It looks like you're going to be out of pocket for a while."

Gavin dug in his wallet and pulled out R500 in R100 notes. "If you need more than that you're drinking too much!" he snapped, slamming it down on the bar of the Blue Porpoise.

Dean picked up the crisp blue notes and rolled them into a wad before stuffing them into Gavin's shirt pocket. "Come on, mate," he said. "I'm as disappointed as you are that he didn't turn up. I don't want your money."

"A deal's a deal," said Gavin handing it back.

Dean shrugged and took the money. "Would it make you feel better if I gave him a ring tonight?" he asked. "See if I can sort things out with him."

"No," said Gavin. "It wouldn't." He looked up. "I really thought I knew him better than that. I was so sure he would be back."

Tristan began to shake again. Hot black coffee slopped from the plastic cup onto his wrist. The woman reached out and steadied his hand, gently easing the cup from his grip. She placed it on the blue metal chair next to him.

He picked it up again. He didn't want the coffee, he wanted something to do with his hands. His mind wrestled with sticky images of Andre's body, landing like a sandbag and slamming into his chest. He still had Andre's blood on the front of his shirt.

"It was my fault," he said. "It should have hit me. I sh..."

The woman shushed him firmly, but gently. He wasn't sure who she was. He'd given a statement to two police officers earlier and he'd been examined by a doctor who had given him an injection to calm him.

Again the woman asked for the details of someone she could contact for him.

"No!" he said. "I..." He couldn't find the words to tell her what he wanted to say. "Could I use the bathroom please?" he asked, instead.

The woman ushered him down the corridor. "It's just through

there," she said. "Come back when you're done and we'll try to get you home."

He nodded and pushed open the swinging double doors. Beyond the doors was another long white corridor. The toilets were to his left but he turned right and followed the arrows to the exit.

He stepped outside the hospital and breathed in the heavy, salt scented air. It was dark and pouring with rain. He wondered if his mother would be worried yet, or if it was still early enough for her to think he'd gone home with Rico and then straight to training. He did that sometimes.

Rico, he thought. It took him over an hour to walk to the house. When he got to the door he hesitated. He was soaked to the skin and filthy. He wondered what Rico's parents would think but he was cold and thirsty and desperately tired. He knocked.

Rico's mother opened the door. "Tristan!" she exclaimed. "Sweetie, what happened to you?"

Lorna Martins took his hand and led him into the kitchen. "Sit down and I'll make you a hot drink" she said, guiding him to a chair.

"Rico will you come in here a minute please?" she called. "Tristan, what happened to you?"

He knew he was being rude but he found himself unable to answer.

Rico came into the kitchen. "Did you call me, M... Tris!" He stopped dead in the doorway.

"Rico, go and run a hot bath for Tristan and get him some clean clothes to put on," said Lorna. "I'm going to phone his mother."

"No!" shouted Tristan. "No, please don't, I don't want to go home."

Rico and Lorna exchanged glances. She pulled up a chair and sat facing him, taking both of his hands in hers. "Sweetie," she said. "You don't have to go home. You can stay as long as you want to, but I do have to let your mom know you're here. She'll be worried sick."

Tristan sniffed. "Please don't," he begged. "She thinks I'm at training, I sometimes stay late. She won't be worried. I'll call her later."

"Tristan, my boy." A rich baritone boomed behind him. He leapt to his feet and turned to face Edward Martins. He had always been a little afraid of him, though he was never sure why. The complete opposite of the small, bird-like Lorna, Rico's father was a robust, fleshy man with a loud voice and an even louder laugh.

"Good grief," he said, eyeing Tristan's bloodied shirt. "I would hate to see what the other guy looks like."

"He's dead!" blurted Tristan. "I killed him."

Elize opened the front door. "Oh!" she said and immediately felt foolish. "Can I help you?"

The two young police officers looked at each other.

She felt an uneasy knot begin to pull at her stomach.

The taller of the two cleared his throat. He ran a hand over brush cut, reddish hair. "Ma'am," he said. "Are you Mrs," he consulted his note book. "Are you Mrs Elize Steyn?"

"Yes," she said. "What is it? Is it Tristan?"

"Ma'am, is your son home at the moment?"

She breathed a sigh of relief. "No," she said. "He's not."

The two officers looked at each other again.

Relief turned to a cold hard stone in her belly. "What?" she asked. "What is it?"

Brett came up behind her. "Who are you keeping on the doorstep at this time of night?" he asked. "Oh!"

Elize turned to him. "They're looking for Tristan," she said.

He invited the officers into the house. "What's he done?" he asked.

"Sir, Ma'am," the shorter of the two took charge. "As far as we know, your son is fine."

Elize pressed herself against Brett. *As far as we know?*

"But, there was an accident this afternoon, a boy was hit by a motor vehicle. Your son was with him. He was very upset and he left the hospital before they could contact you. We were hoping he came straight home."

Elize looked at Brett. "Oh my God, Brett," she said covering her mouth with her hand. "Rico. He would have been with Rico."

"Ma'am?" queried the officer.

She shook her head, trying to clear her racing mind. "Rico Martins," she said. "Tristan's best friend. They're always together."

"Ma'am, no," said the tall officer. "The boy's name ..." He consulted his book again. "Turner, Andre Turner."

"I'll call Lorna," said Brett. "See if Tris went there."

Tristan sat at the kitchen table in a pair of Rico's pyjamas. They were ridiculously big. He fiddled with the sleeve, rolling a cuff to just above his wrist.

Lorna sat beside him, her hand on his arm. She had gently coaxed the details of the accident from him and now they all sat in silence.

Tristan had refused Edward's offer of something to eat but had managed half a glass of fresh orange juice.

"Can I tempt you with some of mom's apple pie, at least?" asked Rico.

He shook his head. "No thanks.".

"You have to eat something," said Rico. "You swiped my breakfast this morning because you were starving and then you pitched it at a tree."

Tristan looked up from his sleeve. "Sorry about that," he mumbled.

"Leave him, Rico," said Lorna. "He'll eat when he's ready. I'll make us all a drink."

She filled the kettle then placed it on the drainer when the phone began to ring. "Sort this will you, love," she said to Rico, and went to answer it.

Hello?... Oh, hi there." She turned to look at Tristan. "Yes,

Brett," she said. "Don't worry, he's here."

Brett and Elize sat on Tristan's bed. He hadn't spoken since they had picked him up. Elize took his hand in hers and gently caressed his fingers.

The dark bruise on his pale face twisted at Brett's conscience. "Tris," he said. "It wasn't your fault." He turned to Elize. "Could I have a minute with him please?"

Elize hesitated. Tristan gripped her hand, his eyes widened, pleading.

Brett dropped his head into his hands and sighed. "Fine," he said, getting up. He walked to the door.

"No, wait," called Tristan. He released his mother's hand and sat back against the pillows.

Elize rose and leaned over to kiss the top of his head. "I'll go and make you some Rooibos," she said. "It'll help you sleep."

She closed the door behind her and Brett sat back down on the bed. "Tris," he began. "I'm so sorry I..."

"Dad, don't. Please." Tristan took a deep breath. "I was really stupid. I could have killed myself as well as Tallulah. I deserved a smack in the mouth."

Brett shook his head and touched Tristan's cheek. "No you didn't," he said. "A good hiding, maybe. But never my fist in your face. It was unforgivable." He saw Tristan's eyes glaze and his mind disengage.

"Dad, Andre... I think his..." He dissolved into tears.

Brett was completely out of his depth and wished Elize was back with the tea. "Tris, I'm sure Andre will be fine. He..."

Tristan shook his head, his eyes haunted. "No," he said. "No, he won't, I killed him," he sobbed. "I killed him, Dad. It was my fault. The car should have hit me." He teetered on the brink of hysteria.

Brett caught him by the shoulders and shook him roughly. "Tristan!" he snapped. "Tristan, stop it!" You didn't kill anyone."

Tristan's mouth came open but he closed it again without

speaking.

"Tris, Andre's not dead," Brett said. "Your mom called the hospital. He's in intensive care. He's had surgery and he's still very ill, but he's stable."

He scanned his son's face for signs of comprehension but saw only confusion. He eased him back against the pillows and pulled the duvet up to his chin.

Tristan was asleep before Elize returned with the tea.

Tristan was up early the next morning. He ate a good breakfast and had more colour in his face than he'd had for a week.

"Are you sure you want to go to school?" asked Elize for the umpteenth time. "You really don't have to."

"I'm fine, Mom. I want to go," he said, slinging his school bag onto his back. "I'm taking my bike so I can go to the hospital after school."

"Tris," said Elize. "I'm not sure that's a good idea. Not yet, love."

"Ma, I'm going," he said. "The worst they can do is throw me out."

Chapter Ten

Everyday, as soon as the final bell sounded Tristan went to the hospital. Everyday the sister shook her head sadly.

"Sorry," she would say. "No change yet."

Everyday he sat outside Andre's room and did his homework. And everyday, at 6pm, he left the hospital just before Kathryn Turner arrived.

On the Friday afternoon Sister Napier met him at the door, her face lit by a huge beam. "I've got some good news for you today," she said. "Doctor decreased the sedation this morning and your friend has said a few words."

"Can I see him?" asked Tristan.

Sister Napier tilted her head and looked at him. He saw the conflict in her kindly eyes. "Well, you're not a relative so I shouldn't really let you, but go on," she said. "Five minutes won't hurt."

She led him to the door and stopped, her hand on the handle. He thought she had changed her mind and his heart sank.

"I have to warn you," she said. "He is very ill and you might get a shock."

He nodded.

Sister Napier opened the door and popped her head round it. "Hi, Andre," she said. "I've got a friend of yours who wants to see you." She stepped aside, guiding Tristan through the door with a hand on his shoulder. "Five minutes," she said. "No more."

"Thank you," said Tristan as she pulled the door closed behind him.

He started at the sight of Andre lying in the high intensive care bed. One leg was strung above him in traction, the other inside a metal frame under a thin hospital sheet. There was a tube in his nose and several more in his arms.

Pain and fever had burned the flesh from his body and his skin was like ageing putty.

Andre looked at him for a moment before turning his head

away. "Get out, Steyn," he said. "I don't want you here."

Tristan crossed the room to the bed. The rank smell of illness mingled with disinfectant. He swallowed hard. "Tough," he said. "It's my fault you're in this mess and I'm not going to let you wallow in it and feel sorry for yourself on your own. I need you back at school. I missed my trip to de Lange's office this week."

Andre almost smiled.

"Andre, I'm so sorry. I..."

"Don't Steyn," said Andre, turning to face him. "If you insist on being a pain in the arse and staying here, just sit over there and do it quietly."

Tristan pulled the chair round so he could face him. "Can I bring you anything? Some books or music to listen to?"

Andre looked at him. "What books you got?"

He was suddenly embarrassed by his limited reading tastes. "Mostly martial arts stuff," he said. "But I'll get you anything you want."

"I'll try a martial arts one," said Andre. "When can you bring it?"

Tristan thought a moment before rooting in his school bag. He pulled out his precious copy of Mas Oyama's *Essential Karate*. It was a book he had wanted for years. His mother had finally sourced an original copy in London and paid over R500 for it. He hadn't even finished reading it but he handed it to Andre. "Here's one you can start with," he said.

Andre turned it in his hands. "Thanks," he said, dropping it onto his chest. "I'll have a look later."

Tristan nodded. He could see that Andre was tired. He got up and moved his chair back to the wall then took the book and placed it on the bedside locker and straightened Andre's sheet.

"I'll see you tomorrow," he said quietly. But Andre was already asleep.

A week later Andre was moved out of intensive care. He was in a room on his own and the nurses allowed Tristan to spend the afternoons with him. He began bringing him school work to do and they sat quietly studying together.

"What did you get for number six?" asked Andre. "The one about the anhydrous copper sulphate."

Tristan paged back in his book. "B," he said. "But it was just a random stab with the pen. I haven't got a clue."

"Oh," said Andre. "I thought it was C."

"Yeah?" He scribbled out his B and marked C with a tick."

"Steyn," said Andre. "There's no guarantee it's right so don't blame me if you cop hell from Price."

The two of them finished their homework in silence then Tristan packed the books back into his bag. "Oh, here," he said. "I brought you some martial arts mags. Are you sure you're interested in these? I can get you something else if you'd prefer."

"No, these are cool. Thanks," said Andre, taking the pile.

"Are you still doing karate?" he asked. "It's just that you seem to spend a hell of a lot of time here."

"Nah," said Tristan.

"You should. Michelle thought you were so cool."

Tristan flushed. He looked up from *Martial Arts Illustrated*. "Did your mom let her start training again?"

"No," said Andre. "She still thinks karate makes you violent."

"Shit," said Tristan. "It's my fault. Should I talk to her about it?"

"Oh hell, no! Not unless you fancy a bed in here too."

"But Michelle loved it. And she was coming along so well." He paused for a moment. "How is Michelle? Is everything okay at home?" It was the first time he had brought up the subject of Andre's family.

Andre turned away slightly. "She's fine. Yeah, she's good."

"Andre..."

"Don't," he said. "I don't want to talk about it."

On Monday Tristan arrived with a tub of chocolate ice cream.

"Here," he said. "I thought you must be sick of hospital food so I got you this from the shop downstairs."

"Great, thanks," said Andre. He peeled the lid of the tub back and held it out to Tristan. "You want some?"

"No, thanks," he said. "I don't eat dairy."

"You allergic?"

"Nah. Just a bit of a freak. I can't get past that whole cow's tits thing," he said with a grimace.

Andre laughed aloud. "You know, Tristan, you're a bit of a wuss, really."

He looked up. It was more the fact that Andre had finally used his first name than what he had said.

"I always thought that you were this hard as nails, *skrik vir niks*, kind of guy," said Andre. "When actually you're quite a wimp."

Tristan nodded. "Uh huh," he said. "I guess you could say that."

"Here." Andre held out a spoonful of the ice cream. Try it."

He shook his head and fished in his bag for a banana. Retrieving it he looked up, conscious of Andre's gaze.

"Tristan, thanks for coming here so often. I don't know how I would have come through this if it wasn't for you."

"God, Andre," he said, feeling awful. "You wouldn't even be here if it wasn't for me."

Andre turned and faced the wall.

"You okay?" asked Tristan. "Do you have pain? Must I get a nurse?"

Andre shook his head then turned back to Tristan. "I might have ended up here anyway," he said.

Tristan didn't understand.

"Hell, I might have ended up dead," he said. "It's actually good this happened. I need to be in here."

"But..."

"She's kicked him out," said Andre, with a sigh.

Finally Tristan understood. He nodded but remained silent.

* * *

"Rico, wait up," called Tristan, jogging to catch him.

Rico walked on without slowing. "What's wrong, Tris? Andre throw you out?"

Tristan stopped. "Come on, Rico," he said. "That's not fair." He started after him again.

Rico began to laugh and stopped walking. "Sorry mate," he said. "Couldn't resist. I was pissed at you last week but I've found myself someone better to hang out with now. So, I won't give you a hard time for dumping your best friend and I'll still tolerate your company occasionally."

"Ric, give me a break. What would you do if you were the one who as good as kicked the guy under the car? Anyway, he's pretty cool when you get to know him. You should come with me this arvie."

"No can do, sorry. I'm meeting a chick."

"Chick?" said Tristan. "Where'd you find a chick?"

Rico pointed to the school gate. "You go out there," he said. "Walk to the end of the road, turn left and walk up two blocks." He made little walking movements with his fingers. "There you will find another school, quite similar to this one," he waved his hand with a flourish at the buildings behind him before going on. "But with one major difference. It has girls! Lots of them. Oh, and a sea view too."

"Yeah, Rico, I know where they hang out," said Tristan. "I mean how did you meet one?"

Rico pulled a face. "Actually," he said. "She came round here looking for you."

"For me?" He frowned, he didn't think he knew any girls. Not girls who would come looking for him anyway.

"Who?" he demanded.

"Megan Taylor ring any bells?"

"Oh no," he groaned. "She's probably going to give me a hard time about not training."

"Serious?" said Rico. "You still not going?"

He shook his head.

"And that's where you know Megan from?"

"Yup," said Tristan, rooting in his bag and fishing out a tissue. He blew his nose. "She's from Cape Town. Only started at the dojo beginning of this term."

"If you're getting sick stay away from me," said Rico, pointing to the tissue he was stuffing in his pocket.

"Ag, it's nothing," he said. "Bit of a cold maybe. Listen, Ric, if you're seeing Megan after school just tell her I'm at the hospital everyday and can't come to training. But only if she mentions it first."

Rico shrugged. "So you two aren't... you know?"

"We aren't anything Rico. Go work your Martins magic on her if you're interested."

"Geez, Tris, what's wrong with you? She's a total cherry and she came here looking for *you*."

"Ja, Rico, to see why I'm not at training," he said. "I was supposed to be helping her with her kata."

Tristan jumped. He made a grab for the book before it slid off his desk. He'd hardly heard a word of the lesson and hoped fervently that Miss Price wasn't about to ask him a question.

"Tristan Steyn," she hissed. "Your handwriting is atrocious!" She moved in close. "And how do you spell anhydrous?"

Tristan went cold. *Oh, please, no!* He looked down at the open book. A thick red line encircled the word, along with the note 'spelling' in huge red letters in the margin.

He swallowed. "Apparently not the same way you do, miss," he said.

"No," said Miss Price. "Apparently not." She tapped a long-nailed finger onto the page. "The word anhydrous appears no fewer than four times in the printed text on that page and *still* you get it wrong!" Miss Price was on a roll. Spelling mistakes were her pet peeve and only the very brave or the very foolish didn't double check their homework before handing it in. Tristan wasn't feeling very brave.

Humiliation was Miss Price's weapon of choice. "Steyn, go to the front of the class please."

He slowly stood up. His hands began to shake and his chest squeezed tight, refusing to let in enough air. His knees threatened to buckle and leave him in a hopeless and terrified heap between the two rows of desks.

"Hurry up, boy. We don't have all day."

As he walked to the front of the class, Miss Price slipped into his seat. "Now," she said, folding her hands on the desk. "You can start by telling us all how you spell anhydrous."

Tristan shifted nervously. He felt the colour rush to his face and cleared his itching throat. He tugged at his collar which seemed to have tightened. "Um, how I spell it, miss, or how it should be spelled?" he squeaked.

Miss Price arched an immaculately groomed eyebrow. "Well, Mr Steyn, why don't you entertain the class?" she said. "And start by telling us how you spelled it!"

Suppressed giggles crept round the room.

"Sorry, miss," said Tristan. "I can't remember how I wrote it."

"Oh, my dear boy," snapped Miss Price. "Is there any hope for you? Go on then," she sighed. "Give us the benefit of your vast knowledge and tell us how the rest of the population would spell it."

Tristan's nose began to run again. He rooted in his pocket for the tissue. He sniffed and put the tissue to his nose.

"For goodness sake, Steyn! I'm only asking you to spell a simple word, not recite Tolstoy. I'm sure there's no need for tears."

The class erupted, and by the time Miss Price had called them to order the bell had rung to end the lesson. Tristan had never been so embarrassed in his entire life.

"Right," said Miss Price, raising her voice to compete with the scraping of chairs. "Tomorrow, before we begin, Steyn will teach us all how to spell anhydrous both forwards and backwards. You may leave."

Tristan wanted to rush out of the classroom and disappear

among the other students leaving their lessons, but he had to go back to his desk and collect his bag. He was still shaking as he packed his books into the canvas rucksack. Miss Price came to his side.

"Don't forget," she said. "Forwards and backwards by tomorrow. And while you're at it you can write out a page each way. It might help it stick."

"Yes, miss," he said miserably.

He skulked out of the classroom to find a group of boys hanging around outside. He turned away from them but they came up behind him. Marcus Dedekind seemed to have taken on the role of standard nine bully in Andre's absence.

"Steynie, my man, did you kiss and make up with miss in there?" he teased. He threw an arm across Tristan's shoulders.

Tristan turned sharply, knocking his arm to one side.

"He wouldn't kiss Miss Price," said Brayton Jones. "He's saving himself for when his boyfriend comes out of hospital."

Fuming, he began to walk away again.

"Ag shame," said Marcus. "The little lightie's going to cry again."

He cursed his nose as he pressed the tissue to it once more. He carried on walking.

Brayton caught him by the collar of his blazer, pulling him up short. "What's with you and the creep anyway?" he asked.

Tristan spun round slamming his shoulder into his chest. Brayton yelped and back-pedalled into the classroom wall.

Tristan pinned him there. "Just shut up about him!" he yelled. "Just shut up and leave me alone!"

"Tristan Steyn!" snapped Miss Price, stepping out into the corridor. "Come here, now. You and I are going to have a quiet word with Mr de Lange."

Tristan felt sick.

"Steyn!" said the head. "What is wrong with you? Can you please explain what is going on in that stunted little mind of yours?"

Tristan remained silent.

The head sighed. He turned to the cupboard behind his desk and reached for the cane.

"Steyn, this is the second time in a under a month that you've been in my office for fighting. I will not have it in this school."

He laid the cane on the desk. Softening a little, he continued, "Tristan, if you have a problem we need to get it sorted out. Do you want me to call your parents? Is there anything you'd like to discuss? See the guidance counsellor perhaps?"

"I would prefer you to deal with it, sir," he said.

"As you wish," said the head, picking up the cane.

Tristan followed him to the mat.

"I won't put up with any of your acrobatics this time," he said. "So you'd better behave yourself."

Acrobatics? "Yes, sir. I will."

This time he knew what was coming. This time his self control was tempered by anger, not eroded by fear, and he took the six stinging cuts with no more than a sharp intake of breath.

"That's the last time, Steyn," said the head, as Tristan stepped off the mat. "Once more and you're expelled from this school. Dismissed."

Tristan didn't go to the last two lessons. He ran out of the school gates and headed for the hospital instead. He arrived just as Andre was finishing lunch.

Andre glanced at the wall clock. "What happened?" he asked. "Bomb scare or earthquake?"

"Nah," said Tristan. "Prison break." He dropped into the chair and wished he hadn't. "Ow," he whined, shifting uncomfortably.

"What's up?" asked Andre. "You hurt yourself?"

"Cane," he replied.

"Without my input?" Andre grinned. "You rebel. Hurt?"

"Like a bitch," said Tristan, blowing his nose.

Andre tossed him the banana from his tray. "Here," he said. "It wouldn't be so bad if you had a bit more meat on you. Eat that."

"Thanks," he said, snapping the top off and pulling the skin down into four neat petals.

The door squeaked and began to open. He jumped up and turned to leave as Andre's doctor came in. Andre waved his hand.

"Uh uh," he said. "Don't go."

He looked at the doctor for confirmation.

"You want your friend to stay?" asked the doctor.

"Yes, please," said Andre.

He lowered himself back into the chair. He was uncomfortable with the doctor's presence. He'd sensed a tension as soon as the man walked in.

Andre's face was strained, his lips a thin white line against his pale skin.

The doctor flipped through his file for a third time before placing it on a stainless steel trolley next to the bed. He cast a nervous glance at Tristan and then back to Andre. "Would you prefer me to come back when your mother's here?" he asked.

Doctor Woodlane, Tristan read on his badge. He played with the name in his head. Woodlane conjured images of pleasant tree-lined walks but the atmosphere in the room was anything but pleasant.

"No," said Andre. "I want to know now."

Doctor Woodlane picked up the file and opened it again. He adjusted the rimless glasses on his nose and cleared his throat.

Tristan never understood why people wore rimless glasses.

"Andre," said the doctor. "The results of the latest tests show that we have about a six month window. If we don't operate within that time, then the pressure in your spinal cord may do permanent nerve damage."

"Which means?" asked Andre.

"It means you won't be able to take part in sports or any strenuous activities and..." He cleared his throat again. "And it may mean you being wheelchair bound."

Tristan's mind was reeling. It was his fault. He had caused the accident and now Andre was being told that he might never walk again.

Andre remained impassive. "Will I be able to play the guitar?" he asked.

"Oh yes," said the doctor. "You'll be able to do that."

"Good," said Andre. "I couldn't before."

Tristan bit his lip. The doctor frowned. Tristan couldn't help it, he covered his mouth with his hand to stem his giggles. Andre glanced at him and sniggered too.

"Right," said the doctor. "I see." From the look on his face he didn't see at all. "I'll come back when your mother's here. I really need to discuss this with her."

He closed the door behind him and Tristan and Andre dissolved into laughter.

The boys passed a quiet afternoon doing homework and reading. Tristan had tried to talk about the operation but Andre wouldn't be drawn, so no more was said. At quarter to six he began to pack his bag.

"Can you stay a bit longer?" asked Andre.

Tristan glanced at the clock. "Your mom's going to shoot a coronary if she sees me here."

"She's not coming," said Andre. "She doesn't get here that much anymore."

He sat down again. "Sure," he said. "You fancy a game of cards?"

"You think we could get the nurses in on a couple of rounds of Bullshit?" asked Andre.

They both shook their heads.

"Nah," said Tristan. "Chinese Patience?"

It was after nine o'clock when the nurses finally kicked him out.

Chapter Eleven

Tristan slept through his alarm. By the time his mother dragged him out of bed he was already late for school.

"Are you sick?" she asked.

"I'm fine, just a bit of a sniffle." He hopped round the kitchen, slice of toast in one hand, pulling on his shoe with the other.

Elize sighed. "Should you be visiting Andre if you have a cold?"

"Mom," said Tristan, round a mouthful of toast. "Stop fussing. I got it from the hospital in the first place."

In truth, he didn't know where he had picked up the cold and he knew it was irresponsible to expose Andre to the virus. But the hospital had become something of a refuge to him and he couldn't face not going.

"Yes but, Tris..."

"Mom, I'm late, see you tonight." He grabbed his bag and another slice of toast and shot out of the door.

"Come home straight after school today, please," Elize called after him. "It's not healthy you spending all your time at that hospital."

He waved as he ran out of the gate. He was over half an hour late already, and with double chemistry the first two periods, he just knew he'd mess up spelling anhydrous.

He turned right instead of left at the top of Sea View Drive. Whatever his mother thought, this morning the hospital seemed the healthier option. It was certainly the more appealing.

Tristan waited until there were no nurses in the corridor before slipping quietly into Andre's room. Andre was asleep. He sat in the chair and pulled out his chemistry book and began to write out the word anhydrous.

Andre woke with a start, making Tristan jump. "God, what time is it?" Andre blinked at him.

"Sorry," he said. "I didn't mean to wake you. It's still early. I'm doing a bunk."

"Careful, Tris, I don't want you getting into trouble."

"I won't. You okay? You don't look too great today."

"Ah, it's nothing. A bit of pain in that knee." Andre pointed to his left knee. The leg was still in traction though it had been lowered.

"You want me to get a nurse?"

"If they see you in here they'll kick your arse straight back to school," said Andre. "Anyway, I had something not that long ago."

"Okay, just relax and close your eyes," said Tristan, getting up and moving to the bed.

Andre looked at him with suspicion.

"I'm going to teach you something I do when I'm in pain. It's a sort of relaxation thing. You..." He turned as the door opened and Dr Woodlane and Kathryn Turner came in.

"You!" shrieked Kathryn. "What are you doing in here? Get out now!" Kathryn flew at him.

"Mom, don't," cried Andre. "Please!"

Tristan found himself manhandled out of the door before he could say a word. Stunned, he stood in the corridor outside the room. He needed his school bag but didn't dare risk knocking on the door and asking for it. He decided to wait.

Dr Woodlane came out of the room first. "Young man," he said, removing his glasses and placing them in the breast pocket of his white coat. "I really think you should leave before Mrs Turner comes out of there."

"Yes, but..."

"Anyway, shouldn't you be in school?"

Tristan pushed his hands through his hair. "Yes," he said. "But my bag is in there and..."

Kathryn Turner stepped into the corridor.

He took a deep breath and walked up to her. "Mrs Turner," he said. "I'm sorry, but..."

Kathryn Turner leaned close to his face. He could smell her lipstick mixed with toothpaste and coffee. He backed off but she moved in again.

"You stay away from here," she hissed. "If I ever see you here again I'll have you thrown out and reported for harassment."

"Mrs Turner, I..."

"Don't you dare, Tristan Steyn!" she said. "My son is lying in there in agony because of you." Her hand shook as she pointed to the side ward door. "We've been to hell and back and it's a long way from over. My boy will probably never walk again." Kathryn Turner's anger turned to grief. "You've destroyed our family," she sobbed. "Just get out!"

Dr Woodlane turned the weeping woman away and pointed firmly to the exit.

Tristan fled.

All of the guilt he'd so carefully buried in a dark corner of his mind came out to haunt him. He felt a sense of utter revulsion for his very existence.

He ran as hard as he could from the hospital. He thought about going to Jonno but he knew he hadn't the strength for the journey or the lecture about skipping school. Then he remembered Jonno and his father played golf on Tuesdays and his mother would be out until at least midday. He ran for home.

By the time he reached Sea View Drive he was cursing his lack of peak fitness. So hard to gain, so easy to lose. He slowed to a brisk walk and and began to cough violently.

He unlocked the house and sat on the cool kitchen floor to regain his breath. All he wanted to do was rebury the guilt. All he wanted to do was erase the image of Andre's body tumbling, falling, sliding. All he wanted to do was forget.

Chapter Twelve

Tristan had never felt so ill in all of his life. Every time he moved the violent retching would begin again and he would cling to the toilet bowl. His mouth was dry and tasted foul, but he couldn't summon the strength to get to the basin for water.

Something squeezed his brain at regular, pulsing intervals. His muscles ached and fatigue, siding with gravity, pinned him to the floor. Then there was the nausea, oh God, the nausea.

He leaned over the bowl again, heaving, convinced that at any moment his entire gut would slide from his mouth and disappear under the scum-topped water in the toilet.

There was a knock on the bathroom door. He groaned and slid to the floor. The door came slowly open.

"Oh sweet heavens," said Elize.

Brett and Jonno arrived, Brett still clutching a golf club, as Dr Louw came out of Tristan's room. He gave them the once over and turned to Elize.

"Will he be all right?" she demanded. "What's wrong with him?"

"He'll be fine," said the doctor. "Nothing that plenty of water and the rest of the day in bed won't cure."

"But what is it?" she insisted. "Is it contagious?

"Hardly," he replied. "Mrs Steyn, your son is drunk!"

Elize's mouth fell open.

"Right, that's it! I'll kill him," said Brett. "Enough is enough," He marched up the passage.

"Easy, tiger," said Jonno, stepping between Brett and the bedroom door. "You going off on him now is not going to fix this. And you're not going in there with that!" Jonno caught hold of his wrist, pushing the 5-iron under his nose. "Let me talk to him first."

Brett looked long and hard at Jonno. "J," he said. "What the hell do you know about raising kids?"

"Not a damn thing. But I've been on his side of this fence and I've got a better idea than you have of how he's feeling right now." He pushed the golf club against Brett's chest. "Come on, Bru. Please?"

Brett sighed. "Okay," he agreed.

Jonno pulled the curtains wide open. Tristan moaned and covered his face with the duvet.

"No, you don't, sunshine," said Jonno, gripping the edge of the quilt and yanking it to the floor. He sat on the bed and rolled his wayward nephew onto his back.

"Oh, nice," he said, turning away. "Eau de Captain Morgan. Welcome to hell kiddo, you couldn't have made a better choice."

Tristan rolled back onto his side. He began to retch again. Jonno handed him the bucket Elize had put by the bed but there was nothing left to come up.

"Sit up," he said. "And talk to me."

"Jonno, piss off. Leave me alone."

He rolled him over again and hauled him upright. "Listen, sunshine," he said. "Your old man is outside in that passage," he jerked a thumb at the door. "He's armed and dangerous and we've got about five minutes to sort this out before he comes in here swinging. It's me or him. Your call."

Jonno handed Tristan the glass of water from the bedside table. He sipped just enough to wet his mouth then leaned back against the headboard clutching a pillow to his stomach.

"Well?" said Jonno, taking the glass.

He opened his eyes and squinted at Jonno. "I hate her," he said.

"Right," said Jonno. "Not a good start. You've lost me at first base. Who's her? Teacher? Girlfriend? Mother?"

"Andre's mother," he said. "She's a total cow. Andre is stuck in that bed all the time and I'm the only person who ever visits him and now she's thrown me out."

"Why? She must have a reason."

"She just hates me because it's my fault Andre's in there. She said I destroyed their family."

"Well," said Jonno. "I'm not saying I agree with her, but I can see why she might be upset with you."

"Yes, okay," snapped Tristan. "I know it's my fault. I know he wouldn't be there if it wasn't for me. Do you think I feel good about that?" He slammed his fists into the mattress. "But it's not fair," he wailed. "I want to help. I want to do something and she just throws me out. It's not even as if she goes there herself! She's never there!"

"Oh, for God's sake, Tristan. Have a bit of insight can't you?" snapped Jonno. "Has it ever occurred to you that maybe she can't afford to sit by his bed all day?" He snatched a handful of CDs from Tristan's bedside table. "Do you know how hard your dad works to keep this fancy roof over your head? And to pay for your training and to buy you all this stuff?"

He tossed the CDs onto the bed. "Think boy! Not only is that poor woman worried sick about her son, she's probably having to work all the hours God gives her to pay for his medical treatment." He stood up. "Now, why don't you stop bitching about how hard this is for you and think about how hard it is for Andre and his family?"

He leaned down and caught Tristan's chin in his hand, forcing him to make eye contact. "And if you really want to do something to help, I suggest you sort yourself out and go and give Mrs Turner a reason to change her mind about you. Grow up Tristan! All this self pity really doesn't suit you."

Jonno released Tristan's chin and backed away. He could see his words had hit home but decided to put the boot in one more time. "And I think you should get yourself back in the dojo," he said. "As much as I love you, Tris, I can't say I like you very much these days. You've turned into a self centred little brat since you stopped training."

He opened the bedroom door. "Oh, and if you know what's good for you, you'd better get yourself tidied up then get out here and apologise to your mom and dad."

Tristan stumbled into the kitchen. His shirt was open up the front and the button of his jeans was unfastened. Water from his dripping hair soaked the back of his shirt and ran down his chest.

"Ehem," said Jonno. "I thought you were going to tidy yourself up!"

Tristan looked up at him. "I had a shower."

"So I see," said Jonno. "But clean and tidy are not synonymous."

Elize shook her head. "Tristan, we do have towels in this house," she said.

He still felt nauseous and unsteady and didn't want to get into an argument. "Sorry, Ma," he said.

"Is that it?" asked Jonno, sipping from his coffee mug. "Is that all you can say? Your mother comes home to find you blind drunk. You scare her half to death and all you can say is sorry ma? I don't think so, sunshine."

He glared at Jonno who went on, "Tris, you owe her an explanation at least."

Tristan sat at the kitchen table and rested his head on his arms. Elize stood behind him and rubbed his shoulders. "Are you feeling a bit better now?" she asked.

He shook his head without lifting it from his arms.

Jonno grinned at Elize. "Sis, you can't even imagine how bad he's feeling," he said. "And it's going to be another day or two before he fully recovers."

He flicked the kettle on. While he waited for it to boil he tipped up the coffee jar over a large mug.

"Jonno," said Elize. "We have spoons as well as towels in this house. What's wrong with you Steyn men?"

"Sorry," he said taking one from the drawer and adding an extra spoonful to the mug for good measure.

He poured on the almost boiling water then sat next to Tristan. "Here," he said. "Get that down your neck. It'll either kill you or liven you up a bit."

Tristan lifted his head. The smell of the coffee caught in his throat. "Uh uh, please," he moaned. "I can't drink that."

"Suit yourself, I can. Now, explain yourself to your mother while I go and persuade your old man not to break your neck."

Tristan came upright. "No!" he said. "Let me rather talk to him first. You didn't do a such a great job last time." He took a sip of the strong black coffee. It made him shudder. "Mom," he said. "I'm really sorry. I've been evil recently and I..."

Elize shushed him. "No," she said. "You're not evil, Tristan. And I know things have been difficult for you, but please, don't do anything like that ever again. I was so worried about you and I felt like such a fool when Dr Louw said you were drunk."

"I'm sorry, Ma."

"In fact," she went on, "I think you should phone him and apologise for wasting his time. And then you'd better go and see your dad. He's working in the study."

Tristan wasted another twenty minutes of Dr Louw's time with monosyllabic responses to a lecture on what alcohol would do to his young liver.

He replaced the receiver then buttoned his shirt and tucked it into his jeans. He knocked on the study door.

"Yes?" called Brett. He opened the door and went inside.

Brett looked up from a document. "What is it, Tristan?" he said. "I'm busy." He pushed his glasses up his nose and went back to the papers in his hand.

"I just wanted to say I'm sorry. I..."

"Tristan," Brett interrupted. He removed his glasses and laid them on his desk. "You've been doing a lot of that lately. Perhaps you could try modifying your behaviour instead?"

Tristan avoided his father's eyes. "Yes, he mumbled. "I'm sorry,"

"Tristan, sit down," said Brett.

He fell gratefully into the chair.

"I've tried really hard to be tolerant with you but lately you've made it more and more difficult for your mother and I to understand what's going on inside that head of yours. Now, I know you're having a hard time, what with your friend and all, but I'm not going to put up with you getting drunk in this house."

Brett leaned back in the black leather office chair. "I would have thought that what happened with the surfboard would have had a bit more of an impact. Please, Tristan, don't force me to make a more lasting impression."

He leaned forward and rested his elbows on the desk. "Now," he said. "You can get outside and wash and wax the cars, mine, your mother's and Jonno's. And use a bucket, not the hose. Once you've done that, you can mow the lawn then clean the swimming pool."

Tristan's mouth fell open. He felt terrible. All he wanted to do was collapse on his bed. Working outside in the hot sun would kill him, he was sure.

He was about to protest but thought better of it. *It'll serve you right if I do collapse and die*, he thought.

"Now, off you go," Brett said. "I've got work to do."

Tristan got up and walked to the door. "I'm really sorry, Dad," he said, opening the door.

Brett waved him away, then called him back. "Oh, Tristan," he said. "Better check with Jonno first. I'm not sure what's holding that heap of his together."

Tristan closed the door behind him and leaned on it until the fresh wave of nausea passed.

"No," said Jonno. "It's fine thanks. And it's got nothing to do with what's holding her together. It's more about what's holding you together. Anyway," he added, "Her sun roof leaks like a cumulonimbus."

Tristan groaned as he hoisted the bucket of water.

"I'll tell you what," said Jonno. "You wash, I'll wax." He stripped to the waist and tied his T shirt in his dreadlocks.

"Thanks," said Tristan. "But he'll kill us both."

"What he doesn't know about won't piss him off."

Jonno had washed and waxed Brett's Mercedes in the time it took Tristan to throw up three times in his mother's Strelitzia and lift the wipers on her Corolla Conquest. Jonno finished the job while he sat groaning over a bucket.

"Right, come on, Tris, I'll mow this grass at the front but you'll have to pull yourself together and do the back."

"No," he moaned. "I can't, I'm going to die." His head was pounding and the harsh light from the mid afternoon sun pinned his eyelids closed. He felt as if his gut had been wrenched out of his mouth and still he was paralysed by nausea.

"Tris, believe me, I know how rough you feel. I've been there more than once. But you have to do this." Jonno squatted in front of him. He was leaning like a rag doll against his father's car door.

"You have to cut the grass at the back and do the pool. He can see out of the window back there."

"I can see perfectly well out here, thank you very much," boomed Brett.

Jonno jumped and leapt to his feet. "Ah, Brett," he said.

"And exactly who's done what out here so far?"

"Well, technically..."

"Technically, you've done it all. I ought to belt the pair of you."

"Brett, come on, look at him," said Jonno. "Don't you think the way he's feeling now is enough to put him off for life?"

"Coming from a person who's just mentioned being there more than once, I'm not convinced," Brett said.

"Tris is not as stupid as me," said Jonno. "And, he still has the hangover to come. That's going to be rough. Besides," he added, "None of this makes any sense. If you really want to punish him why not wait until he's sober enough to appreciate it?"

Chapter Thirteen

Andre refused his food again. His leg hurt and he was frustrated to the point of tears with lying on his back in bed. The doctors had lowered the traction and had spoken about operating again. He knew it wouldn't happen.

He had slipped down in the bed. There was no one there to help him up. He was miserable and he missed Tristan's company. He had been convinced that, despite his mother's threats, Tristan would come back. But he hadn't. Andre was hurt.

Tristan ignored the knock on his door. He turned onto his side and tossed the duvet off him. He was hot again.

Other than frequent trips to the bathroom, he hadn't been out of bed for three days. The hangover smacked him round the head every time he moved, his stomach steadfastly refused all but the smallest sips of water and, to top it all, his sniffles had become a full blown cold. He wanted to die.

Again the knock. This time the door came open and Rico burst in. "I hope you're decent mate 'cause Megs is coming in," he said.

Tristan groaned and pulled the pillow over his head.

Megan popped her head around the door. "Okay if I come say hello?"

"Hi," said Tristan, lifting the pillow. "I'm contagious, you'd better go."

"Nothing could live in here, not even a virus," said Rico. He pulled the curtains back and threw both windows open, then sat on the bed. "Geez, bru," he said. "You must have had full on flu. You look like death."

Tristan sat up and pulled his knees to his chest. He was embarrassed having Megan in his room. She had stepped over several magazines and a pile of dirty laundry to get to his martial arts wall and was examining his trophies. She ran her fingers over the coloured belts hanging from a dowel on the wall. Her touch lingered on the green belt, her next goal.

"No," he snapped, as she lifted a photo frame that was lying face down on a shelf.

She pulled her hand away quickly. "I'm sorry," she said. "I didn't mean to be nosy."

He blushed. "No," he said. "It's okay. You can stand it up. I'm sorry I was snappish."

"What's the big deal?" asked Rico, craning to see, as Megan stood the photo upright. "It's just some bloke in a karate suit."

Megan and Tristan gasped in unison.

"He's the founder of our style of karate," Tristan explained.

Rico looked unimpressed.

Megan came and joined them on the bed. "Why was he face down?" she asked.

He felt himself blush again and dropped his head back onto his knees. "I didn't want him to see me like this," he mumbled.

Rico roared with laughter.

"Don't," said Megan, slapping his shoulder. "You don't understand. It's a symbolic thing for us. His photo in the dojo is a reminder to train hard and keep our body and mind in shape."

"And in the bedroom?" asked Rico, jabbing Tristan with his elbow.

"I train in here too," he snapped, indignant. "Well, I used to."

"Does that mean I have to call you Sempai in here too?" asked Megan with a grin.

"As I recall," he snorted, "You don't have to call me Sempai anywhere. The last time I was in a dojo 5th kyu ranked higher than white belt."

Megan screwed up her nose. "Sorry," she said. "I forgot about that."

"I miss something?" asked Rico. "If you're going to talk karate at least do it in Rico speak."

Megan looked at Tristan.

He inclined his head towards Rico. "Go ahead," he said. "It's not a state secret."

Megan briefly explained.

"That sucks," said Rico. "Is that why you don't go anymore?"

He shook his head. Then he thought about it for a moment. "Well," he said. "I didn't think it was, but maybe it has something to do with it."

"The kids miss you, you know," said Megan. "They're always asking Sensei when you're coming back."

Tristan wasn't sure he wanted to have this conversation. "I'm not coming back," he said. "I'm taking up tiddlywinks instead." He was beginning to feel cold again. He shivered and hugged his knees to his chest.

"Here," said Megan, ignoring his comment. She jumped off the bed and pulled the duvet up for him.

"Thanks," he said and began to cough. He held his head in both hands and buried his face in the duvet. Coughing was a nightmare of pain in his head and throat.

Megan took the glass of water from the bedside table and handed it to him. He mumbled his thanks and took a sip. He was still having difficulty with his stomach's urge to reject whatever he offered it. He didn't want to puke in front of Megan for the second time in the few short weeks he'd known her.

"Ag shame," said Megan. "You still look really sick. Come Rico, I think we should let him sleep."

"Good idea. I'm having second thoughts about catching whatever it is he's got.

"Guys," said Tristan. "Could you maybe do me a favour?"

"Anything mate," said Rico.

"Please will you go and see Andre?"

"Oh come on, Tris. No!"

"You said anything!"

"Okay, anything but that."

"Forget it then," he said, rolling onto his side.

"Tris, come on. Don't do this to me."

"Andre?" asked Megan.

"Turner," said Rico.

"The guy in the hospital? Rico, don't be such a beast," she

snapped. "Of course we'll go."

Rico was unhappy. He walked up to the first nurse he saw. "Um, hi," he said. "We're friends of Andre Turner. We were wondering if it would be okay to see him."

"Well," said the nurse. "He hasn't been too well the last couple of days but I'm sure a few minutes won't hurt."

"Hello," said a voice behind them. He turned.

"I'm Sister Napier," she said with a smile. "I think the two of you are just the tonic Andre needs right now."

I'm not so sure about that, thought Rico. He felt a pang of guilt none the less.

"Come," said Sister Napier. "I'll show you where you need to be."

Rico and Megan followed. He didn't like hospitals. The closer they got to the side room the more his stomach knotted. The smells and the sounds on the wards were almost as awful as the prospect of getting up close and personal with Andre Turner.

They walked into the room and he gripped Megan's hand. He felt faint as he looked at the ghost of a person in the bed. He turned to tell Sister Napier that there had been a mistake but she was gone.

He moved a little closer. Andre's face was ashen and the bones stood out, the colour of his skin and the angular features turning his face into some bizarre alien landscape. Megan hugged his arm and leaned against him.

Andre opened his eyes. There was no mistake. The piercing blue was instantly recognisable. His eyes came wide as he saw them.

"Hi, Andre," said Rico. "This is my friend, Megan."

Andre blinked at them but didn't speak. He tried to push himself up in the bed but collapsed, exhausted, against the pillows.

"Here," said Megan, moving to the head of the bed. "Let me help you." She gently helped Andre to sit up higher and adjusted the pillows behind his back.

Rico knew he was staring but he couldn't help himself.

"Thank you," said Andre, his voice dry and harsh. Megan poured water from the carafe at the side of the bed and helped steady the glass as he drank.

"Thank you," he said again, leaning back against the pillows and closing his eyes.

Megan looked at Rico. She waved him closer to the bed. "Talk to him," she mouthed.

"Um, so, Andre," he said. "Did Tristan give you the geography notes from Mr Pike?"

Andre's eyes flickered open. "Yes," he said. "Thanks for getting them." He regarded Rico for a moment. "Did Steyn send you here?" Rico and Megan exchanged glances.

"It's fine," said Andre. "You don't have to stay. Steyn came because he was on a guilt trip. You have no reason to be here at all."

"Andre, that's not true," said Megan. "Tristan likes visiting you."

"Actually," said Rico. "It was true."

Megan elbowed him hard in the ribs.

"Ow, would you let me finish, please," he said, rubbing his side. "Tris did start coming out of guilt, but he's been trying to get me to come for ages now. He said if I got to know you that I'd like you. He thinks you're actually a pretty cool guy."

"So where is he then?" asked Andre. "I know my mom went ballistic on him but I didn't think he would scare that easily."

"Shit, sorry," said Rico. "Someone should have let you know. Tris is as sick as a parrot. We went to see him today and he almost looks as bad as you. Hasn't been in school all week."

Andre brightened. He reached over and opened the bedside drawer. "Here," he said. "This is full of chocolate and mints. I'll never get through them if I spend the rest of my life in here."

Rico saw a shadow pass over Andre's face and instantly felt the pang of guilt again. Megan pulled the chair round and they both perched on it the best way they could.

Rico was surprised to find that he and Andre had a similar sense of humour, and that they were both passionate armchair surfers. They both read all the local surfing magazines but neither had ever been on a board.

"Hey," Rico said. "Tristan's dad's a surfer. He gives lessons too." The three of them made a deal to book a taster session with Brett as soon as Andre's health would permit.

They spent the afternoon laughing, joking and munching chocolate while Rico filled Andre in on the latest news from school.

Rico and Megan left with a promise to be back the next day.

Andre laid back on the pillow. He had thoroughly enjoyed Rico and Megan's company.

Despite the clawing pain in his lower back and the ache in his knee, Andre was happier than he had ever been. He had friends.

For the first time in his life he felt like he was a part of something. He felt like he belonged.

It was Saturday. Tristan had been in bed since Tuesday afternoon. The hangover was long gone but, along with the fever, congestion and pain of the cold, it had left a weakness in its wake. He stepped out of the steaming bathroom and gratefully gulped the fresh morning air. He rubbed the towel over his wet hair then draped it over the foot of the bed. He still felt unsteady on his legs as he made his way to the kitchen.

"Good God," said Jonno. "It lives." He was leaning against the kitchen counter sipping from a giant black and white mug shaped like a soccer ball.

Tristan knew he was there as soon he ran into the smell of coffee from half way down the passage. "Howzit, J," he said. "Hi, Ma, Dad."

His parents were sitting at the kitchen table finishing off a leisurely breakfast of croissants and fresh fruit.

"Welcome back," said his mother. "I thought we'd never get you out of that flea pit of a bedroom."

Brett waved over the *Independent*.

"You feeling better now?" asked Jonno. "I thought your folks had buried you under the garage floor, I haven't seen you for so long."

"I'm fine thanks," he said, taking the mug from Jonno's hand. "This is cool. Where'd you get it?"

"Out of my car," said Jonno. "Your mom doesn't have big enough mugs."

Tristan took a sip. The hot strong coffee seemed to soothe his still sore throat. "Ag won't you make me a coffee like that, please," he asked.

"Tristan, *jy kan dit self maak*," you can make it yourself, said his mother.

"Course I will," said Jonno, flicking on the kettle.

Elize shook her head. "There's no wonder you're his favourite uncle."

"Yeah," said Jonno, "That's until Danie lets him ride that damn quad bike round the farm. How do I compete with that?"

"You can show me how to get dreads when I leave school."

"Don't you dare," said Elize.

Jonno swatted him. "Hey, I'm working damn hard to prove to your mother that corrupting you is not my sole aim in life. Save that conversation for my place, okay?" he said with a wink.

"I never thought I'd say it, Jonno, but you're doing a good job," said Elize. "Now, sit down and get some breakfast, both of you."

"Thanks, 'Lize," said Jonno. "But I ate already. I'm going to go surf the Rock."

"Watch out for that guy with the green hair."

Jonno laughed. "That would be Arno Bekker, good guy," he said. "Damn good surfer, but he doesn't tolerate idiots in the water."

"I noticed," mumbled Tristan.

Brett laid the newspaper on the table. "I've got work to do," he said, and left the kitchen.

Tristan sighed and bit his lip. "I guess I'd better get the lawnmower out."

"No," said Elize. "You're not overdoing it. I want you to stay in and rest today. Your dad will be fine, just stay out of his way for a day or two."

Tristan had managed a mashed banana on toast with no ill effects. Apart from his throat, he felt better than he had in over a week and decided a bit of sun would do him good.

He was wandering round the front garden when Rico came up the driveway. "Howzit, *boet*," he said. "I was hoping you'd be up. I have inside information. Mrs T is out of town for the weekend. So if you're up for a trip to the hospital, the coast's clear."

"Great, let's go," said Tristan, pleased to hear the enthusiasm in his own voice.

In truth he was afraid. Afraid of Kathryn Turner's wrath, and afraid of his own poisonous guilt.

Chapter Fourteen

They could see Andre was upset.

"Um, I'll go and get us something to drink," said Rico. "Leave you guys to catch up."

Tristan waited for the door to close then pulled the chair up to the bed. "What's up?" he said. "And no bull, I know something's wrong."

Andre sniffed. "We can't afford the operation I need," he said. "My mom's gone to Jo'burg to see if my dad's folks can help out, but I know they won't help her."

"How much?"

"About thirty five grand,"

Tristan held Andre's gaze. He took a deep breath and laid a hand on his wrist. "Don't worry," he said. "We'll get the money. I have an idea."

"What? Where the hell do you think you can come up with money like that?"

"Andre, I put you in here and I'm going to do everything I can to get you out."

"How?"

"Give me some time to get things started then I'll tell you my plan. For now, just trust me."

Andre sighed.

"You've got nothing to lose," said Tristan.

"They're taking me out of traction on Monday," said Andre, brightening a little. "I'll be in plaster though, but at least I can get out of this damn bed."

"Cool, that means you can come too."

"Come where?"

"To help get the money," he said. "You'll see."

Rico came back with three cans of Fanta Grape. "You two caught up yet or do you want more time?"

"I was just about to tell Steyn he looks like crap," said Andre. "Then we're done."

"Cool," said Rico. "Where's the pack of cards? Megs showed me this excellent new game last night."

Tristan was worried about raising the money for Andre's operation. He'd had an idea but he was rapidly losing faith in his ability to pull it off.

He rolled onto his belly on the warm cement and dipped his arm into the swimming pool. The water felt cold again. The 100 lengths he'd already done had left him hanging onto the side of the pool, breathing hard. He'd immediately abandoned the idea of following up his swim with a run on the beach. He knew he had to get back in shape.

"Hey, you okay?"

Tristan looked up as Brett sat down and dipped his feet into the water.

"Damn, that's cold. You been in?"

"Yeah," said Tristan. "Nearly killed me."

"You still look a bit peaky. You need to take it easy for a day or two."

"Can't," he replied. "I have to get fit again, and fast too."

"You have to get well first or you'll do more harm than good. Swimming's about the best exercise to get you back into the swing of things. Come on, get in."

"Too cold." He turned his head away from the harsh sun reflecting off the water.

"Wimp!" Brett slid slowly into the water.

Tristan heard him gasp as it lapped around his middle. "Told you," he said.

Brett swam a couple of lengths then came back to the side. "It's not so bad once you're in."

"Umm, if you say so."

Brett scooped up a handful of water and slopped it onto Tristan's sun-warmed back.

"Noooo!" he yelped. He tried to roll away but Brett caught his arm and pulled him into the pool.

He surfaced and sucked in air. "I can't believe you did that!"

Brett laughed. "Come on, you lazy devil," he said. "Get that blood pumping." Brett challenged him to 100 lengths.

It took him a while to warm up but he had soon pulled five lengths ahead of his father. When he finished he sat on the steps waiting for him to catch up.

Panting, Brett slid up and sat next to him. "Damn," he said. "I thought with you being sick and not training that I could take you."

"Dad, you're old. Not a chance."

Brett caught him round the neck and shoved him under the water.

"Okay, truce," he yelled, as Brett pulled him up for air. "You're not old." He kicked away from the step to the middle of the pool. "You're ageing."

Brett hit the surface of the water and sent it spaying into his face. "I'll get you later," he said.

Tristan raised his hands above his head. "Okay, I surrender," he said, venturing closer. "Can I ask you a favour?"

"A favour?" said Brett. "You just called me old. You might want to reconsider your timing."

"It's not for me, it's for Andre. I need some legal advice on fund raising."

Tristan smoothed his hair with a sweaty palm and knocked on the door.

"Come!" called the head.

He gripped the handle and pushed open the heavy wooden door. He closed it quietly behind him and silently moved to stand before the desk. Clasping his hands behind his back, he waited.

The head looked up from the book he was writing in. He put his pen down and held out his hand. "You have a note, I presume?" he sighed.

Tristan swallowed. "No, sir," he said.

"Well who sent you, then? And what have you done this

time?"

"Um, no one, sir. I haven't done anything. I..." He cleared his sore throat. "I wanted to ask you something, sir," he said.

The head removed his glasses and laid them on the book. "Well, you'd better sit down then. What can I do for you?"

He was surprised to find his hands were shaking as he pulled the chair out and sat down. "Sir, I... It's about Andre Turner. He needs an operation and..."

"Tristan, relax, I don't bite. And unless you've done something you shouldn't have, I'm really not the ogre I might seem to be."

"Sorry, sir," he said. "I want to help raise the money they need for the operation. I have an idea but we would need somewhere to do it. I was wondering if we could use the school sports field?"

"Well," said the head. "I would obviously need to know a bit more about it."

"I know, sir," said Tristan. "My dad's a lawyer. He's going to find out about all the insurance and legal stuff. I just want to know, if I write up a plan with the details and everything, if you would look at it and at least think about it?"

"Yes," said the head. "Of course I will."

Tristan found Rico under the Jacaranda tree. There were still ten minutes of the break remaining and he wanted to get to Miss Price before the rest of the class came in.

"Hey, Ric," he said. "I have to shoot off to see Chemcow but will you meet me here after school?"

"Okay," said Rico. "But I'm meeting Megs at two thirty so don't be late."

"Oh crap, I was hoping you'd come to the hospital."

"We will. We were going to anyway."

"Oh, okay, cool. I'll catch you here later then." He looked at his watch and made a run for the science block.

He found Miss Price at her desk marking books. The classroom door was open but he knocked and waited.

"Ah, Steyn," she said. "I thought I'd frightened you away

100

permanently."

"You almost did, miss," he said. "But my mom wanted me to come back and she's even more scary."

Miss Price smiled. "So, can you spell anhydrous yet?"

"Yes, miss. But my public speaking still needs work and I thought maybe I could rather just spell it for you?"

Miss Price closed the book she was marking and set it on the pile with the others. Tristan pushed his hair behind his ear and tugged at his collar.

"It's all right, you don't have to do it. Just check your spelling from now on," she said. "Before you hand in your homework."

"Yes, miss. Thank you."

Tristan sank deeper into the chair as Megan stood up.

"Come on," she said. "You can't put it off forever." She held out her hand to him.

He sighed and let her drag him out of the chair. "You have no idea what torture this is," he said.

"Well, it won't go away unless you fix it. Now, come on, don't be such a baby!"

"Good luck," said Andre. "I hope you're not in too much trouble. I feel really guilty about this."

Tristan gaped at him. "Are you mad? I nearly kill you and *you* feel guilty because I got myself into trouble at training."

"Yes, but you should have gone back ages ago, instead of always being here."

"I wanted to be here, Andre. I put off going back because I'm gutless," he said. "But I'm going to do something about it this time."

"Rather you than me," said Rico. "I'm going to stay here and drink Coke, eat chocolate and play cards while you two go and get yourselves kicked round a yoyo."

Tristan frowned. "Huh?"

Megan laughed. "Dojo," she said. "Not yoyo!"

* * *

Tristan straightened his dogi and secured the white belt neatly around his waist. He came out of the changing room and bowed into the dojo. There was no sign of Sensei or Shihan so he went to the back of the mat room to warm up.

Shihan Dean arrived and was chatting to one of the brown belts. Tristan approached but kept a respectful distance. Dean finished the conversation and turned to him.

"Osu!" said Tristan. "Could I speak to you please, Shihan?"

Dean studied him before responding. His eyes falling to the white belt and immaculate dogi. "You may," he said. "Come to the office."

Tristan followed.

Dean closed the door. "Sit," he said.

"Thank you." Tristan perched on the edge of the chair.

Dean took a seat behind the desk. "So, you wanted to speak to me?"

"Yes, Shihan," he said, looking down at his hands, folded in his lap. "I'm sorry. I behaved like a child the last time I was here and I made it worse by not coming back to training and..." He looked up at Dean. "I would like to start again. If you'll have me back in the dojo I promise I'll behave better and I'll work really hard."

"Of course I'll have you back," said Dean. "And I know you'll work hard."

"Thank you, Shihan."

"How's your friend?" asked Dean.

Tristan breathed a sigh of relief. He'd been dreading being asked why he hadn't been to training. "He's getting better," he said. "But it's hard for him."

"I'm sure it's not easy for you either." Dean pushed his chair back and stood up. "Well, Sensei Gavin will be pleased to see you back. You'd better go and do some warm ups before he starts the class."

"Thank you, Shihan. I won't let you down again."

"You didn't let me down, Tristan," said Dean. "We could both have done things differently."

Gavin's delight at seeing Tristan back in the dojo was overshadowed by the fact that he was clearly struggling. Twice during warm ups he had pulled out of a stretch because of cramp. He was also breathing hard after some basic aerobic work.

He watched him closely throughout the session. He was putting in the effort but his fitness was well below par.

After the session Gavin knocked on the office door. Dean called him in.

"Hell," said Dean, banging the receiver back on the cradle. "I've been on that bloody phone all night. I wanted to get out there and see how Steyn was coping training with the juniors."

Gavin sighed. "He struggled."

Dean frowned, "Damn it," he said. "I thought he'd had a bit of an attitude adjustment when we had a chat earlier."

"Uh uh, no. No problem at all with the attitude. He was brilliant. Never questioned a thing. Took instructions from his seniors, whatever their grade. Not even a peep when a blue belt, rightly I might add, corrected his fist position. He just really seemed to struggle physically, which surprised me. I thought he would have kept up some training."

"He'll soon get that back," said Dean. "But I did want to see how he coped with the juniors. I'll give him that belt back tomorrow night if he behaves."

Gavin shook his head. "I'll be honest with you," he said. "I think you'd be better giving him a week at least with the juniors just to get his fitness back up to scratch."

"That bad?"

"Yes, that bad!"

The next night Gavin approached Tristan in the mat room before the session. He was pale and looked tired even before they began.

"Osu!" said Tristan.

"Are you all right? You really don't look well."

"I'm fine, thank you, Sensei. Just tired."

"I was worried about you last night. You seemed to struggle quite a bit."

"I was sick last week," he said. "I only went back to school yesterday, but I really want to get back into shape as soon as I can."

"Be careful," said Gavin. "I don't want you pushing yourself tonight," He raised a hand to stem Tristan's protest. "If you really want to show Shihan that your maturity has improved, you need to know your limitations. Now, don't push it!"

"Yes, Sensei."

Tristan didn't push himself. He couldn't. And he began to worry. After the session he went into the mat room and worked on his flexibility. Stretching hurt and he couldn't remember ever being unable to get his head onto his knees.

"I think you should go home, don't you?"

He jumped. "Osu! Yes, Shihan," he said.

"Come on," said Dean. "I'll give you a lift. You can throw your bicycle in the back of the *bakkie*."

"Thank you," he said. He wanted to protest but he didn't think he could ride home anyway. He really didn't feel well.

He leaned back against the headrest and closed his eyes.

"I want you to take at least another week off from training," said Dean. "You're obviously not over whatever you had."

Again, he wanted to protest but couldn't. "Yes, Shihan," he said.

He knew he would never get a better opportunity to ask Dean about his idea to raise the money for Andre's operation. But he also knew his current physical condition gave good grounds for an instant no. He decided to approach him with part of the plan.

"Shihan, have you picked a date for the demo yet?"

Dean slowed for a yield sign and didn't immediately answer. "Don't worry," he said. "You'll be fit enough to take part in that. And if you behave like you have the last couple of nights you'll have your obi back too."

"Thanks. But that's not what I was thinking."

"Oh," said Dean. "What then?"

"Well," he said, wishing he hadn't brought it up. "I wondered if we could do it as a fundraiser again this year."

Dean blew out a long breath. "Organisation was a bit of a nightmare last time," he said. "That's one of the reasons we never did it again. What were you thinking of raising funds for?"

"My friend Andre needs an operation and they can't afford it. I know we raised over R100 000 last time and he only needs about R35 000. So I thought maybe we could do it partly for his op and then donate the rest to the hospital towards a scanner they need."

Dean stared straight ahead and nodded. "Well," he said. "That might work. But we would need to check up on the legalities of fundraising for an individual."

"My dad's on to that. I asked him to look into it."

Dean smiled. "Determined little thing, aren't you?"

"I..." He was stunned to find himself on the verge of tears. "It was my fault," was all he could manage.

Dean pulled the car onto the driveway, behind Meryl, and stopped the engine. He turned in his seat to face Tristan. "What was?" he asked. "The accident?"

He nodded.

"Tristan, I don't..."

"I ran in front of the car," he snapped. "It swerved to miss me and it hit Andre. It's my fault he's in there and it's my fault he can't walk. It should have been me! I sh..."

"Stop it!" said Dean. "I know that's a pretty rough position to be in, but torturing yourself about it won't make Andre better. And it certainly won't do you any good. Getting in a state about it is probably how you've made yourself ill. Now, come on, let's get you inside and we can talk about doing something constructive instead of wallowing in self pity."

Tristan opened his mouth to object. First Jonno and now Dean accusing him of self pity. "I think..." he began.

Dean raised an eyebrow.

Tristan shut his mouth then opened it again. "I think you have a point," he mumbled.

Dean lifted Tristan's bicycle out of the back of his pick up and leaned it against the garage door.

"Thanks," Tristan said. "You want to come in for a coffee or something?"

Dean looked at his watch. "Well, I don't want to impose if your folks have guests," he said, indicating the Beetle with his thumb. "But I would like to have a word with your dad about the fund raising."

"Cool," said Tristan. "You won't be imposing, it's just my uncle Jonno."

He led Dean into the lounge. Brett and Jonno stood to greet him. "I'll make coffee," Tristan said, leaving the three of them to talk.

Dean settled onto the large cream sofa. This was his first visit to the Steyns' house, though he had met Brett before and they got on well. He felt an instant rapport with Jonno too.

"Well," said Brett. "I take it Tris has mentioned the fund raising idea."

"Yes," he said. "He has. We did one a couple of years ago and raised money to promote sports for disadvantaged kids but I'll be honest with you, it was a bit of a nightmare getting it all organised. Insurance was the biggest issue because we need a bigger venue than the dojo."

"Excuse me a sec," said Brett. "I've got some paperwork in my office that might help." He got up and left the room.

"So," said Jonno. "Is Tris behaving himself now he's back at training?"

"Apparently. I haven't had a chance to watch him the last couple of nights but his Sensei is pleased with him. We're a bit concerned about his health though. I don't think he's over that bug he had."

"Hmm." Jonno examined his thumbnail. "He didn't look that great when he came in."

Tristan entered with coffee on a tray. He looked unsteady and Dean was concerned. He put the tray on the coffee table and sat down hard on the floor. Dean and Jonno rushed to his side.

"No," he said, waving them both away. "I'm fine, don't fuss."

Jonno placed his palm on Tristan's forehead. "You're far from fine, sunshine. You're burning up."

As Tristan slumped forward Jonno caught him just before he hit his head on the coffee table.

Chapter Fifteen

On his mother's orders, Tristan spent the next three days in bed. He felt awful and he was disgusted with himself. He had been so determined to get back into training.

Dr Louw had diagnosed acute tonsillitis and put him on a course of antibiotics.

On the Saturday morning he got up. He couldn't bear another day in bed. He wandered into the kitchen, sat at the table and raided the fruit bowl.

"Are you feeling better?"

He jumped. He hadn't heard his mother come into the kitchen. "Yes, I'm okay now, thanks," he said.

"Shall I get you some breakfast?" Elize asked.

"No thanks." He shook his head and held up a half eaten banana. "I've got this."

"What do you think to a quiet day on the beach today? Jonno's coming for lunch and then going surfing. Do you feel up to a bit of fresh air?"

"Maybe this afternoon," he said. "I'm going to the dojo this morning."

"You are not! You..."

"Chill, Ma, dad's taking me and I'm not training. We're going to talk about the fundraiser." He poked an antibiotic into the last of his banana and swallowed it.

"You're supposed to drink those with water," said his mother. "Here," she filled a glass and handed it to him. "Drink!"

Tristan was nervous. He knew it was now or never. He had to put the other part of his plan to Shihan today. He was still nowhere near fit enough but he had time to get there. The antibiotics were doing the job and he knew he could get back into shape.

He knocked on the office door. Sensei Gavin let them in and the four of them settled round the desk.

Dean examined the papers Brett had given him. "It looks

good," he said. "A couple more phone calls and we should be sorted. But you'll have to let us know for sure about the school sports field." He looked up at Tristan.

"I'll speak to Mr de Lange on Monday," he said. "But he already said it's okay if we cover the insurance."

Dean nodded.

"I've spoken to a few people about food and other stalls," said Brett. "There's been quite a bit of interest. Plenty of people seem to be willing to work at the event and donate a percentage of their profits. I just thought a bit of something for everyone would give us more scope than a straight forward martial arts demonstration."

"Good idea," said Gavin. "We'd want to keep people there as long as possible."

"Um," said Tristan. "I just wondered if I could do something too." He shifted uncomfortably. "I was thinking maybe I could get sponsored to do kumite with the kyu grades and shodan that would be interested in fighting me?"

As much as he wanted to, Tristan didn't dare ask to fight anyone higher ranked than himself. Dojo etiquette demanded you never ask a senior grade to spar but you never refuse if asked by them.

Dean sat back in his chair and steepled his fingers. "I would say that would be most of them," he said. "You do know that over the four dojo we have over 300 members?"

"We could put him up against the yudansha instead," said Gavin.

"Sensei," said Dean. "You want me to put my youngest, smallest shodan up against the rest of the yudansha?"

"Some of them," he said. "We'd have to work out how many and how we'd pick them, but under dojo rules, it makes more sense. Why not?"

"Because he'd get creamed, is why not."

"Um, sorry," said Brett. "Yudansha?"

Dean turned to him. "Sorry, Mr Steyn," he said. "The black belts."

Brett paled. "And how does it make more sense for him to fight black belts rather than the, um, less qualified ones?" he asked.

Less qualified ones? Tristan cringed.

"Well," said Gavin. "Under dojo rules, the senior grade is responsible for the safety of both fighters. So they moderate the level of contact to suit the opponent's ability and level of experience. If we let him fight the juniors, he'll be pulling his punches but he may have to defend against full contact in every fight. If he fights the seniors, his ability will dictate the level of contact. In theory, he'll only take full contact from the shodan, the same grade as him."

Brett nodded. "I see."

"All of whom are bigger and older than him," said Dean. "Sempai." He turned to Tristan. "Honestly now, if I put you up against say, Sensei Jason, what do you imagine the outcome would be?"

Sensei Jason Swart, sandan, one of the best knockdown fighters in the country. He began his karate in a tough dojo in Cape Town, before going to train in Europe and Japan. He returned to South Africa three years ago and was now senior instructor at Shihan Dean's North Beach Dojo.

Tristan hadn't seen him fight but he knew his reputation well. "Worst case scenario," he said. "Would probably involve an undertaker."

"Hmm," grunted Dean. "And best case scenario?"

"Um, something along the lines of bow, get kicked in the head and collapse in a snivelling heap?"

Nodding, Dean turned to Gavin. "At least the boy's not deluded."

He knew he shouldn't but he couldn't help himself. "I meant him," said Tristan.

Gavin grinned. Dean's eyes flew wide and he spun his chair to face Tristan. Tristan looked away from Gavin, now shaking with silent mirth.

Dean leapt to his feet. "Sempai, just when I think..."

Gavin snorted with laughter. Tristan sucked in his lower lip and bit back giggles.

Dean looked from one to the other. "Okay, you two," he snapped. "Very funny. You had me going for a minute there."

Brett poked Tristan's shoulder. "Behave!"

He put on his serious face. "I'm sorry, Shihan."

Dean sat on the edge of the desk. "You can have a taste of Sensei Jason next weekend, you young pup. He'll be here working with the guys going to Cape Town for the dan gradings in June. Now," he went on. "If we decide to go ahead with this how are you going to feel when you're exhausted and hurting and you're being dropped by every new fighter within seconds of them stepping up to fight? Think about that before you answer."

Dean stood up and began to pace. "Remember, there will be a lot of your school friends watching this. People who don't understand karate at all."

He perched again. "Now, I know while you're fresh you're capable of winning fights. But when you start to get tired these guys are going to take you down, not maybe, not sometimes, every time. Every time a fresh fighter comes up, you are going to hit the deck. What do you think your friends will say if Sempai Helen's first attack puts you on the floor?"

Tristan held Dean's cool green eyes but remained silent.

"You see my point, Sempai?" he asked. "They will have no idea how tired you are, no idea of the focus and effort you need, no idea of the guts it takes to just step out there and face some of those fighters. They don't know more gold bars means a higher rank, all they are going to see is you getting your butt kicked by a bunch of guys *and girls* wearing the same colour belt as you."

"It's a good point, Tris," said Brett.

"It's not about what they think. This is for Andre. It's about raising the money and..." Tristan paused.

"And?" asked Dean.

Tristan plucked at his thumbnail then looked up. "Shihan, I've messed up. I missed the chance to find out if I was good enough for the national team and I don't know where I am as a karateka anymore. I need this challenge."

Dean nodded slowly. "Tristan, you're going to have to give me some time on this. Assuming the legalities and the venue check out, I'm happy to do the demo as a fundraiser. But I don't know about letting you fight. I will give it some thought though."

"Okay," said Tristan. "Thank you."

Tristan went back to training on the Monday evening. He worked hard but stayed within his limits. He still had two days on the antibiotics and didn't want to take any risks.

After training Sensei Gavin called him into the office. "How are you feeling?" he asked.

"I'm much better, thank you."

"Good," said Dean, entering the office behind him. "You might want this back then." Dean handed him his black belt. "But it doesn't mean you can slack off."

"Thank you, Shihan," he said. "I won't."

Tristan trained carefully all week and by the weekend he was feeling much stronger. He bowed into the dojo on the Saturday morning and found himself face to face with Sensei Jason Swart.

Tall and well built, Sensei Jason cut an imposing figure. His boyish face and thick blond hair, pulled back into a ponytail, made it hard to judge his age.

Based on his track record as a competition fighter and coach, Tristan guessed he must be older than he looked.

Sensei Jason acknowledged him. "So, you're the one who wants to fight the yudansha at the demo, yes?"

"Osu!" he said. "Yes, Sensei."

"Excellent," said Jason. "I admire your spirit and, if you've got what it takes, I've asked Shihan for permission to coach you."

"Thank you, Sensei," he said. "I would appreciate that. I need to put in some serious training."

Jason looked him up and down. "Yes," he said. "You need building up too. You're a bit on the weedy side."

Tristan passed no comment.

"Hopefully you make up for what you lack in power with speed," said Jason. "I want to get a good look at you today. Can you stay after the session?"

"Yes, Sensei."

Jason pushed the class hard. Several students had trouble getting back to their feet after kneeling for the final formalities.

Tristan was feeling a little sore but he knew he still had a lot of work to do.

Crap, he thought. Rico was meeting him after training and they were going home for lunch and then to the hospital. He wouldn't dare turn down Sensei's request but he did need to let Rico know.

He approached Jason. He was busy with another student so he hung back and did some stretches to keep himself warm.

Sensei Jason finished and came over to him. "Right," he said. "Let's get you on the bag and see what you can do."

"Osu! Yes, Sensei. But my friend is waiting outside. Is it okay if I tell him I will meet him later please?"

"You can invite him in to watch if you like. I'm not going to work you to death today. I just want to see what you've got so we won't be long."

"Thank you, Sensei." He made his way quickly to the door. Rico and Megan were both outside.

"'Bout time," said Rico. "Is it okay if Megs comes for lunch too?"

"Sure," he replied. "But Sensei wants to work with me a bit longer. You guys can come in if you like. But take your shoes off, Rico."

"Cool," said Rico.

"Go," said Megan. "I'll make sure Rico does the right thing."

"Thanks." He hurried back into he dojo.

Jason was waiting by the heavy bag hanging at the end of the room. "Right," he said. "Show me what you've got."

"Osu!" said Tristan. He went in hard and Jason had to adjust his stance more than once to keep the bag steady. By the time he stopped him they were both breathing heavily.

"Good," said Jason. "Now, pad up. Let's see how well you can fight."

His hands shook as he pulled on the shin pads. It was only partly due to the recent exertion. Sensei pulled on pads too. Tristan had never fought with them before. He didn't like them.

"Okay Sempai. You go as hard as you can and you shout up if I come on too rough."

"Osu!" said Tristan. "Yes, Sensei." They both knew Jason would have to do some serious damage before Tristan would tell him to back off. They bowed to each other and began the bout.

Nervous, Tristan held back. Jason came in with a low kick. He saw it coming and lifted his leg to block. He used the momentum to try and push Jason off line and didn't even see the fist that landed firmly against his ribs. Jason had caught him with a simple distraction.

He gasped and stumbled to one side, the power of the blow taking him by surprise. He quickly got his foot back to the ground and stepped aside to recover his composure.

Jason let fly with another punch but he saw it this time. He stepped into the attack and deflected the blow and, at the same time, he landed a hard palm heel strike to Jason's breast bone. He heard Jason exhale sharply and immediately followed through with a powerful punch to the stomach.

Jason stepped sideways avoiding the blow. He came in with another low kick and caught Tristan squarely on the thigh.

His leg buckled but he stayed on his feet. He stepped back and to the side, breathing hard. His leg hurt and he was fast losing confidence.

Get a grip, he told himself. Jason was playing with him and he knew it. He could take him any time he wanted. He knew Sensei

114

wouldn't play with him for long and expected to end up on the floor at any moment.

No! thought Tristan. *I can do this.* He moved in closer to his opponent and let loose a barrage of punches to the stomach and chest. Jason dodged the attack with well practised footwork.

Jason moved back and Tristan only just saw it. Jason's foot was flying towards his head. He ducked and the foot sailed over him. Tristan came up quickly with a high block, catching Jason under the knee and slamming him hard onto his back on the dojo floor.

Tristan was stunned. He fell to his knees beside his Sensei. "I'm so..."

"Don't you dare!" Jason's finger shot towards his face. "If you even think about apologising I'll kick you from one side of this dojo to the other."

Tristan said nothing. He stood and helped his Sensei to his feet.

"Well done, Sempai," said Jason. "I'd have you on my team any day of the week. I'd like to coach you, so you've just earned yourself your fight at the fundraiser. You'd better start getting some sponsors."

"Thank you, Sensei," said Tristan.

Jason knocked on the office door. It came open and he stepped inside. Sensei Gavin closed it behind him. Dean indicated the chair opposite him and Jason sat down. Gavin crossed the room and perched on the window sill.

"How did he do?" asked Dean.

"I want to coach him." said Jason. "There's potential there, for sure."

Dean looked up sharply. "Do you really think you had long enough with him to see that?" he asked, looking up at the wall clock.

"He put me on the floor in under twenty seconds," said Jason. "Bloody embarrassing it was too, there were a couple of his friends watching." He beamed good naturedly. "I underestimated him hopelessly. He needs work, a lot of work, but the potential is definitely there."

"He put you on the floor?" asked Dean. "Tristan Steyn? Are you sure you had the right kid?"

"Little guy." Jason held up his hand exaggerating Tristan's lack of stature. "Might just manage 50kg in a soaking wet dogi and looks like he couldn't fight sleep."

"That's the one," said Dean. "And he put you on the floor?"

"He did," said Jason. "Ducked under a damn head kick, parried my leg and pitched me straight onto my rear."

Dean and Gavin both laughed aloud.

"Well, I wish I'd seen that one," said Dean. "Okay, he can fight and you can coach him. But I want you to test him over the next few weeks. He's still a kid, I don't want him getting hurt. Test, but don't push too hard. And if you think I need to pull him out, say so. We'll still do some kumite for the fundraiser but it doesn't have to be all on his shoulders if you think he's not ready."

"Will do," said Jason. "By the time I've finished with him, he'll be ready. But I'll say this now, there's not a chance in hell we can pit him against too many fighters."

Dean sat back and steepled his fingers. "Go on," he said.

"Let's be realistic, he's fifteen, he's a runt and the only really heavy contact he's experienced was at his grading.

Dean was nodding. "You won't hear any arguments from me," he said. "So what do you propose?"

"I say we put all the names in a hat and, for a small donation, let the spectators pull them out. All the names go in but he only fights ten at two minutes a bout," said Jason. "That's twenty minutes fighting at the most and none of us will know who the next opponent will be until the name comes out of the hat."

Dean nodded and looked at Gavin.

"Sounds good to me," he said. "It's tough enough to be a good show but it's not going to kill him."

* * *

"It was amazing," said Rico. "There was this monster of a guy. Muscles like you wouldn't believe and Tris just up and flips him onto his back. You should have been there."

"Damn," said Andre. "I wish I could come too. I'd love to see you fight, Tris." Andre's leg was in plaster and he was sitting out of bed. He leaned forward in his chair towards Tristan.

Tristan was subdued and didn't feel much like talking. "Rico's exaggerating," he said. "Anyway, the club is organising a fundraiser. I'm going to get sponsored to fight some of the black belts and you'll be there to see them kick the crap out of me."

"That will be so cool," said Andre.

"Gee, thanks mate!"

"No, I didn't mean the bit about them kicking the crap out of you. I meant the watching in general."

Tristan grinned. "I know," he said.

"They won't kick the crap out of you," said Rico. "Look what you did to that third belt, or whatever he was, today."

"Rico, I'm going to get tooled," said Tristan. "And it's third dan."

Megan took Rico's can of Coke and sipped from it. "Yes," she said, handing it to Tristan. "You are. And I think you're mad. Why can't you organise it differently? Do something that involves other people fighting too, like a tournament or something?"

He took a drink from the can and passed it to Andre. "Because people are more interested in blood and gore than a fair fight," he said. "The idea of me getting smashed to a pulp will be far more appealing than a few people taking part in a tournament."

"God, Tristan, you make it sound like you're really going to get hurt," said Andre.

"He is," said Megan.

Tristan shrugged. "I might," he said. "But I can always pull out if it gets too rough."

"Yes," snapped Megan, leaping to her feet. "But you won't! I have to go now," she said. "I'll see you on Monday, Andre."

"That's my cue," said Rico, getting up. "See you guys

tomorrow or Monday, I'll give you a ring, Tris."

The door closed behind them and Andre turned to Tristan. "I hope it's for a good cause," he said. "I wouldn't get myself kicked around like that for..."

"It is," interrupted Tristan. "It's for your op and that scanner thingy the hospital needs."

Andre stared at him. "Tris, thank you. I really appreciate you doing it but I can't let you get hurt. I know how miserable it is to be in pain and I..."

"Yes, thanks to me, you do," said Tristan. "And I'm not going to change my mind. I put you here and I want to fix it. If I have to suffer to do it then it's no more than I deserve."

"Tristan, no one else blames you for this. It's not your fault. You can't punish yourself like this."

"Your mom blames me," said Tristan.

"My mom is looking for someone else to blame so she doesn't have to blame herself. If I'd been in school that day, like I should have been, then neither of us would have been there at that time."

"Come on Andre," said Tristan. "Your mom was just trying to protect you from your dad."

Andre's eyebrows shot up. "Oh God, Tris," he said. "You'll never understand, so just drop the subject."

Tristan frowned. "Understand what?"

Andre looked away. "My dad might be a lot of things but I don't need protecting from him."

"Andre! He beats you, of course you need protecting from him. You can't fight back by yourself."

"My dad has never hit me!"

"But what about..."

"Tristan, just drop it, okay!" Andre struggled out of the chair and grabbed his crutches. "I'm going to the bathroom," he said.

"Andre, wait!"

"I need a leak. I can't wait." He hobbled off to the bathroom, leaving Tristan feeling hollow and confused.

Chapter Sixteen

Tristan was at the dojo early on Sunday morning. Sensei Jason had asked him to train with him.

"Come on," said Jason. "In the car. We're going to the beach for a workout today."

Tristan enjoyed working outside and was looking forward to the session. He hoped it would wake him up a bit as he had spent most of the night worrying about Andre.

"Right," said Jason. "I don't know this area that well so we can either go over to North Beach or you can direct me to a good place to park the car close to where we can train.

"Our house," said Tristan. "We're on Sea View Drive, just across the road from the beach. You can park on our driveway."

Jason pulled up in front of the garage doors. "You sure no one is going to want to use that garage?"

"No," said Tristan. "But I'll ask my mom."

Elize came down the front steps. "Are you okay? Did you get hurt?"

He shook his head. "We're going to train on the beach. Can Sensei leave his car here?"

"Yes, of course."

Tristan introduced Elize and Jason.

"You know he's been sick, don't you? You won't push him too hard?"

"Ma!" hissed Tristan. "I'm fine." He immediately regretted bringing Jason to the house.

"Why don't you both come back for lunch when you've finished?"

Tristan was about to protest but Jason got in first. "Thank you, Mrs Steyn," he said "That would be great."

Tristan and Jason crossed the road to the beach. Jason had a small cooler bag containing bottles of water.

"We'll have to leave these somewhere safe until we get back from the run," said Jason.

"Okay," said Tristan. "I'll take it to Mark in the lifeguards' control room." He carried the bag up the beach.

"Hi, stranger," said Mark. "I haven't seen you around for ages. What are you doing on the beach in your pyjamas?"

Tristan frowned. "It's not my PJs, Mark," he said. "We're training on the beach today."

"Hell," said Mark. "You'll cook in that outfit. You be careful."

"Can I leave the water with you while we go for a run?"

"Some of it, yes. But you'd better carry a bottle each if you're going to run in that get up." Mark took two bottles out of the cooler bag and handed them to Tristan.

"I mean it," he said. "Be careful. I don't want my guys treating you two lunatics for sun stroke."

Sensei Jason had come up behind Tristan. "Don't worry about it," he said. "We'll be fine. We'll be wet most of the time anyway."

"I hope you're a better swimmer than you are surfer, Tris," said Mark.

Jason looked quizzically at Tristan. He quickly introduced Jason to Mark, hoping to avoid any further mention of the surfing incident. His adventure with Tallulah had spread like wildfire among the regular beach goers. To his horror, Mark briefly filled Jason in.

Jason grinned. "I'll pull him out if he gets into trouble. I do a bit of life-guarding at North Beach some weekends," he said.

Mark nodded. "That makes me feel better," he said. "There's a bit of a back and side wash out there today."

"Right, I'll keep an eye on him. Come on you," said Jason. "We've got work to do."

The two of them jogged down the beach to the water's edge.

"You follow me, okay?" said Jason.

"Yes, Sensei."

Jason jogged into the water until he was waist deep. Tristan followed. They turned parallel to the beach and pushed through the water as hard as they could. His heart rate soon went up but he kept pace with Jason.

Jason turned back towards the water's edge and ran hard though the knee deep surf. The breaking waves forced them to lift their knees high but Jason kept up a brisk pace. Tristan refused to fall behind.

Making a quick turn to the left, Jason sprinted up the sloping beach into the soft sand. The two of them ran hard for about two kilometres.

Hampered by his soaking dogi, Tristan was beginning to struggle but Jason showed no sign of letting up. They ran on and then turned again, down to the water. They ploughed back in, waist deep.

"Okay," Jason called. "Walk it out and get some water down you."

They turned back in the direction they had come and walked through the water. Tristan struggled against the rolling surf but managed to maintain his balance. He gulped the cool water from the bottle. His head ached and his heart was still pounding.

He screwed the cap back on his bottle.

"Back up on the sand," said Jason. "Push ups, 100, you count."

The two of them dropped onto their fists on the sand. Tristan began the count.

"*Ichi, ni, san...*" The hot sand abraded his knuckles and and he struggled to keep his wrists level on the soft beach. By the time he reached fifty, he was ready to collapse. Jason was still going strong and Tristan was determined not to give up. At the count of 100 Jason leapt to his feet. Tristan resisted the urge to fall in a heap on the sand and got up too.

"Am I working you too hard, Sempai," asked Jason.

"Osu! No, Sensei!" said Tristan firmly.

"Liar," grinned Jason. "Come on then, on your back on the sand. 100 sit ups, 100 crunches and then on your feet for 100 squats. I'll count the sit ups."

Tristan was grateful not to be counting. He was having enough difficulty breathing. His stomach muscles were burning and they were only on 75. He focussed on his breathing and got through the rest of the sit ups.

"Your count," called Jason as they shifted into position for the stomach crunches. Tristan began the count and with a monumental effort he made it to 100 without collapsing.

"On your feet," said Jason. "And into the surf. Nice deep squats, I'll count."

They were deep enough to be knocked around by the waves and to get soaked but not deep enough for the water to support their body weight. Balancing against the waves and the weight of his wet dogi made the squats torture. Jason made every one seem effortless while Tristan found himself holding his breath against the pain in his legs.

"Breathe, Sempai," said Jason. "Come on, nice sharp exhalations with the effort."

"Osu!" yelled Tristan, forcing the air out of his lungs. He was horrified when Jason began the count where he had left off even though they had done at least ten squats while he had been talking.

At Jason's call of 100, Tristan's legs were shaking and he could hardly stay on his feet.

"Am I working you too hard now, Sempai?"

"No, Sensei," said Tristan, with a little less conviction.

"Fine," said Jason. "Sprints up to the top of the beach and back down into waist deep water. We'll zigzag back to the lifeguards' tower."

Tristan turned and ran up the beach. It hurt. Turning at the top, he felt a tightness in his hamstring. He sprinted back down and into the water, running out to waist deep.

Turning again, he headed back up towards the beach but, as he stepped forward, his foot went into a dip in the sandy seabed. He was neck deep in water as the next swell broke over his head, knocking him down, face first.

He held his breath and struggled to regain his footing. His hamstring cramped and, had his head been above water, he would have yelled out loud. He felt Jason's hand catch the shoulder of his dogi and pull him up. He broke the surface, and sucked in the sweet air.

Jason dragged him up the beach and rolled him onto his stomach. He coughed and gasped as Jason pushed his fists hard into the cramping hamstring.

"Does that feel better?"

Tristan nodded. "Yes, it's okay now, thank you," he said, desperate to stop Jason digging into the painful muscle. Jason eased the pressure off and it immediately went back into spasm.

"Ow!" yelped Tristan.

Jason flipped him onto his back and pushed his knee up under his chin. Grabbing his ankle he pulled his leg up over his head stretching the cramp out of the muscle.

"Better?"

"Uh huh," Tristan managed, as Jason let go. He sat upright with his legs straight out in front of him. When the muscle threatened to cramp again he dropped his head onto his knees and held the stretch for a while.

"Okay," said Jason, laying a hand on his shoulder. "That's enough for today. Let's get you home and out of that wet gear."

Tristan stood up and gingerly tested his leg. "I'm fine now," he said and broke into a trot. Jason followed and the two of them jogged back to the lifeguards' tower to retrieve their water.

Tristan gulped down two bottles.

"Careful," said Jason. "You want some electrolytes now, especially if you cramp easily."

"I don't normally."

"You don't normally work as hard as I'm going to work you either," said Jason.

Tristan frowned as they approached the gate. It was closed. "Sorry," he said. "They don't usually close this."

Tristan pressed the buzzer and waited for a response.

"Ma, we can't get in," he said, when his mother's voice came over the intercom.

The gate buzzed and slid open. Tristan and Jason trudged up the driveway.

Elize came down the steps to meet them. "Oh goodness. Look at the state of the two of you."

"It's okay, Mrs Steyn," said Jason. "I'll get changed in the car."

"You most certainly won't," said Elize. "Lunch will be ready in about half an hour so you can have a shower in the guest bathroom and get yourself comfortable, And please, call me Elize."

"Thank you," said Jason.

"Why was the gate closed?" Tristan suspected his mother had done it so she would know when they got back.

"What? Oh," said Elize. "The neighbour's dog was out again and I didn't want him in the garden."

Tristan excused himself and hurried to his room to shower and change. He was unhappy about Jason and his mother being alone for too long. He hated it when his parents got too familiar with his school teachers and his karate instructors.

He soon forgot his hurry as the hot shower soothed his hurting body. The salt water and the heavy fabric of his dogi had rubbed his skin raw in places, and the hot water burned before easing the sting.

Tristan turned the shower on full and let the sharp little needles of water massage away the aches and pains of a hard training session.

Elize handed Jason a glass of ice cold orange juice as he came into the kitchen. He was wearing an official Greenview Bushido Kai club tracksuit and his wet hair was hanging loose over his shoulders.

"There you go," she said. "That should make you feel better."

"Ah, thank you," he said. "Perfect."

"Did Tristan behave himself?"she asked.

Jason nodded and swallowed a mouthful of juice. "He's going

to be sore later," he said. "Sorry, but I think I may have pushed him a bit hard. Beach work is tough if you're not used to it, but he kept up well. He's certainly got determination."

"Yes," sighed Elize. "I wish he would apply it to other areas of his life too."

Tristan wandered into the kitchen, his hair still dripping. He poured a glass of juice and drank it quickly and then filled his glass with water from the tap.

"Hey," said Jason. "Go easy on the water. It's good to stay hydrated but you need electrolytes too. Get something salty down you before you drink anymore."

"Yes, Sensei," said Tristan, putting the glass on the drainer.

Elize looked from Tristan to Jason. "Well," she said. "If you ever need a place to stay, you're more than welcome to move in here. I've never seen Tristan obey an order so fast and without objection."

"I find if you kick them hard enough right from the start, they'll usually jump when you tell them to," said Jason, grinning.

"Hmm," said Elize. "I might have to try that."

Tristan glared at his mother.

"You might have left it a bit late," said Jason.

They both laughed.

"Okay," Elize said. "Lunch is ready. Tristan, show Jason through to the dining room please. And give your father a shout. He's in the study."

Tristan struggled through the meal. He had always found it hard to eat so soon after training but he didn't want to appear rude while Sensei Jason was there.

"Oh, Tristan," said Elize, looking at her watch. "Rico called this morning. He's coming round at two to go and see Andre with you."

"Okay," said Tristan. Jabbing at the last of the carrots on his plate, he became aware that everyone seemed to be waiting for him to finish. He quickly ate the vegetables and placed his cutlery neatly on the plate. "Sorry," he mumbled.

Tristan was glad to escape with Rico but he was concerned that Sensei Jason had retreated to the study with his father.

"Tris, will you just chill," said Rico.

"But don't you worry that if your folks get together with your teachers and coaches that they'll all end up knowing too much about you?"

Rico stopped and folded his arms across his chest. "You're kidding, right?" he said. "Tris, first of all, I'm really not that deep. I have nothing to hide from my folks or my teachers. And secondly, I'm not that paranoid. I know my place in the family hierarchy and if there are people or things to be talked about, I will be the last in line."

"Ja, well you've got hundreds of brothers and sisters," argued Tristan. "I'm the only one my folks have to worry about and I know they ask questions about how I do at school and training and I hate it."

Rico shook his head. "Four," he said. "I have three brothers and a sister. And in case you hadn't noticed, none of them still live at home. So what if they ask questions anyway? At least you know they give a damn."

Tristan kicked at a stone and sent it tripping across the footpath. He didn't respond.

"You're lucky you don't have parents like poor Andre," Rico continued.

"Yeah okay, Rico," he said. "I know, I'm a spoilt brat."

"That's not what I meant, Tris. But if you're going to put words in my mouth then at least you picked something appropriate. That's exactly how you're acting today."

"Fine, do you want to go and see Andre on your own?" asked Tristan, turning back towards home.

"Tristan, stop it!" snapped Rico. "What's wrong with you today?"

Tristan didn't know what was wrong with him. He felt irritable and angry and he didn't want to go to the hospital.

He shrugged. "Sorry," he said. "I'm a bit sore and ratty from training this morning."

Rico thumped him on the arm. "What you need is junk food," he said. "You eat all that rabbit food and healthy stuff and you nearly kill yourself training and then you wonder why you're ratty." Rico became quite animated. "We'll go via the Spar and get chips and Coke and cake and whatever other rubbish we can sneak into the ward and we'll have a feast. It'll make you feel much better, you'll see."

"Rico, I just ate!"

"No," said Rico. "You didn't eat, you grazed. I'm talking proper food. Besides, I'm starving. I didn't have lunch today." Tristan sighed and followed him to the shop.

They arrived on the ward armed with two plastic packets of snacks and fizzy drinks. Rico and Andre played Chinese Patience and happily munched away at the chips and chocolate, while Tristan easily managed half a packet of marshmallows. He hated to admit it, but their sweet softness did seem to ease his mood.

He shifted uncomfortably in the chair. He was beginning to seize up and wanted to move.

"Do you fancy a walk down the corridor, Andre?" he asked.

"No," said Andre, not looking up. "I had my walk earlier."

He watched the two play cards for a while longer and then stood up. He felt like a spare part and wanted to go home.

"Sorry guys, but I have homework to do," he said. "I'll see you tomorrow."

Andre waved a hand.

"Oh, okay," said Rico. "See you at school then. You want to take some chips?"

He shook his head. "No, thanks," he said. "You guys eat them." He hobbled miserably out of the room.

Rico laid his cards down on the table.

"Are you going to tell me what that was about?" he asked.

"What?" asked Andre.

"Come on, the atmosphere in here was like a deep freeze in the Antarctic. Did you and Tris have a fight?"

"No," said Andre. "We're fine. He just doesn't know when to shut up sometimes."

Tristan started walking home but his anger got the better of him and he turned into Marine Park Road.

He marched up the garden path and knocked on the door of number 242. Michelle opened the door and almost shut it in his face.

He put his foot in the door and pushed it open. "Michelle," he said. "I really need to talk to your mom. Is she in?"

She opened her mouth to speak but was interrupted by Kathryn Turner's voice from somewhere in the house. "Who is it, Michelle?"

Michelle stood aside and waved Tristan in.

Kathryn came into the hallway wiping her hands on a tea towel. "Michelle," she said. "Would you please go to the shop and get me some milk? My purse is in the lounge."

Michelle left and returned with the purse.

"You can get yourself some sweets while you're out," said Kathryn. "But don't be too long."

"Okay," said Michelle. She pushed roughly past Tristan and out onto the verandah.

"What do you want?" asked Kathryn, once Michelle was out of earshot.

"I need to talk to you, Mrs Turner," he said. "Please."

"In the kitchen then." She inclined her head towards the end of the hall. He followed her into a large airy kitchen. The back door was open with a screen door in place to keep out the flies.

He stood close to the screen, the cool breeze soothing his nerves. "Mrs Turner," he began. "I'm so sorry. I never wanted Andre to get hurt. I just..."

"Oh for heaven's sake, Tristan," Kathryn snapped. "What

difference does it make how sorry you are? If you hadn't tried to interfere in something that was never your business none of this would have happened."

He looked down at his feet. "I know," he said. "But at the time, I didn't think I was interfering. I just wanted to help Andre. I still want to help him." He looked up at Kathryn.

She frowned. "I think you've done enough damage, Tristan. I would prefer you to just leave us all alone."

He took a deep breath and looked her directly in the eye. He spoke before his courage failed him. "Mrs Turner, I know Andre needs an operation and I know it's expensive. I want to help to raise the money for it. It's my fault he..."

"Are you suggesting we can't take care of our own family?" asked Kathryn, her voice low and even.

"I... No!" he said. "I'm just saying I want to help. It was my fault so I should help."

Kathryn moved closer to Tristan. He resisted the urge to back away.

"Did Andre tell you about the operation?"

"Yes," he said and immediately wished he hadn't.

"Stupid boy!" hissed Kathryn.

Tristan wasn't sure whether she meant him or Andre. "He..." began Tristan.

"Shut up," snapped Kathryn. "I've told you before, I don't want you anywhere near that hospital and I don't want anything from you. And neither does Andre!"

"Well I'm still going to do it," he said. "I'm doing it for Andre, not you. If you want to fight with him about it then you can do what you want. But you can't stop me from doing it!"

"Don't you dare speak to me like that!" said Kathryn. "You don't know anything about us. Just get out of this house. Now! Before Michelle gets back."

"Fine," said Tristan. "I will, but I'm not going to stop seeing Andre unless he asks me to." He was shocked by his own audacity but he was angry and went on. "You have no right to make his decisions for him!"

Kathryn Turner lunged at him. She caught him by the collar and drew back her arm. He raised his hand and blocked the slap that flew towards his face. He caught her wrist and pushed her arm to one side.

Stunned, Tristan stared open-mouthed at her. He released her wrist and took two steps backwards. "You," he said. "It was you who hit Andre." He turned and fled through the hall to the front door.

"Tristan!" Kathryn called after him. "Tristan, wait."

Arriving home, Tristan ran up the driveway and took the steps two at a time. The door came open and he almost knocked Sensei Jason off his feet.

"Whoa, steady on," said Jason. "You should be resting. You've got another tough session at the dojo tomorrow night."

"Tristan," said Brett. "Be careful!"

"I'm sorry," he said. He turned to Jason. "Sorry, Sensei."

He just wanted to get to his bedroom. "Um, Dad," he said, backing into the house. "You might be getting a phone call from Mrs Turner. You won't like it, but please let me explain before you kill me."

Brett and Jason watched Tristan disappear into the house.

"Hmm," grunted Brett. "That sounds ominous."

"Yes," said Jason. "I think I'd better leave you to it. Thanks again for these papers," he tapped a large brown envelope. "I'll get them to Dean tonight. We'll be able to get most of the organisation behind us now, and then I can focus on getting Tristan ready for his fights."

"That's if I haven't killed him by morning," said Brett. "I'd better go and see what he's been up to."

Brett waved Jason off and went to find Tristan.

He knocked on his door and went in. Tristan was lying on the bed, sound asleep. He hadn't even removed his shoes. Brett eased them from his feet and folded the double duvet over him. He never moved.

Tristan woke up in the same position he had fallen asleep in. He was stiff and sore and could hardly turn onto his side. His back always ached if he slept on his stomach. He eased his knees up to his chest and was surprised to see he was still fully clothed.

He blinked in the bright sunlight and lifted the alarm clock off the bedside table, 5:35am.

He remembered now how tired he'd been when he got home. He had intended to lie down for five minutes but had slept for a full twelve hours.

He hauled himself upright and swung his legs off the bed. Every muscle in his body ached. He stood up and dragged himself into the bathroom.

The hot shower eased the aches while he stood under it but the pain came back with a vengeance as he pulled on his school uniform.

It was far too early to leave for school but he knew if he let himself lie down again he would go straight back to sleep. He hobbled into the kitchen.

Elize was sitting at the kitchen table. "Good morning," she said. "You're up early."

"Morning," said Tristan. "Well, I was in bed just after five yesterday but I still feel like I could sleep for a week." He slipped into a chair opposite his mother. Folding his arms on the table he rested his head on them.

Elize sighed. "I warned Jason not to work you too hard," she said. "You've only just got over tonsillitis. Tristan, you really should be more careful. And I don't like the idea of this fight you want to do. You could get hurt."

"Ma," he said. "I got hurt playing rugby far more than I ever have in karate and you moaned at me when I gave that up."

"I know, Tris," said Elize. "But I worry about you."

He raised his head. "If I was going out at night and stealing cars then you would have a reason to worry," he said. "But I'm doing something healthy and constructive, so why are you fussing?"

Elize raised her eyebrows. "How is someone smacking you round the head and aiming to knock you unconscious healthy exactly?" she asked.

"It's not like that, Mom! I've been training for almost eleven years and I've never been knocked unconscious!"

"Hey, hey, hey, what's going on in here?" asked Brett, entering the kitchen and taking a seat at the table. "Are you back chatting your mother?"

Tristan didn't answer.

Elize took Brett's hand in hers. "I'm just worried about him fighting all those black belts," she said. "I hate the idea that we have to sign papers to give consent. It just seems like we're giving them permission to beat him senseless."

Brett sighed. "It's Tristan's decision, love," he said. "He knows better than we do what it's all about. If he wants to do it then I'm happy to give my consent."

"Thank you," said Tristan. "Ma, it's not like it's a street fight. I have choices. If I can't handle it I can pull out. Besides, Shihan has no faith in my ability to do this. He'll probably pull me out anyway," he added moodily.

"Fine," said Elize, raising her hands. "But don't come crying to me if you get hurt. You'll get no sympathy at all, but if it's really what you want to do then I'll sign the papers."

"Thanks, Ma," said Tristan, leaping up from the table and planting a kiss on the top of his mother's head.

"I'm going to school and the hospital and then straight to training. See you later."

"What about food?" asked Elize. "You haven't even had breakfast."

Tristan grabbed an apple and two bananas from the fruit bowl and waved them at his mother.

"Breakfast," he said. "*Moenie jou bekommer nie*, Ma!" Don't worry!

"Oh, come on, Tristan," said Rico. "What's wrong with you? You've been walking around like an old man all day. Andre will think we're not coming."

He walked faster and came up alongside Rico. "Sorry," he said. "I'm stiff as hell from training on the beach yesterday. I have no idea how I'm going to survive karate tonight."

"Can't you do a bunk for one night?"

"Not unless I have a death wish."

"I thought hobbies were supposed to be fun," said Rico. "I really don't understand you guys."

"You and everyone else who doesn't train," said Tristan. "You have to do it to get it."

Tristan opened the door to Andre's room and stopped dead. Rico walked into the back of him, shoving him forward and further into the room.

Kathryn Turner turned towards the door. Tristan would have backed out of the room but Rico was still directly behind him.

Kathryn smiled. "Hello boys," she said. "Come in. I was just leaving."

Tristan remained rooted to the spot as Kathryn rose from the chair. She took Andre's hand in hers and told him she would be back later, then she turned and made for the door.

Tristan stepped aside and Rico followed suit.

"Tristan, may I have a word?"

He indicated to Rico that he should go inside and then stepped out of the room with Andre's mother. The door closed, leaving them alone in the corridor.

"Tristan," said Kathryn. "I want to apologise to you. Things have been difficult for us and..."

"You don't have to explain anything to me," he interrupted, his tone cool. "I'm sorry if I was rude to you yesterday. But I feel horrible about what happened. Andre is my friend and it's important to me to be able to do something to help. I want him to get well again," he said. "And I want him to be safe, Michelle too!"

Kathryn nodded. "I know," she said. "They will be. Both of them."

Tristan placed his hand on the door handle and pointed to the door. "May I?"

"Of course," said Kathryn. "I didn't realise how much your visits mean to Andre."

"Thank you," he said. He breathed a sigh of relief as Kathryn turned and walked down the corridor. He opened the door and went in.

"You okay?" asked Rico.

He nodded.

"What was that about?" asked Andre, his face pale and drawn. "Did she tell you to leave again?"

"No," said Tristan, perching on the wooden chair arm. "We've sorted out our differences for now, I think."

The chair arm was uncomfortable so he stood up and leaned against the end of the bed. "We really need to get another chair in here," he said.

"No," grinned Andre. "We don't. I'm going home tomorrow!"

"You are? That's great," said Tristan. "But what about the op?"

Andre pulled a face. "I have to come back for that when we can get everything sorted out," he said. "I have to be in a damn wheelchair most of the time until I've had the surgery, but it's better than being stuck in here."

Tristan was genuinely happy for Andre but he felt a stab of concern about him going home to his mother. "Will you be okay?" he asked. "I mean, will you manage at home, with the wheelchair and everything?"

He didn't want to say too much in front of Rico.

"If you need help, we'll be there,"said Rico.

"Thanks," said Andre. "Tris, don't worry about us. Everything will be fine." Andre held his gaze.

Tristan bit down on his lip then nodded. "Right," he said. "But if you need anything, call me, okay?"

"Thanks," said Andre. "I might need your help next week. I'm coming back to school."

Rico frowned. "Will you manage the steps?"

"Yeah," said Andre. "I only have two classes up top and the doc says I'll be fine on the crutches."

"So what's up then?" asked Tristan.

Andre lowered his eyes, his cheeks colouring as he fiddled with the hospital ID band around his wrist. "Well," he said. "I wasn't exactly the most popular person in school, was I?" He looked up at Rico then at Tristan. "I'm scared, you guys. I feel totally defenceless like this." He waved a hand over his plastered leg.

"Don't worry," said Rico. "We'll look out for you."

"Yeah," said Tristan. "You'll be fine."

The trio spent the afternoon out in the hospital gardens, all thoughts of homework forgotten as they basked in the sun and enjoyed the fresh air.

Tristan and Rico took it in turns to push the wheelchair as they explored the entire grounds.

By the time they went back inside the sun was low in the sky and Tristan realised he had left it too late to eat before training. He was angry with himself. It would be a hard session and he would need all the energy he could get, but to risk eating now would mean, at best, severe stomach pains and, more worryingly, the possibility of throwing up in the middle of the dojo.

As soon as the warm ups were over Tristan knew he was in trouble. Sensei Gavin had worked them harder than usual and he was feeling shaky and sore.

"Right," said Gavin. "*Kihon* today. Basics." He reminded the newer members of the meaning. "And Sempai Tristan and Sempai Jabu, step out please. Sensei Jason would like you both in the mat room."

"Osu!" They acknowledged the order in unison, then both stepped back and walked behind their row towards the mat room.

Tristan bowed out of the dojo and stood alongside Sempai Jabu. They looked at each other but neither spoke as they waited for Sensei Jason.

Tristan was nervous. Jabulani Mhlophe had a reputation as a dedicated and hard trainer and an even harder fighter. He regularly trained at both Sensei Gavin and Sensei Jason's dojo just to get in the extra hours.

Sempai Jabu was working towards his second dan grading and would be taking the test in June.

Though almost ten years his senior, at 5'7", Jabu wasn't much taller than Tristan. However, he was well built and could pack a powerful punch. Tristan didn't even want to think what one of his kicks would feel like.

Sensei Jason entered the mat room. "Right," he said. "In case you're wondering why you're in here, I'll fill you in. Jabu, you need as many fights as you can get and Tris, you need toughening up for your kumite at the demo."

Tristan wasn't sure how to interpret toughening up. *Was Sensei suggesting he was a wimp?* Looking at Sempai Jabu, he realized the true magnitude of the task he was taking on. It occurred to him that he may, indeed, be a bit of a wimp.

"Okay," said Jason, "I want to see good hard fighting." The two of them faced each other and bowed.

"*Hajime!*" begin, Jason called.

Jabu was surprisingly fast for his build. He stepped to one side and before Tristan knew what had happened he was on the floor gasping for breath.

He got to his feet immediately but it was another few seconds before he dare take his hands from his ribs and and face his opponent again.

"Okay?" asked Jason.

He nodded. He sucked in his lower lip and made eye contact with Jabu. He inclined his head slightly, acknowledging his opponent's strike.

Jason began the bout again.

Tristan ploughed in and landed a hard kick. The intended target was Jabu's ribs but he had seen it coming and closed his guard. Tristan's foot slammed Jabu's arm against his ribcage causing him to gasp and step away. But Jabu's elbow had hurt his foot and he shied away from kicking with it again.

He blocked a punch to his stomach and brought his knee round, catching Jabu's hip. Momentarily off balance, Jabu hopped back on one leg. As he did so, he lifted the other, slamming the ball of his foot up under Tristan's solar plexus.

Tristan let out a small choking sound and fell to his hands and knees. He sat back on his heels and pushed his fist up into his diaphragm.

"Get up," yelled Jason, "You're not hurt."

"How do you know I'm not hurt?" he choked.

"Because I said you're not," said Jason. "A little whack like that doesn't hurt. Now get up!"

He got to his feet, swallowing against rising nausea.

"Let's go again," said Jason. "Ready?"

"Osu! Yes, Sensei." The pair waited for Jason's call to begin. "Hajime!"

This time Tristan landed the first blow. He went in hard with a roundhouse kick to Jabu's right thigh and, as his leg buckled, he followed up with a heavy punch to the ribs. Jabu went to ground but was up before Tristan could catch his breath.

Tristan was struggling. He was still winded from Jabu's kick. He backed away from a barrage of punches Jabu threw at him.

Don't, he thought. *As soon as you back away you lose.* Jabu was on him in a flash. He pushed him back and further off balance and, at the same time, he slammed his elbow into Tristan's already hurting sternum.

"Urgh!" he grunted. He stayed up, but he knew he was finished. He felt the strength go from his arms. The healthy respect he'd had for his opponent turned to fear as he realised he was utterly defenceless against Jabu's next attack.

Tristan wasn't even sure what hit him where. He simply became aware of lying on his side on the cold, hard floor.

Sensei Jason helped him to his feet. "Ready for another bout, Sempai?" he asked.

"Osu! Yes, Sensei," he said. He took a deep breath and tried to steady his nerves. He was hurting, afraid and humiliated, but he wasn't going to give up.

Jason started them for a third time.

Tristan's fist shot out and smashed into Jabu's chest.

Jabu back-pedalled a couple of steps but immediately recovered. "*Kiai!*" he yelled, as his retaliating kick smacked into Tristan's left thigh.

Tristan gritted his teeth against the pain and transferred more of his weight to his right. He knew he was off balance but his left leg felt heavy and useless.

Jabu's left foot came in at head height. He avoided it with a bit of deft footwork but it cost him dearly. His leg, still deadened by the kick, refused to support his weight and he stumbled like a drunkard.

Jabu capitalised on the opportunity. Using the momentum from the missed kick, he continued to turn. Planting his left foot firmly on the ground, he brought his right foot up, the spinning back kick catching Tristan squarely on the side of the jaw. He went down like a sack of flour.

Tristan sat up, dazed and confused. Sensei Jason was kneeling beside him. He took hold of Tristan's chin and gently tilted his head to the light. He blinked.

"Are you okay?"

"Yes, I'm fine thank you," he responded. He rubbed his eyes then rested his head in his hands. The dizziness was beginning to fade. He stood up.

Jason draped an arm over his shoulders and led him to a bench at the side of the room. "Sit there for a few minutes," he said. "Sempai Jabu's bringing you some water. I'll be back just now."

Jason left as Jabu returned with a bottle.

"Thank you," said Tristan. He unscrewed the cap and took a drink, then offered the bottle to Jabu.

"Thanks," said Jabu. He looked quickly round the room and gulped some of the water. They both knew that eating and drinking in the dojo was forbidden. Jabu handed the bottle back. Tristan took another quick swallow then capped it and placed it under the bench.

"Sorry," said Jabu. "I didn't mean to kick you that hard. I was a bit off balance. I should have pulled back."

Tristan shrugged. "Sensei said to go hard."

"I know," said Jabu. "But I didn't mean to knock you out. It's one thing in a tournament, but damaging your training partner is not good. Are you all right?"

He nodded. "I'm fine," he said. "But my mom is going to kill me. I only told her this morning that I'd never been knocked out before."

"You're lucky you get your mom," said Jabu. "It looks like Shihan is going to kill me."

"Wanna swap?" asked Tristan.

Jason and Dean bowed out of the dojo and came into the mat room.

"Are you all right, Sempai," asked Dean, catching Tristan's chin in his huge hand and looking into his eyes. He placed his other hand behind Tristan's neck and turned his head from side to side, still checking his eyes.

"Yes, thank you, Shihan," said Tristan. "It was only a bit of a knock."

"I don't want you getting knocked unconscious," said Dean. "You can't afford to take the risk."

Tristan frowned. "Meaning?" he asked.

"Tristan, you're fifteen years old. You're still developing," snapped Dean. "You could do some permanent damage."

"Oh, okay," he said. "I thought you meant I didn't have enough brain cells."

"Don't put words in my mouth, Sempai," Dean said. "I might be tempted to use them." He turned to Jabu. "Are you all right?"

"Osu! Yes, Shihan. I'm fine thank you."

"Good," said Dean, "You can go and join the class in the dojo. Tristan, I'm taking you home."

He opened his mouth to protest and immediately changed his mind. Arguing with Shihan was not a good idea.

"Thank you," he said, instead.

Dean was angry. He had expected Tristan's parents to be concerned but he was wholly unprepared for Elize Steyn's fury. He was even less prepared for the fact that she had directed it at Tristan and not, as the adult responsible for her son's safety, at him.

Brett had quickly ushered him out of the door with the assurance that he would sort things out. But Dean was worried. He had wanted to stay and fight Tristan's corner.

Gavin and Jason both stood as Dean barged into the office. He waved a hand at them. "Sit," he said, and turned on Jason.

"Sensei, what the hell were you thinking?" he yelled. "That kid is fifteen years old. I told you to test him, not kill him."

Jason shot back to his feet. "That *kid* is also a shodan!" he flared. "And if he can't fight with the big guys then he either shouldn't be wearing that belt or he should be training in a non-contact martial art!"

Dean threw up his hands and turned to Gavin. "Hallelujah!" he said. "Finally, someone who agrees with me. I told you when we graded him that he was too young!"

Dean's anger was now directed at Gavin. "And as of right now the rules of this dojo have changed." Dean banged his fist on the desk. "No one under the age of eighteen will be allowed to even think about grading to shodan! No matter how talented they are!"

"Actually," said Jason. "I don't agree with you. Not entirely."

"Excuse me?" Dean frowned at Jason.

"Well," he said. "I agree that if he can't hold his own against the adults then he shouldn't have the grade. But I think he's more than capable of taking the dings and I think it's your lack of faith in him and you mollycoddling him that's knocked his confidence."

Dean and Gavin stared, agape, at Jason.

"I'm sorry if I'm speaking out of turn, Shihan," said Jason. "But I think you are underestimating his capability and I think you're holding him back. He's never going to be good at kumite while you are trying to protect him because of his age. You seem to think that just because he's young, he's going to cave taking a bit of heavy contact from guys at his own grade."

"He was just knocked unconscious by someone his own grade!" snapped Dean.

"Yes," said Jason. "He's being treated like a kid so he's acting like one. He was frightened to death of his opponent and his focus was shot!"

Tristan poked miserably at his cereal. His head ached and his mother was banging around the kitchen, making it perfectly clear she was still angry with him.

After Dean left last night she had blasted him with a lecture on the stupidity of his chosen pastime. He objected to the word sport.

After that, what bit of sleep he'd managed had been plagued by nightmares of broken bones, ruptured organs and losing fight after fight in front of a crowd of jeering schoolmates.

For the first time since he'd asked to do it, he doubted his ability to manage the fights. And worse, he doubted his worthiness to wear a black belt.

He pushed the bowl of cereal aside and stood up. "I'm going to school," he said. "See you later."

Elize didn't look up from wiping the drainer and he slammed the door hard behind him.

Tristan went straight from school to the dojo. He needed to speak to Shihan Dean. He kicked his school shoes off in the mat room and shoved them under the bench. He crossed the mats in his socks and bowed into the dojo.

Sensei Gavin came out of the office. "You're eager, Sempai," he said. "Training doesn't start for another four and a half hours.

"Osu!" he acknowledged Gavin. "Sensei, I need to speak to Shihan," he said.

"He won't be in until after three."

Tristan glanced at his watch; another twenty five minutes.

"Could I practice kata until he gets here, Sensei?" he asked.

"Of course," said Gavin. "The dojo is all yours."

He changed into his dogi and did some dynamic stretching to warm up. He decided to begin with Taikyoku Sono Ichi and work his way through the kata until Shihan Dean arrived.

He loved kata and was soon so absorbed in his practice that he lost all track of time and place.

Gavin and Dean watched Tristan perform Yantsu kata. So great was his focus it was clear he unaware of his audience.

"Beautiful," said Gavin. "I wish my kata was as good as his."

"Watch and learn," said Dean. "That's a karateka who truly loves kata. It's a real shame he missed the try outs for the national team. He would be our best bet in the kata competition, I'm sure of it."

"Yes," said Gavin. "I'm not sure about his kumite though. I think kata is where his talent lies."

"I disagree wholeheartedly."

Gavin and Dean turned as Jason came up behind them.

"We know that, Sensei," said Dean.

"I'm not saying his kata's not good," said Jason. "It's a joy to watch. I'm just saying, if he wasn't so terrified of the big guys, his kumite could be that good too. And if he can't fight, he may as well be doing ballet."

Dean sighed. "We'll see about that," he said. "I've decided to let you carry on coaching him. But!" He pointed a finger in Jason's face. "If that boy gets any permanent damage *you* will be the one standing between him and his mother. And me and his mother, for that matter," he added. "Gav, let him finish what he's doing then tell him he can come in and see me."

Tristan was embarrassed when he realised he was being watched. He stopped what he was doing and dropped to his right knee to adjust his belt.

Gavin came over. "I'm impressed," he said. "I can see you work hard on understanding your kata, not just performing them. Anyway, Shihan is here now. He's waiting in the office for you."

"Um, thank you, Sensei," said Tristan, his mind on his meeting with Shihan.

He removed his belt and straightened his jacket before knocking on the office door.

"Come in," called Dean, after a short pause.

Heart hammering, Tristan opened the door and entered. He stood in front of the desk.

"Sempai," said Dean, frowning. "Where is your obi?"

He placed the belt on the desk pushing it towards Dean. "I don't think I'm good enough to wear it," he said. "You told me that wearing a black belt in your dojo was a privilege we have to earn, not a right. Well, I think it's a responsibility too, and I don't think I can live up to it."

Dean inclined his head and looked deep into Tristan's eyes. "Go on," he said. "Tell me what you mean by that."

"Shihan, I know shodan is only the beginning and I still have so much to learn, but I'm also supposed to set an example and to teach what I do know to the juniors," he said. "I don't think I can. Some of those kyu grades are a lot older than me and bigger than me and they could probably put me on the floor in a fight without even blinking. I'm supposed to be the same grade as Sempai Jabu and I didn't last 60 seconds against him."

Tristan's carefully thought out speech was long forgotten and he babbled on. "Basically I'm rubbish at kumite and I don't think I deserve to be ranked shodan."

"Is that what you think?" asked Dean.

"Yes," mumbled Tristan. "I think you should keep my belt and let me grade to shodan when I'm good enough."

"Sempai, sit down." Dean picked up the belt. "And let me tell you what I think."

Tristan pulled out the chair and sat. He tugged at his dogi jacket and pulled it tightly around him.

"I think," said Dean. "That you are taking yesterday's little incident totally out of context. So you took a bit of a pounding. But you have to remember, Sempai Jabu is one of our Provincial knockdown competition fighters. He trains for, and wins, tournaments on a regular basis and he's preparing for his nidan grading. You, on the other hand, focus most of your attention on kata and kihon. You slack off when it comes to kumite, you always have. You've only ever done enough to get through your next grading! And that is one of the reasons I was reluctant to let you fight for this fundraiser."

Tristan opened his mouth but Dean raised a hand to silence him.

"Now, I suggest you put this back on, find a way to soothe your bruised ego and get out there and do as Sensei Jason tells you. That way you'll just about be in fighting shape in time to help your friend." Dean held the belt out to Tristan.

He resented Dean's words and his anger got the better of him. "I don't think it has anything to do with my ego or with slacking off," he said, folding his arms across his chest and refusing the belt. "I just don't think I'm good enough."

"Well then, Sempai," said Dean, laying the belt back on the desk. "I find your thinking highly insulting!"

Taken aback, he looked up at Dean and frowned.

"You are implying that your Sensei and I, with many years more experience than you have, exercised poor judgement in grading you to shodan!" said Dean.

Tristan flushed and looked down at the desk. "I'm sorry, Shihan," he said. "I didn't mean it like that. I... I never thought about it that way."

Dean leaned forward and rested his arms on the desk. "Sempai," he said. "That is precisely your problem. You're far too impulsive, you don't think!" Dean stood up and threw Tristan's belt at him. "I will not tolerate my students speaking to me the way you did today. Especially not my junior yudansha! Now put that belt on and get out into the mat room."

Tristan stood and tied the belt round his waist.

"Right," said Dean. "Go and warm up, and make a good job of it. You'll train with me this afternoon and we'll see once and for all whether or not you're good enough!"

"You're coasting, Sempai!" Dean moved in and walked behind him. "Stop working to the count," he said jabbing him roughly between the shoulder blades.

"When we do kihon in the dojo that count is timed for the white belts. I want to see more from you. The faster and more powerfully you perform those techniques, the harder you're working. Now work!" he said.

Shoving a hand under Tristan's belt, Dean twisted it, pulling the knot hard into his abdomen. "Work as if keeping this belt depends on it."

Dean moved back in front of him. "*Mae keage*," high front kick, he said, and began the count. "Ichi, ni, san..."

Dean had doubled the speed of the count but Tristan still lengthened the time between his kicks by delivering them with as much power and speed as he could.

Dean drilled him hard on basic and advanced techniques, insisting on maximum focus and explosive speed and power. If he was unhappy with the performance he would restart the count at one. After hundreds of blocks, punches and kicks Tristan was tired, sore and hungry but he knew Dean wouldn't let up.

"On your back, Sempai," said Dean. He joined him on the floor. They interlocked their feet and did 150 sit ups.

"Crunches," said Dean. This time he counted two hundred and

then rolled onto his belly. Tristan followed suit.

"Push ups! 100 on your fists and 10 on your finger tips. Go!" he yelled.

Tristan's right hand was still sore from his fights with Jabu. He struggled with the finger tip push ups and dropped to his palms after only five. He immediately corrected his position and completed the set of ten, hoping Dean hadn't noticed.

"On your feet," said Dean. He jumped up and the two of them did 100 squats.

"Okay," said Dean. "I think you need to catch your breath for the next round." Dean crossed the mat room and returned with three small dumbbells, each weighing 1,5kg.

Dean tied one to the loose ends of Tristan's belt and placed one in each of his hands.

"*Kiba dachi*," said Dean. "Arms out to the sides and hold it until I get back."

Tristan stepped sideways and into the low, wide horse stance. Working against his body weight and the extra weight on his belt, the muscles in his legs began to protest almost immediately. Loosely gripping the weights in his hands, he stretched his arms out to the sides. More pain and trembling from overworked muscles.

He focussed his attention on a tree outside the window and tried to relax. Breathing deeply he attempted to empty his mind. He knew that either Dean or one of the Sensei would be watching and he refused to give in and drop his arms or shift his stance.

He was almost sobbing with the effort of holding his position when Dean came back in. Dean took the weights from Tristan's hands and untied the one from his belt.

"Okay?" he asked.

He nodded, not trusting his voice.

"*Yasume*," relax, said Dean, gently pushing his arms back to his sides. He eased himself up out of his stance and walked a few paces to stretch his knotted muscles.

"Let's work those kinks out shall we?" asked Dean.

"Osu!" yelled Tristan.

Dean meant it too. He tested Tristan's punching and kicking techniques on the focus pads and the hanging bag. Twice he slipped in his own sweat and fell heavily on the wooden floor.

After almost two hours of relentless pushing Tristan was gasping for air and water.

"Okay, take a break," said Dean. "Come with me." He followed Dean back to the office on shaking legs.

Dean rummaged in his training bag. "Here," he said, opening a bottle of water and tipping a sachet of rehydration powder into it. He capped the bottle and gave it a good shake. "Drink this."

"Thank you, Shihan," said Tristan, gratefully gulping at the fluid.

"Careful," said Dean. "I don't want you being sick when we start again."

His breathing had slowed in the five minutes they had been in the office.

"Right," said Dean. "Outside!"

Tristan followed Dean outside, across the car park and onto the adjacent golf course.

Dean had a friendly agreement with the owners allowing him to use the section close to the dojo for training. In return, Dean agreed to replace any dojo windows, broken by the occasional rogue golf ball, at his own expense.

"Right," said Dean, pointing about 200 metres ahead. "To that tree and, for your own sake, try to keep up."

Dean took off at a full sprint along the side of the golf course, his long legs flying. Tristan tried his hardest to keep up but he didn't stand a chance.

Dean reached the tree a full 15 seconds before Tristan did. He glanced at his stop watch. "Again," he said. "Back to the start." He raced away.

By the time Tristan arrived back at the starting point he knew why Dean had told him to try and keep up. He was timing thirty second rest stops between his sprints but, because he was so much slower, Tristan was lucky to get 10 seconds.

"Go!" yelled Dean almost as soon as Tristan had stopped. He gave everything he had but there was nothing left in the tank. He staggered up to the tree and fell, heaving and gasping, at Dean's feet. Dean dropped down next to him and helped him to his knees, supporting him as he retched violently and vomited onto the grass.

Dean let him stay on the ground until his breathing had eased. After about five minutes he slapped him on the shoulder.

"Come on, Sempai," he said. "Up you get." He dragged him to his feet and helped him back to the dojo.

Taking him into the office, he sat him in one of the chairs. "Here you go." He took a towel out of his kit bag and draped it over Tristan's shoulders, then placed three bananas and a bottle of water on the desk. "Get some rest and make sure you eat and drink something now." Dean looked up at the wall clock. "Sensei Jason will want you in the mat room in an hour."

Dean found Jason in the dojo talking to Gavin. "Slight change of plans tonight," he said. "Gav, I'll be wanting to borrow some of your seniors. I want two 3rd and 2nd kyu students, three 1st kyu, four shodan, a couple of nidan and you." Dean pointed to Sensei Jason.

Gavin raised an eyebrow. "I'll do my best," he said. "It depends who comes to training."

"Fair enough," said Dean. "In that case, I want 13 of the best fighters you've got in tonight." He turned to Jason. "Sempai Tristan's training tonight, I want fifteen fights at a minute and a half each. Start him with the green belts and work your way up. You and I will finish it."

Jason gaped at Dean. "Hang on," he said. "Yesterday you told me to go easy and tonight you want me to hammer him?"

"You're the one who said I treat him like a child and mollycoddle him. Well, today he behaved like a child so I'm testing your theory. From now on I'll push him the same way I would an adult and we'll see if he starts acting like one. He told me today he doesn't think he's good enough to be shodan."

Gavin sighed. "Of course he's good enough, he more than proved himself at his grading," he said. "You don't need to put him through another one tonight."

Dean turned to Gavin. "I know that, but apparently he doesn't. It's just a crisis of confidence over yesterday's little stinger with Sempai Jabu," he said. "Anyway, I won't have my juniors implying that I used bad judgement in grading them."

"Oh!" snapped Gavin. "That's rich. You didn't want to grade him anyway."

"Sensei, you know damn well that had nothing to do with his ability as a karateka. I just don't like young kids taking too many knocks and I don't like that boy's attitude!"

Gavin narrowed his eyes and shook his head. "Excuse me," he said. "I have things to do." He stalked off.

"Hang on, Shihan," said Jason. "I've got a lot of work to do to get him ready for this fundraiser. I need to pace him."

"Tonight," said Dean. "You need to wipe the floor with him. You can start pacing him tomorrow."

Tristan was hunched forward in the chair clutching an empty water bottle. Gavin closed the door quietly and squatted beside the chair. He slid the bottle from his hands and placed it on the table. "Tristan?"

He looked up, seeming to notice Gavin's presence for the first time. His face was flushed a deep red, his lips were dry and he was breathing through his mouth. His untidy hair clung damply to his forehead.

"Osu!" he said and moved to stand.

Gavin held up a hand to stop him. "No," he said. "Stay there. Are you all right?"

He nodded. "Yes, thank you, Sensei," he said.

"Good," said Gavin. "I'd eat those if I were you," Gavin pointed to the remaining two bananas on the desk. "I think you're going to need them."

"Sempai Jabu again?" he asked.

149

"Among others," said Gavin, watching him closely. If the boy was concerned, he didn't show it. "Now eat please, and drink." Gavin took the empty bottle from the desk and replaced it with a full one from a cabinet by the window. "I'll leave you to prepare yourself."

Tristan stood up as Dean entered the office. Dean looked him up and down. He tugged self-consciously at his grass stained and filthy dogi. He knew he looked a mess.

"Sempai, do you want to go home tonight and get cleaned up and have a rest? You can work with Sensei Jason tomorrow."

"No, Shihan," said Tristan. "I want to train tonight." He knew the question was as much a part of his test as the brutal workout had been.

"Come on then," Dean guided him out of the door with a hand on his shoulder.

Gavin was warming up the class.

"Wait here," said Dean and went to Gavin's side. Gavin called Sempai Kathy Mason out of the front row to continue the warm up routine.

"Just send them through after warm ups," said Dean. "I'll send them back to you as we're done with them."

Gavin nodded and looked across at Tristan.

Tristan was watching the class warm up. He studied the black belts closely and noticed the ones who really put the effort into their techniques. Most of them were ranked nidan and above and all of them were considered to be among the best in the club.

He realised he had been coasting. Kihon and kata came naturally to him. He had the gift of grasping new techniques quickly and easily, and he performed them well.

What he didn't do was try to improve. He considered a well executed technique to be just that. Today he'd learned that there was more to it. Any technique, no matter how well executed, could always be performed with more speed and more power.

He thought about his kumite. Shihan was right, he did slack off. He was capable of so much more, and he knew it.

Tonight he was going to prove it. To his Shihan, to himself and to anyone who tried to underestimate him on the mats.

Chapter Seventeen

Dean was hoping for a miracle but expecting a disaster so he was delighted when Tristan quickly dispatched all of the kyu grades without too much trouble. He had taken a couple of hard knocks though, and was clearly tired.

Dean watched as he stayed loose and mobile against Sempai Kathy Mason, the first of the shodan. He was alert but relaxed and content to let his opponent make the first move.

Sempai Kathy moved fast and came in with a roundhouse kick to Tristan's head. He stepped in close, avoiding the flying foot and catching Kathy's inner thigh with his elbow. She tried to pull her leg back but she was too late. Tristan swept her balancing leg out from under her and finished with a pulled punch to her sternum.

Tristan took a heavy blow to the stomach in his next fight and dropped to his knees. His opponent, Sempai Chris Potter, a gorilla of a man, was twenty years his senior and at least twice his weight.

Jason came to his side. "You okay?"

He struggled to his feet and nodded. "Osu!" he said. "Yes, Sensei."

Jason restarted the bout and Sempai Chris went straight for Tristan's stomach again. He was so desperate to avoid another punch that the first he knew of Chris's kick was a blast of agony in his right shin. Chris put the full weight of his body behind the kick and Tristan's leg shot backwards pitching him, face first, towards his opponent.

He snatched at Chris's dogi in an attempt to break his fall but Chris stepped back and he slammed onto the mat.

Jason gave him a moment before calling Sempai Jabu ahead of the next in line, forcing him to face his most feared opponent immediately after his first defeat. Sensei Jason was not going to go easy on him.

Tristan was still badly shaken as Jabu stepped up to face him.

Out of respect for his opponent he made eye contact but quickly looked away, afraid he might telegraph his fear.

Still in pain, his first instinct was to back away. But Jabu moved in a blur and planted a side kick right into Tristan's aching gut.

The impact hurled him across the mats, sending him sprawling onto his back. He rolled with the momentum and came back to his feet.

Pain clawed at his belly. He could barely breathe and standing upright was an impossibility, but he moved quickly back into the fight. Jabu came at him again. Tristan blocked the elbow strike and a low kick but his counter attacks were woeful.

With a mighty yell, Jabu smashed his instep into the side of Tristan's right thigh. His mouth came open but he made no sound. Staggering to his left he sank to the ground. He got back to his feet but his leg was useless.

Tristan looked tired and drawn. He was exhausted. Not only had he lost track of the number of people he'd fought, he realised, with dismay, he had no idea how many more he had to fight.

Did Shihan have a number in mind or was he just going to work him until he dropped? He made up his mind that he wasn't going to drop until he had absolutely nothing left to give.

Jason looked over at Dean. Dean gave a little nod. "Take a breather, Sempai," said Jason.

Dean came over and offered Tristan some cool water. "Not too quickly," he said. "But get some fluid into you."

"Thank you, Shihan," he said sipping the water carefully. He replaced the top and held the dewy exterior of the bottle against his flushed face.

Jason rested a hand on his shoulder and gave him a gentle shake. "Ready?" he asked.

"Osu! Yes, Sensei." Tristan thanked Dean and handed him the water bottle before taking his position on the mats.

Tristan was surprised how much the short break and the water had revived him.

Both fought hard, but he stayed on his feet against the last of his shodan and, to his amazement, the first of his nidan opponents.

The fights cost him his new found energy and Sempai Mandla Zulu, the second of the nidan, thrashed him convincingly. Mandla's merciless pounding forced Tristan to constantly defend and he never landed a strike.

Dean came forward to start the next fight as Sensei Jason stepped onto the mat. Tristan felt a heavy fear settle in his chest and he forced his mind to recall his last fight with Sensei.

He played it over in his head but the feeling he'd had when Sensei Jason had gone to ground had not been one of victory, it had been one of shock, one of fear.

He shook his head trying to focus on the present moment. "Osu!" he bowed to his opponent.

"Hajime," called Dean, starting them off.

Jason went straight for Tristan's right leg. He suffered two hard kicks before he could even react. He staggered sideways staying out of the direct line of attack but Jason moved with him planting a fist firmly into his ribs.

Tristan swayed slightly, sucking in air and trying to remain upright. But his knees buckled and he sank to the floor.

He hauled himself back to his feet and flew at his Sensei. His punch smacked into Jason's breastbone but it lacked power and control. His fist slid sideways, skimming the skin from his knuckles, leaving a smear of bright blood across the front of Jason's jacket. He fell forward against Jason's chest. Jason caught his dogi and held him up, letting him go only when he had found his balance.

Again, Tristan ploughed in, but his punches were erratic and uncoordinated. Jason caught him with a low kick, knocking him to the floor, and finished with a tap to his stomach.

This time he stayed down.

Jason hauled him to his feet. Placing a hand behind his neck he pulled Tristan towards him. He leaned down resting his forehead against Tristan's. "Got anymore in there?" he asked, tapping his fist against Tristan's chest.

"Osu! Yes, Sensei," he said, pulling away and standing ready, waiting to face his next opponent.

Shihan Dean stepped onto the mat and the colour drained from Tristan's face, leaving him pale and expressionless. He stood, on the point of collapse, facing his toughest opponent yet. Jason began the bout.

Breathing hard, fear kept Tristan rooted to the spot. With a gargantuan effort he managed to sidestep Dean's first punch and, instead of a powerful whack to the chest, he took a glancing blow to his biceps. His arm hung limply at his side. Dean ended the fight quickly and decisively. Spinning round he lifted a long leg and hooked his knee behind Tristan's neck. Using minimum force he hurled him face down onto the mat.

Battling utter exhaustion, Tristan came to his knees and tried to stand. His foot slid out to the side and he fell back to the floor. He tried again and came up onto all fours. He had the will but he had no fight and no strength left in him.

Dean waved everyone out of the mat room and into the dojo then sank down beside Tristan. He placed a hand on the back of his sweat soaked dogi. He could feel Tristan's heart thumping wildly.

He waited for it to slow before speaking. "Come on," he said. "Up you get." He helped Tristan to stand.

Tristan leaned forward, resting his hands on his knees before managing to come upright.

Dean put an arm around his shoulders and tugged at the knot on his belt. "Now, don't you ever let me hear you say you're not good enough to wear that belt," he said.

Tristan hobbled into the dojo, still supported by Dean.
Sensei Jason came over and ruffled his damp hair. "Good going, Sempai," he said.

Completely overwhelmed, Tristan hadn't spoken a word since the fight had ended and he found he still couldn't. Jason squeezed his shoulder as Dean led him into the office.

He fell into the chair and took the bottle and the banana Dean held out to him but made no effort to eat or drink.

Dean took the bottle back and unscrewed the lid. "Come on now," he said. "Get something inside you or I'll be picking you up off the floor again."

He put the bottle to his lips. As soon as the first trickle of cool water slid down his parched throat he began to gulp and didn't stop until he had drained the full half litre.

The water revived his spirits and the exhaustion was replaced by a feeling of euphoria. He had survived his toughest test yet and, though the fundraiser would be more pressure, there would be fewer fights and he would be fresh when he started. For the first time, he knew he could do it.

"Okay," said Dean. "I'm going to tidy up a bit and then I'll be back. Will you eat that banana, please?"

Dean returned fifteen minutes later, freshly showered and wearing a club tracksuit.

Tristan quickly peeled his banana.

"Right," said Dean. "Are you ready for the really tough bit?"

Tristan almost choked on the fruit. He looked up at Dean, pale and wide eyed.

Dean grinned then laughed out loud. "Don't worry," he said. "All you have to do is stand behind me. I'll tell your mom why you look like you've been in a war zone."

He swallowed the banana and rested his elbows on his knees and his head in his hands.

"That gave you a scare, didn't it?" said Dean.

"Hmm, with good reason," sighed Tristan.

Tristan slid from the high seat of Dean's Toyota Hilux and stood, barefoot, on the wet block paving.

The heavy downpour had stopped almost as soon as it had begun but water stood in pools on the lawn and the driveway. Sheet lightning flickered in the night sky and thunder still grumbled in the distance.

Tristan splashed, ankle deep at times, to the front steps. Dean took the steps two at a time and placed Tristan's school bag and training holdall on the verandah by the front door. He came back and helped him up the steps.

Tristan wondered how he would ever get out of bed tomorrow, let alone walk. He bent down stiffly and rolled up the legs of his sodden dogi pants.

"*Eina!*" Ouch, said Dean, looking down at his shin.

Tristan followed Dean's gaze. He hooked his big toe into the turn-up and flicked it back down. He would rather drip on his mother's floor than let her see the state of his leg.

"Looks like I won't be swimming for a while," he said.

"Not unless you wear a full wetsuit," said Dean, taking his hands and turning his arms to reveal deep bruises from wrist to elbow.

Tristan opened the door and went in. He stuck his head round the lounge door but there was no one there. "Ma?" he called, not wanting to trail water through the entire house.

"In here," said Elize. "Dining room."

Frowning, he glanced at the display on the hall telephone and was surprised to see it was only 8pm, a full hour before training should have ended. His surprise must have shown.

"I thought you could do with an early night," said Dean. He placed Tristan's bags neatly beside the dining room door as Tristan opened it and went in.

"You're early, did... Good grief," said Brett. "Have you been playing rugby?"

Elize turned, her eyes widening as she took in her filthy and dishevelled son.

"I'm really sorry," said Dean "I don't want to disturb your meal. Perhaps I could talk to you later?"

"No," said Elize. "It's fine. I was just about to get dessert. There's plenty, so why don't you join us?"

"Thank you, Mrs Steyn," said Dean. "But..."

"No buts," said Elize. "Sit, I'll bring you some lemon tart and then we can have coffee in the lounge and talk. And please, call me Elize."

Dean flashed her his best smile. The one he reserved for pushy parents and belligerent authority figures.

"Thank you, Elize," he said, removing his jacket and hanging it on the back of the chair Brett had pulled out for him.

Elize turned to Tristan. "*Gaan stort dan kom eet*," she said. Go and shower then come and eat.

Tristan obeyed without a word. When his mother spoke Afrikaans she meant what she said.

"Sorry about that," said Brett, clearly embarrassed.

"Not to worry," said Dean. "Lemon tart sounds pretty good actually."

Lightning brightened the dimly lit room. A rush of cool air entered, sweeping the curtain aside and bringing with it the smell of wet earth. Brett got up from the table and closed the window. Thunder rolled overhead and the rain began again, performing a lively dance on the roof.

The scent of fresh coffee drifted through from the kitchen. Were it not for the thought of facing Elize, Dean would have looked forward to a cosy evening in with the Steyns.

He cleared his throat. "I think I might be in trouble again," he said.

"Looking at the state of Tristan, I think you might," said Brett with a grin. "Don't worry though, we've had a chat about last night, given her a different perspective, she'll be fine. And her bark's worse than her bite anyway."

Tristan stepped, shivering, out of the shower. Wrapping himself in a thick towel he hobbled painfully to the bedroom.

He wanted to get into his pyjamas and crawl into bed but he knew he couldn't leave Shihan and his parents alone. He was terrified his mother would order Dean to stop teaching him karate.

He sat on the edge of the bed. The storm had cooled the air and he was reluctant to remove the towel.

He carefully dried his battered body and pulled on a pair of soft tracksuit pants. He slipped the drawstring into the loose elastic waistband, unable to bring himself to tie it round his aching middle.

He examined his bruised arms and slipped the tracksuit top over his clean white T shirt. A quick glance in the mirror revealed no obvious sign of injury.

Tristan headed back to the dining room trying his best not to limp. He reached the door at the same time as his mother. She was carrying two plates, each one holding a large slice of fluffy lemon tart, garnished with fresh strawberries and slices of orange and lime.

"Go and sit down," she said to him. "I'll bring you your food."

He followed her through the door and took his seat. She placed the desserts in front of Brett and Dean.

"Thank you," said Dean. "I'm glad you insisted I stay. This looks delicious."

"Tristan," said Brett, as Elize left the room. "You look worn out. Are you okay?"

Tristan glanced at Dean before responding but Dean made no effort to speak.

"Hard lesson at the dojo," he said. "I'll live."

Elize returned with Tristan's meal and her own dessert. She sat down and laid her napkin on her lap. "Please," she said. "Start, no need to wait."

"So, Tris," said Brett digging his spoon into the dessert. "Tell us about training."

Tristan shrugged, mashing rice and pumpkin together. He poked a few peas into the mix and shovelled some onto his fork but couldn't summon the energy to bring it to his mouth. "Tough session, that's all," he said.

"Um," said Dean. "It was a bit more than that."

Elize looked up sharply. Tristan turned to Dean for help.

"Let's just say," said Dean. "That Tristan proved himself more than worthy of his grade today, and he's convinced me that he'll do a good job at the fundraiser."

"You mean you roughed him up a bit?" said Brett with a grin.

"You could say that," said Dean. "But I'm pleased to say, he remained conscious throughout."

Elize said nothing. She finished her dessert in silence and then gathered the plates. "Tristan, please eat that before it gets cold," she snapped.

He sucked his fork and looked down at the plate. Since the storm had passed, the air in the room had become warm and heavy. He had managed half of his supper but he was beginning to overheat and feel nauseous. He knew he would have to remove his tracksuit top before he could eat anymore.

He waited for Elize to take the crockery to the kitchen then stiffly worked his arms out of the top and lifted it over his head.

He pushed another forkful of rice into his mouth and chewed slowly before dropping the fork onto his plate and pushing it away.

"Thanks, Ma," he said, when Elize returned. "But I really can't eat anymore. I'm sorry."

"Okay," said Elize looking at the mess on the plate. "But, Tristan please don't play with your food if you can't eat it. Now, coffee's ready. If you go to the lounge I'll bring it through."

She reached down and took Tristan's plate. "Tristan!" She let the plate drop back to the table with a clatter and lifted his arm. "Look at this," she said, turning his wrist. "You're full of bruises. You look like a rotten apple!"

"It's nothing, Ma," he said, pulling his hand from her grip. "I'm okay."

Elize sighed and shook her head. "I'll never understand you men," she said. "Barbarians, all of you."

Dean was both surprised and pleased that Elize had barely made a fuss. He followed Brett through to the lounge feeling much more relaxed.

Brett and Dean sank into the two deep leather armchairs and Tristan curled up on the sofa.

Elize set the tray on the coffee table. She handed Tristan a mug of Rooibos tea and poured three cups of coffee. "Cream and sugar?" she asked Dean.

"Just black, thank you," he said. Elize handed out the coffees and sat on the sofa next to Tristan.

"So," said Brett. "When do you think Tris will be ready for the fundraiser? Have you set a date yet?"

Dean shook his head. "No date yet," he said. "But we're thinking after the Easter holiday."

"Why so long?" blurted Tristan.

"Because you still need to work on your preparation and there's a lot to organise," said Dean. "Besides, it's not that long."

"Can I take part in the *tameshiwari* demo this year?" asked Tristan.

"No!" snapped Dean. "You can't even think about *tameshiwari* until you're at least sixteen."

"I'm almost sixteen," he said.

"How almost?" asked Dean.

"Sixth of May."

"In that case," said Dean, narrowing his eyes. "You can't even think about it until you're at least eighteen."

"What is it?" asked Elize.

Dean looked at Tristan. "Well, go on," he said. "Tell your mother what it is."

"Breaking things," he said.

"You mean like they do on that awful video you've got? Breaking bricks with their heads and those huge ice blocks with their elbows?"

"Uh huh," he grunted.

"Forget it," said Elize. "You can wait until you leave this house before you think about it, or I'll break you."

Dean smiled at Elize. "I'm with you on that one," he said. "It's not for youngsters."

Dean looked back at Tristan hoping he wouldn't push the point but he was in no state to argue.

Dean leapt out of the chair and was at the sofa in an instant. He caught the falling mug before even a drop of the amber liquid could spill. He placed it on the table. "I think he needs to be in bed," he said.

Both Elize and Brett sat in startled silence. Tristan was slumped against his mother breathing deeply and evenly.

Chapter Eighteen

Tristan groaned.

"What have you done now?" Rico asked.

"I have no idea. But I guess I'd better go and find out."

"Rather you than me," said Rico as they parted company outside the school hall.

Tristan limped towards the admin block. His mouth was dry and his heart was pounding harder now than it had when the head had first called on him to report to the office after assembly.

He ran through the last few days in his mind but couldn't think of one good reason the head might want to see him.

He had been a few minutes late getting to assembly but when the prefect saw the trouble he was having walking he said he would let him off, so it couldn't be that.

He had missed handing in his maths homework on Tuesday but so had Rico, and Mr Pietersen would never have reported him for it.

He had also taken the day off school yesterday, at his mother's insistence, but she had contacted the school and let them know.

He knocked on the office door but, as he expected, there was no answer. He stood in the passage outside and waited.

Quickly straightening his blazer and tie, he stood to one side as Mr de Lange approached. "Ah, Steyn," he said. "Step inside please."

The head entered the office and held the door for Tristan. "Thank you, sir," he said meekly and limped in.

"Sit," said the head, rounding his desk and moving a pile of books to one side. He sat down and rested his arms on the blotter, leaning towards Tristan.

Tristan lowered himself stiffly into the chair.

The head frowned. "Are you all right?" he asked.

"Just a bit stiff, sir," said Tristan.

"I see," he said, still frowning. "Well, I had a phone call from Mr Stander yesterday afternoon, about the use of the school sports field."

Tristan released the breath he hadn't realised he was holding and relaxed in the chair.

The head continued. "It's all organised and it's going to take place on the 6th of May."

Gee, thanks, Shihan, thought Tristan.

"So now all you need to do is publicise it. And you can start by taking the stage after Monday morning's assembly and telling the school all about it."

"Me?" blurted Tristan. "Sir, I can't!" He felt the blood drain from his head and he gripped the sides of the chair.

The head raised an eyebrow. "Nonsense," he said. "Of course you can. If you can get up in front of crowds of people and fight, then you can get up in front of the school and speak."

Tristan felt sick and it wasn't just the prospect of Monday morning's assembly. It was the first time he had considered that there would be a crowd of complete strangers watching him fight.

Mr de Lange held out a green slip to him.

"Thank you, sir." His hand shook as he took the hall pass. The colour left his face as he stood up a little too quickly. He steadied himself against the desk and pushed his chair back under it.

"Are you sure you're all right?" asked the head.

Tristan pushed his hair behind his ear. "Yes, thank you," he said quietly and left the office.

He took advantage of the hall pass and went the long route to his chemistry lesson. Moving around was better than sitting for easing his stiffness. He breathed deeply hoping to steady his nerves. The scent of freshly turned soil, dampened by a recent shower, soothed him.

"*Sawubona*," I see you, he said, acknowledging the presence of the school gardener.

"*Yebo, sawubona*," yes, I see you, the man responded. Tristan pondered the complexities of the Zulu language, anything to keep his mind off Monday, as he walked past the well tended flower beds towards the science block.

* * *

Miss Price waved him into the classroom and over to her desk before he had time to knock on the open door. "I'm sorry I'm late, miss," he said. He handed her the hall pass and waited for permission to go to his desk.

"Okay," she said. "We're working from page 38 of the textbook. Oh, and please see me after class." She handed him his homework book.

"Yes miss," he said. He took his seat and quickly flicked through the book checking for spelling errors or any other reason Miss Price might want to see him after class. His homework was all correct.

He worried throughout the lesson, though it was more about Monday than about facing Miss Price. At the end of the period he stood before her desk and waited for her to speak.

She looked up and studied him closely. "Are you feeling unwell?" she asked.

"No, miss," he said, frowning.

"You were very pale when you came in," she said.

Tristan managed a weak smile. "Mr de Lange wants me to talk to the school about something on Monday," he said.

"Ah, and you're a little nervous about it."

"A lot nervous, miss," he said.

"You'll be fine, I'm sure," she said. "Now, I believe Andre Turner will be joining us again on Monday. Are you likely to see him before then?"

"Yes, miss. This afternoon."

Miss Price picked up a file and an exercise book from her desk. "Would you mind taking these to him, please?" she asked. "I've made some notes for him to read so he's not too far behind."

Tristan took them and put them in his bag. "Thanks, miss," he said. "He should be fine. We've been working on stuff together so he could stay on top of things."

Although the stiffness had eased a little throughout the day,

Tristan struggled to keep up with Rico and Megan. "You guys go on," he said. "I'll get there sometime before we have to leave."

"We're not leaving you," said Megan. She hung back and, as he caught up, she slipped her arm through his and walked alongside him.

Rico dropped back too, draping a defensive arm over Megan's shoulders.

The three of them arrived to find Andre sitting in the front garden in his wheelchair. He grabbed his crutches and, with a huge beam, walked to meet them.

"Are you supposed to be doing that?" asked Megan.

"The doc says it's good to walk as long as I don't tire myself out," he said.

Andre frowned at Tristan. "What happened?" he asked. "You wanna borrow these?" He held the crutches out in front of him.

"No thanks," said Tristan. "But if the wheelchair's not in use I might consider that."

"Why are you limping?" asked Andre.

Tristan leaned down and pulled up the leg of his school pants. Andre gasped. "Ouch," he said.

"Wow," said Rico. "Now that's a bruise!"

"Tristan!" cried Megan. "That's awful. Was that one of those fights? What happened?"

"Got kicked," he said.

"By what," asked Andre. "A horse?"

"He was built like one," said Tristan. "Hey," he added, changing the subject and cutting Megan's next comment off. "Why don't you guys all come to my place tomorrow? We could spend some time on the beach in the morning then have lunch and go to the dojo in the afternoon." Tristan looked at Andre. "You could bring the wheelchair so it wouldn't be strenuous. And if you got tired my mom could bring you home."

"Would we be allowed at the dojo?" asked Rico.

"Sure," said Tristan. "This Saturday is a bit of a free for all. People can come and watch to see if they want to join, stuff like that. Anyway, Shihan says I'm not allowed to train until Monday so I can sit with you guys and we'll watch Megs sweat."

Megan aimed a swipe at Tristan's head. He tried to dodge but his stiff muscles wouldn't move fast enough.

"Ow," he whined, as her fingertips caught him behind the ear.

"That would be so cool," said Andre. "I'd love to come. I don't know if my mom will let me though."

"She will," said Tristan. "I'll go in and ask her nicely."

"Ma?" Tristan yelled, standing in the passage. He figured, if he shouted loudly enough, his mother would hear him from anywhere in the house.

"Yes, Tristan?" said Elize, coming out of the kitchen. "Don't shout in the house please."

"Sorry, Ma. Is it okay if Andre, Rico and Megan come round tomorrow and stay for lunch?"

Elize wiped her hands on her apron. The smell of fresh bread drifted from the kitchen. "Yes, of course it is," she said.

"Thanks, Ma," said Tristan. "We'll be going to the dojo after lunch so we'll be out of your way all afternoon."

Rico and Megan rode their bicycles up the driveway at the same time Kathryn pulled up in the car.

Rico lifted the wheelchair out of the boot and Tristan helped Andre out.

Elize came out and Tristan introduced her to Kathryn.

"Lovely to meet you," said Elize. "Come in for a coffee."

Kathryn and Elize were sitting at the kitchen table enjoying coffee and fresh muffins when Tristan burst in from the back garden.

"Is it okay if we go to the beach now?" he asked. Elize had packed them a picnic lunch to eat at the beach but it was still only 10:30am. He looked at Kathryn. "We'll look after Andre and bring him straight back if it gets too much."

"I'm not sure," said Kathryn. "I..."

He held her gaze.

"Oh, I suppose it won't hurt," she said.

"Tristan," said Elize, looking him up and down. He was wearing a pair of navy and white baggies and a lime green T shirt. The brightness of the shirt seemed to suck the colour from his already pale face.

Elize wondered where on earth her son got his taste in clothes. "Please cover yourself up before you go out in public. Those bruises look terrible."

"Ma, it's only to the beach," he said. "I'll fry in long pants and sleeves."

Elize shook her head. "Yes, I suppose you will. Okay," she sighed. "But I don't want people to think I'm raising a masochist."

"They won't," said Tristan, "They'll think you beat me."

"I might if you're not careful," said Elize. "Now get off to the beach."

He left the kitchen letting the screen door swing closed with a bang.

"Don't forget sun lotion." Elize called after him. "And take plenty of water with you, it's hot."

"Kids," she sighed, turning back to Kathryn. "Sometimes I... Kathryn?"

Elize pulled her chair round to face Kathryn who had buried her face in her hands and begun to sob.

Tristan helped Andre up the step and into the dojo while Rico lifted the wheelchair in. They folded the chair and placed it against the wall.

As he wasn't training Tristan had changed into his official club tracksuit and would be on hand to help out if they received any visitors.

Dean rotated the open days between his four centres across the city, so each group was only disturbed once a month.

Some open days were quiet but others saw several people dropping in during the session, either for information, or just to watch the training and see if they felt it was right for them.

Megan began warming up in the mat room. Tristan got Rico and Andre to remove their shoes and took them into the dojo.

"Back in a sec," he said after seating his friends in the visitors' area. He knocked on the office door.

"Yes?" called Dean. "Come in."

He pushed open the door and closed it softly behind him.

"Sempai," said Dean. "What are you doing here? I thought I told you not to train again until Monday."

"I'm not training, Shihan," he said. "I couldn't if I wanted too. I'm so stiff I'd be rubbish."

"Good," said Dean with a grin. "So what brings you to the dojo?"

"I thought I could help with the open day. And..." Tristan paused and looked down at his feet. It was hot in the small office but he hadn't removed his jacket. He thought it better to keep his bruises hidden from any potential new students.

"And?" asked Dean.

"It's about the fundraiser," he said, poking at the leg of Dean's desk with his big toe. "Mr de Lange wants me to announce it to the school on Monday."

"Good," said Dean. "We need all the free publicity we can get."

"No, Shihan, I..." The colour left Tristan's face. He began to shake violently and he could hardly breathe. Dean was staring at him as if he were a raving lunatic. "I can't," he blurted. "I just can't do it."

Dean continued to stare, his mouth half open, one hand suspended above a pen as if he had been about to pick it up.

"Sempai, sit down," said Dean, his hand coming to rest on the desk.

Tristan pulled a chair out and sat. He wiped at the beads of sweat that were forming on his forehead with the back of his hand.

"Do you have any idea how much work people have put into organising this fundraiser?" asked Dean, his voice was low and calm but his jaw was tight. Two spots of high colour appeared on his cheeks as he leaned towards Tristan.

"Sempai, doing this demo as a fundraiser was *your* idea," he said. "*You* specifically asked to take part, you let people reschedule their working hours to cater to *your* training needs and now you're refusing to..."

"I'm sorry," wailed Tristan. "But I'm terrified. I just can't. Shihan, please!" he begged. "Can't you do it for me?"

"What?" roared Dean, leaping to his feet. "You want me to fight your fights?" Dean stepped round the desk and towered over Tristan.

Stunned, he rocked back in the chair and gaped, wide eyed, at Dean. Adrenaline surged into his bloodstream, tensing his muscles and making his heart pump wildly. He opened his mouth but nothing came out.

He tried again. "I... No!" he said, gripping the arms of the chair and sliding it back on the vinyl tiled floor. Dean advanced again.

"No, I want you to tell the school about it." Tristan's voice shook as he spoke. His terror, coupled with Dean's reaction, had left him close to tears.

Dean frowned. "I'm sorry?" he said. "You want... Oh, I see," He perched on the edge of the desk. "It's not the fundraiser you don't want to do, it's the talk at school?"

Tristan nodded and Dean burst into gales of laughter.

Adrenaline let down left Tristan feeling physically weak and even more emotionally vulnerable. His lower lip trembled and he trapped it between his teeth.

"Oh my," said Dean. "You really are frightened, aren't you?"

He nodded again and kept his eyes fixed firmly on the floor.

"I'll tell you what," said Dean. "I can't make it on Monday, I have to be in Jo'burg for a meeting. But I'll have a word with Sensei Gavin."

Andre and Rico were full of enthusiasm for what they'd seen in the training session and both were in awe of Dean.

Tristan's main motivation for bringing them to the dojo was to introduce Andre to everyone working on the fundraiser. He wanted Andre to feel involved and he wanted his instructors to get to know the person they were raising funds for.

While the group were chatting, Gavin took Tristan aside. "Sempai," he said. "Shihan mentioned that you want me to announce the fundraiser at your school on Monday morning."

Tristan went pale at the mere mention of Monday morning. "Yes, Sensei," he said. "Mr de Lange wants me to do it but I think I would have a heart attack if I had to stand on that stage." He put his hands behind his back and interlaced his fingers to disguise his trembling.

"Have you asked Mr de Lange if someone else can do it for you?"

Avoiding Gavin's eyes, he shifted his weight onto his left leg and lifted his right heel off the ground. Pushing his knee forward and curling his toes against the floor, he felt a jolt in his badly bruised shin. The pain gave his mind a focus point and the rising panic ebbed.

"No, Sensei," he said.

"Well, don't you think you should?"

"But, Sensei, I won't see him until Monday and then it will be too late."

Gavin frowned at his obvious distress. "All right," he said. "I'll pick you up on Monday morning and we'll go and see him before assembly. But, Sempai," he added, "I really think you should make an effort to do it. If you're ever going to be a good karate instructor you'll have to be able to speak to groups of people."

Tristan swallowed hard and moistened his lips. "Thank you, Sensei," he said. "I'll try to get my head round it."

Kathryn's car was still in the driveway when they arrived back at the house. Rico and Megan collected their cycles and said their goodbyes.

Tristan helped Andre into the house.

"Did you have a good day?" asked Kathryn.

Andre enthused all over again about his afternoon. "That was so cool. I can't wait for the demonstration. Can I go, Mom? Please?" he asked.

Kathryn beamed at his excitement. "Of course," she said. "It's partly in your honour."

Kathryn looked across at Tristan. A shadow crossed her face but he couldn't read it. He frowned. They walked out to the car and he helped Andre in while Brett lifted the wheelchair into the back.

Kathryn thanked Elize for her hospitality then walked to the car. Standing for a moment at Tristan's side, she slipped her hand around his and gave it a gentle squeeze. "I'm sorry, Tristan," she whispered, and got into the driver's seat.

Confused, he frowned and watched the car reverse out of the driveway.

Brett came up alongside him. "Go to my study please," he said. "We need to have a little chat."

"You can't hit me with that!" exclaimed Tristan.

Brett moved the leather strap from his left hand to his right. "Yes," he said. "I can. But I probably won't."

Probably won't? thought Tristan. "But what did I do?"

"Tristan," said Brett. "The way you've behaved over the last couple of months, very little would surprise me but *blackmail?*"

"Blackmail?"

"Yes, Tristan," said Brett. "Blackmail! That's what it's called when you threaten to expose certain information about someone in exchange for their compliance."

He stared at his father, genuinely confused. "But I don't..."

"Tristan!" snapped Brett. "Shut up. If you lie to me I will use this." He tapped Tristan's chin with the belt. "Now," he continued. "Think very carefully before you open your mouth."

Tristan feared his mother's quick temper and had lied to her more than once to avoid punishment. But his relationship with

Brett had always been one of mutual trust and respect. He had never lied to his father.

"Did you blackmail Kathryn Turner?"

"What? No!" he yelled, his temper flaring. "Blackmail her how?"

Brett placed the strap on his desk. "So you didn't threaten to say that she abused Andre if she didn't allow you to go ahead with the fundraiser and continue visiting Andre?"

Tristan went cold. He felt the colour go from his face. He opened his mouth to speak but had no idea what to say to his father.

Brett picked up the strap. "Why, Tristan?" he sighed. "Why did you lie to me?"

"No!" he said, stepping backwards. "I didn't lie to you. I..."

He turned and marched out of the study, slamming the door hard behind him.

He fled down the passage and into his room, kicking the door closed and throwing himself on the bed. He balled up his pillow and hurled it across the room.

The pillow caught Brett on the side of the head sending him leaping backwards. Tristan sat up and covered his face with his hands. *Oh God,* he thought. *I'm so dead.*

"Dad, I'm sorry," he said, jumping off the bed. "You normally knock. I didn't mean for it to hit you."

Brett recovered his composure and turned to face him. "Is that it for the heavy artillery?" he asked. "Can I come in now, or do I need a white flag?"

"I'm so sorry," Tristan repeated, removing his hand from his mouth.

Brett came in and closed the door. Tristan's heart was hammering. He sank down onto the bed and realised that, this time, he was in serious trouble.

Brett sat on the bed and handed him the pillow.

"I'm sorry," he said, for the third time.

"Yes," said Brett. "I gathered that."

He hugged the pillow to him and buried his face. "Are you going to kill me now or torture me by keeping me waiting?" he mumbled into it.

"Torture," said Brett. "I haven't decided how I'm going to kill you yet."

Tristan raised his head, relieved to see Brett didn't have the strap. He preferred his father unarmed.

"Tristan," said Brett. "If you didn't blackmail Mrs Turner, can you tell me why she thinks you did? She was terribly upset about it this morning."

Tristan sighed and pulled his feet up onto the bed. "I knew someone was hitting Andre," he said. "At first I thought it was his dad but then something happened and I knew it was his mom." He pushed his hair behind his ear. "I told her I knew," he said. "But I never said I would tell anyone."

He twisted his feet in his hands and pressed the soles together but the movement hurt his shin. He pulled up the leg of his track pants and examined the black and blue bump.

He cleared his throat. "I might have implied it," he said, subdued. He looked up at Brett. "But I would never have said anything unless I thought Andre was in danger again. And it wasn't my intention to blackmail her. I didn't lie to you, Dad. I really didn't know what you were talking about at first."

Brett tugged the leg of Tristan's pants out of his hand and pulled it back down over his shin. "That gives me the screaming heebie jeebies," he said. "Get some arnica on it. All right, I believe you, but I want you to apologise to Mrs Turner when you go round on Monday.

"I will, Dad," said Tristan. "I'm sorry."

"Be careful, Tris. You can't go making judgements based on insufficient knowledge. There's more to the story than you know and they'll be getting some help now, so don't you worry about it."

Chapter Nineteen

The head looked at Tristan for a full thirty seconds before he spoke. "Steyn," he said. "I would really rather you did it."

Tristan couldn't speak. He stared blankly at the head, too afraid to open his mouth in case his cornflakes made an emergency exit.

Gavin came to his aid. "What if we went up together?" he asked. "I could talk about the demo in general and, when Tristan was feeling a bit more relaxed, he could talk about the sparring? And if he chokes, I'll do that bit as well."

Paul de Lange sighed. "It looks like that might be our only option," he said. "Steyn?... Steyn!"

Tristan jumped. "Sorry, sir," he said. "Um, yes, okay. I think I can do that."

Tristan stood behind the green velvet stage curtain with Gavin, as Mr de Lange wrapped up the official business of the assembly.

"And finally," said the headmaster, glancing towards the curtain. "One of our students will be taking part in a karate demonstration in May and he and his instructor are going to tell you all about it."

The boys stood to greet the school's guest and the hall erupted with the sound of clapping. Any delay to the start of the school day was worthy of a hearty round of applause.

The head stepped sideways and turned to face Tristan and Gavin. He indicated the dais with both hands.

Tristan had never been so terrified in his entire life, not even when he had become entangled in a sunken tractor tyre wound with baling twine, and held underwater in his grandfather's muddy farm dam.

Gavin started forward. Tristan took a huge gulp of air and caught hold of the back of his jacket. "I'll go, Sensei," he said. "It's okay."

He stepped past Gavin and out onto the stage. The head gave

him an encouraging smile and took his seat with the rest of the staff.

The boys, still standing, began to fidget.

Tristan stood on the step behind the dais to gain a little height. Not daring to look at his audience, he took hold of the microphone and pulled it down to his level.

A piercing howl filled the hall and he let go as if he had been bitten. Leaping back, he stumbled off the low step while the microphone slowly returned to its original position. A ripple of laughter spread throughout the sea of boys.

Panic stricken, he turned to the teachers behind him. Miss Price caught his eye. She smiled and nodded, giving him a double thumbs up.

He turned to the front again and got back up on the step. His hand made another move towards the microphone but he decided against it and pulled back, afraid it might strike again. More laughter.

"Um, hi," said Tristan craning up towards the microphone. The room silenced at the sound of his voice. He swallowed hard and looked out over the hall for the first time.

"Oh," he said, surprised to see his audience on their feet. "I'm sorry, you'd better sit down." He pointed at the curtain to his right. "Sensei is still behind the curtain," he said. "He was too scared to face you lot."

The boys roared with laughter as they took their seats. He waited for them, and his heart, to settle down.

"First of all," he said. "I would like to thank Mr de Lange for giving me the opportunity tell you about our event and for letting us use the school sports field. The karate club I train with is organising a demonstration." He was speaking too fast and forgetting to inhale.

"We do one every year, mainly to show potential new students what we do and to show the public that we're not a bunch of barbarians in training."

He paused and gasped for breath and pushed his hair behind

his ear. "I'd like as many of you to come along and support us as possible," he said. "Because this year it's going to be a bit different. We're doing it as a fundraiser."

Tristan stopped and cleared his throat. He looked across the hall at Andre, sitting in his wheelchair. "A couple of months ago my friend, Andre Turner, was knocked down by a car and seriously injured. It was my fault." There was a gasp followed by a low murmur. Glad of the opportunity to gather his thoughts, he waited until the hall fell silent.

"We are doing this demonstration to raise money for a new scanner as a way of thanking the hospital that treated Andre." There was no way he was going to embarrass him by announcing to the entire school that his family couldn't afford the operation. *It's partly true*, he thought, justifying the bending of the truth to himself.

"Now some of you may not agree," he said, "But I can assure you it's for a good cause. You see, I got to know Andre very well over the last couple of months, and if you can get past the odd time he might have caused you grief, he's actually a really good guy."

More murmuring from the audience.

Tristan was beginning to relax, he no longer felt that he may have to dash to the bathroom with less than a second's notice and he'd lost the urge to wipe his hands down the back of his school pants. In fact, his palms were quite dry.

"But, if you really can't get past the times he caused you grief, I have another incentive for you to come," he said. "You'll be able to see some amazing displays of fitness and technique. Our Shihan will be breaking baseball bats with his shin and cinder blocks with his head." He wanted to appeal to his young audience's sense of the dramatic and thirst for potential disaster.

"And, for the sparring demonstration," he went on. "I am going to be sponsored to fight some of the black belts in the club. Most of them are higher ranked than me and all of them are bigger. Even the girls."

He paused, waiting for the giggles to subside. "So, if you want to see me get my butt kicked, come along to the demo."

"Will there be blood?" called someone from the back.

Tristan heard the head stir behind him. He stretched closer to the microphone. "There might be," he said. "We practice full contact karate so it's possible but, even without blood, I can promise you a few real bone crunching whacks."

A young boy in the front row tentatively raised his hand. "But won't you get hurt?" he asked.

Tristan pressed an elbow into his bruised ribs. "Not horribly," he said, sincerely hoping that he wouldn't. "But these guys are good fighters so we'll all take a few knocks. But as I said, it's for a good cause, so please come along and support us. And if martial arts is not your thing," he added, "I'm sure there will be something to interest you. There will be lots of activities to try out and plenty of stalls that have nothing to do with karate, so there's something for everyone."

He glanced at Gavin, still behind the curtain. "Now I'd like to introduce you to one of the people who might be kicking me around the sports field," he said. "And before he kicks me off this stage, I'd better tell you the truth."

He looked down at the dais and rubbed his thumb against a roughened edge. He looked up again before speaking. "Sensei Gavin is not behind the curtain because he's too scared to face you guys. He's here because I spent the weekend throwing up and lying awake at night thinking about standing up here today. I asked him to talk to you about the demo because I was terrified," he said.

"But while I was standing back there." Tristan pointed to the curtain. "I realised that this is important to me and, if I really want you guys to support us, I should at least have the guts to get up here and ask for that support myself."

He turned to face Gavin. "Thank you, Sensei," he said. "And just so this trip isn't a complete waste of your time, please could you give the details about when and where?"

He turned back to the microphone as Gavin stepped onto the stage. "This is one of my instructors." The boys rose from their seats. "Sensei Gavin Richardson."

The buzz he felt from conquering his second demon in less than a week carried Tristan through the day. But, by the time the final bell sounded, his new found celebrity was beginning to take its toll.

Tristan, Rico and Andre had been surrounded by enthusiastic boys in every free moment from the time they had left the assembly hall until they managed to escape at the final bell.

He had already raised R350 in sponsorship pledges and had promised to bring leaflets about joining the club for several interested parties.

He dropped his school bag and collapsed onto his back on the Turners' front lawn. He covered his face with his hands, elbows and knees pointing skywards. "I am in so much trouble," he moaned.

"Why, what's up?" asked Rico. "The whole school has you elevated to superhero status and you're complaining?"

He slid his hands from his face and pushed himself up on his elbows. "That's the problem," he said. "They think I'm going to win all these fights."

"Aren't you?" grinned Rico.

"Rico, I'll be lucky if I win against some of the shodan. The higher grades are going to make mincemeat of me and then I'll have to leave school and hide out for the rest of my life.

"Oh come on, Tris," laughed Rico. "It won't be that bad. Hide for a week and they'll have forgotten all about you."

"Who will?" asked Andre. He had been inside to change and had missed the conversation.

"Tris is just being a drama queen," said Rico.

Tristan ignored Rico's remark. "Is your mom in?" he asked, sitting up.

"Yup," said Andre. "She's in the kitchen."

He got to his feet and brushed dry grass from his backside. "Okay if I go in?" he asked. "I need a quick word with her."

Tristan stood in the kitchen doorway. Kathryn Turner had her back to him preparing sandwiches. "Mrs Turner," he said.

She jumped and turned, knife in hand, to face him.

"Oh, I'm sorry," he said, his eyes on the knife. "I didn't mean to startle you."

"Tristan, come in," she said, laying the knife on the work surface and wiping her hands on a tea towel.

He looked down at his feet then up at Kathryn. "Mrs Turner, I'm really sorry if I..." He found himself struggling for words. He didn't want to say blackmail, it seemed so wrong. "I didn't mean to make you think I would say anything. I..."

"I know," said Kathryn. "You meant well all along. I was just so wrapped up in my own problems that I couldn't see it. Tristan, I'm sorry," she said. "I hope you weren't in too much trouble after we left. I should have phoned but..."

"It was fine," said Tristan. "My dad's cool. We sorted it out."

"Good," said Kathryn, turning back to her sandwiches. "I've made lunch for you. I thought you'd want to eat it outside." She placed a large plate of sandwiches, a packet of Tennis biscuits and three cartons of LiquiFruit orange juice onto a tray. "The ham salad ones are for Rico and Andre. Yours are just salad, is that okay?" she asked.

"Perfect, thank you," said Tristan, taking the tray.

The three of them sat in the shade of the avocado tree that dominated the Turners' front garden and did their homework while munching on their sandwiches.

Andre and Tristan worked on their chemistry while Rico tackled history.

Tristan closed his textbook with a snap. "I must be thick," he said, sucking a tomato seed off his thumb. "There is no way number eight can possibly work. It's driving me nuts!"

"You're not thick, Tris," said Andre, not looking up from his book. "You're deaf. Miss Price said there was a printing error in the text. The two on the end should be a three. It's aluminium oxide."

"*Ag nee*!" Oh no, he moaned. "I just spent ages trying to figure it out. Look at this mess!" his exercise book was full of scribbles and crossed out attempts to work out the equation.

Rico sniggered. "Maybe you should start paying more attention to the lady," he said.

Tristan tore the page from his book, balled it up and launched it at Rico. "Maybe I should tell Megs you've got the hots for my chemistry teacher."

Chapter Twenty

Dean caught Tristan just as he was about to leave the dojo. "Sempai, do you have a minute?"

He was pleased to delay his exit into the dull and wet Saturday afternoon. He hoped he might see Megan when she arrived for her training session.

He was training exclusively with Jason in the lead up to his fights. Because of the strict work and rest schedule he wasn't training with the group and he hadn't seen her for over a week.

"Osu! Yes, Shihan," he said. He kicked his shoes off and followed Dean back into the office.

Gavin and Jason were seated at the desk and an extra chair had been brought in to the small room. Tristan felt a little flip of panic in his belly.

"Have a seat," said Dean.

Worried, he sat down and trapped his hands between his knees.

Dean took his seat and leaned towards him. "Sempai," he said. "We've just been discussing your progress."

He felt himself tense. He knew he hadn't given his training 100% in the last couple of weeks. His workload at school had been particularly heavy and his mother was pressuring him not to neglect it, so he was neglecting his sleep instead.

He hoped he could hold out until the Easter break before anyone noticed he was struggling to cope. He waited for Dean to continue.

Sensei Jason spoke instead. "You're doing really well so you can relax," he said, prodding Tristan's shoulder. "But I want to try and get your weight up a bit."

"How?" asked Tristan, feeling the tension leave his body. He released his hands from between his knees and sat back in the chair. "I feel like I'm eating all day already. I can't eat any more."

The hard training had increased his appetite dramatically but he was not gaining weight as fast as Jason wanted him to.

"Well," said Jason. "We're going to up the intensity of your workouts for the next three weeks so we're going to have to get some extra kilojoules into you somehow."

"Increase the intensity? Wow," said Tristan. "I guess that's going to hurt."

"Not too much," said Jason, grinning. "We'll be working a lot harder but the sessions will be shorter and then we'll taper off to a steady plod in the run up to the fight."

"So I can pick up weight in the plod part?"

"No," said Jason. "You need to get more into you now." He picked up a large plastic tub from under the desk. "So I want you to drink this, three times a day."

"What is it?" Tristan asked, extending a hand and taking the heavy container.

"It's a protein supplement. You're just not getting enough with not eating meat."

Tristan examined the container. The instructions said to mix with water in a shaker. "Can I make it in the blender and zap a banana with it?" he asked.

Jason grinned. "Somehow I knew you'd ask that," he said. "I tried to get banana flavour but they only had strawberry and that. I thought the vanilla would be better with a banana in it."

"Cool, thanks," said Tristan. "I'll try to eat more as well."

"Great," said Jason. "Get some more carbohydrate down your neck, though," He stood up and tapped the lid of the tub. "And let that take care of the protein. Okay, he's all yours," he added, turning to Dean. "I have to get back to North Beach and torture my afternoon lot."

Jason backed out of the door. "Sempai, tomorrow, on the beach outside your place, 7am," he called. "And get up early and eat. I don't want you losing your breakfast."

Tristan was tense again. He felt like a lab rat under Dean and Gavin's scrutiny. He began to fidget.

Finally, Dean spoke. "Sempai," he said. "I know this is asking a lot from you, and you are at liberty to say no if you think it will be too much, but Sensei Gavin and I would like you to take part in the kata at the demonstration."

Tristan beamed. "I would love to, Shihan," he said. "It won't be too much."

"I thought you'd say that," said Dean, smiling. "Have a word with Sensei Gavin about getting in some practice. Oh, and Sempai," he added, "I hope you're over your stage fright."

Tristan was working on it. Since his talk at the school he had spoken about the event at two youth groups, a local athletics club and the golf club next door. And he had collected another R1 410 in sponsorship money.

He still suffered from a bad case of nerves before each one, but Sensei Gavin had told him to interpret the jitters as excitement rather than fear, a tactic that was serving him well.

"I'm getting over it," he said.

"Good, because I have a little challenge for you," said Dean

"What?" he asked, alarmed.

"Ah," said Dean. "All in good time. I'll tell you later."

It was the hardest workout Tristan had ever had. Forty five minutes of sheer torture.

He was on his back, spread-eagled on the sand, his chest heaving painfully as every cell in his body screamed for oxygen. Jason was lying next to him, he was gasping too.

The sun on Tristan's flushed face took his attention from the burning in his chest. The warmth soothed and his breathing began to slow.

All at once the warmth was gone. He was shivering and choking for air. He rolled onto his side coughing and gagging.

He managed to sit up. Spitting out a mouthful of sandy salt water he sat, bemused, as the ocean sucked back the foamy white water.

"Oh, damn it," he said, examining his sopping dogi. "Where did that come from?"

Jason was high enough up the beach to avoid the rogue wave. Sitting on the dry sand he shook with laughter as Tristan, turning a deeper shade of red, began to cough again.

"Tide's coming in," said Jason scrambling up the beach. Tristan tried to follow but his aching muscles refused to respond.

He found himself sitting in waist deep water, laughing so hard he was unable to get up as the backwash sucked him down the beach. The ebbing water released its grip and he got to his feet.

Covered in sand and dripping he plodded towards Jason, hanging on to his sodden pants. Once he was a safe distance from the water's edge he hitched them up and retied the drawstring at his waist.

"Your mom's going to kill me," laughed Jason. "Look at the state of you."

Elize was not happy and, as was so often the case, Tristan bore the brunt of her displeasure. To his deep humiliation, his mother made him strip to his underwear on the doorstep before allowing him into the house.

He showered and changed into a pair of red Quicksilver board shorts and a torn, almost luminous, orange T shirt.

Elize and Jason were sitting at the table drinking coffee when he padded, barefoot, into the kitchen.

"Good grief, child," said Elize. "Are you colour blind?"

"What? No!" he said. "Why?"

"He has to ask?" said Elize shaking her head and turning to a grinning Jason.

"Nice outfit, Tris," he said, laughing.

Indignant, Tristan took the blender from the cupboard and measured out two scoops of protein powder. He added water, two bananas and a tablespoon of peanut butter.

"Careful with that," said Jason, nodding at the jar. "You don't want too much fat or sugar."

"Uh huh," grunted Tristan, sucking the spoon while firmly securing the lid on the blender. He blasted his creation into a thick shake and poured it into Jonno's enormous soccer ball mug.

He flicked on the kettle and sipped the concoction while he

waited for the water to boil.

"Anyone want another coffee," he asked, downing the last of his shake and throwing two Rooibos teabags into the mug. He poured on boiling water and a greasy film rose to the top while the teabags leached a cloud of pale orange into the murky water.

"Not anymore," said Brett entering the kitchen and peering over Tristan's shoulder. "That disgusting substance is enough to put me off hot drinks for life. What is it?"

"Tea," he replied, dropping a couple rounds of wholemeal into the toaster. "Anyone want toast then?"

"No thanks," came the unanimous response.

Brett sighed then sat at the table and began to talk surfing with Jason.

Tristan brought his plate and mug and sat, cross legged, on the chair next to his mother. He flicked at the scum on top of his tea, sucked his finger then wiped it on the front of his shirt.

"Tristan," snapped his mother. "You have the manners of a beast and we have a guest!" She slapped him on the shoulder, knocking him sideways.

"Sorry, Ma," he said. He righted himself on the chair and began to munch dry toast.

He listened with half an ear as Brett and Jason made plans to drive up the coast with Jonno for a spot of surfing later that afternoon. "Can I come?"

"No," said Elise. "You have homework to finish. Besides, I want you to have some time at home for once."

"But, Mom," he began.

"Tristan, *moenie met my stry nie!*" Don't argue with me, she flared. "Now get this mess cleaned up and go and do your homework."

He wet a finger and poked at the toast crumbs on his plate. He put the finger in his mouth and looked at his mother, weighing up his options.

Brett made the decision for him. "Tris, do as your mother says please," he said mildly. "You can come with us another time."

Tristan pulled his finger from his mouth with a loud sucking sound. He got up and collected the mugs and his plate and took them to the sink. As soon as he had cleaned the kitchen he stalked to his room.

Tristan flopped on his stomach on the bed and pulled his calculus book from the bedside table. He opened it and groaned, remembering why he had abandoned the task in the first place.

He had a flair for art and music. Logic was not his strong point and he was eternally grateful to be in Mr Pietersen's maths class this year.

A man with endless patience and a passion for his subject, Mr Pietersen took great pains to gently guide his less gifted students to achieve more than they ever thought possible. This was in sharp contrast to his previous maths teacher, Mr Venter.

Mr Venter was a cold man who thought nothing of meting out severe punishment for no greater crime than simply not grasping a concept.

After a year in his class, all Mr Venter had instilled in Tristan was a hatred for maths and a debilitating fear of the blackboard compass.

He sighed and put the book back down. He wanted to do well. He wanted to hand in his homework on time, but he just didn't understand it.

He knew Mr Pietersen would sit with him during break and, yet again, patiently explain. But his inability to comprehend still filled him with a dread he couldn't shake.

"Tristan!" Elize called him from the kitchen. He slid off the bed and hurried down the passage.

"Rico's on the phone for you," she said.

"Thanks, Ma." He took the receiver. "Howzit, Ric," he said.

"Yo, bru, you busy?"

"No, but..."

"I'm with Andre and Megs. We're going to Parkway Mall, you wanna come?"

"Hang on a sec," said Tristan. He covered the mouthpiece with his hand.

"Ma, can I go with Rico to Parkway?"

"You can," said Elize. "Whether or not you may is a different question entirely."

He sighed and rolled his eyes. He hated it when his mother did that. "*May* I?" he asked.

"Tristan!" snapped Elize. "I told you I want you to stay in and finish your homework."

"But I have finished," he protested.

"Well I still want you at home for once."

"But, Ma," he said. "I'm bored."

"Tristan, don't argue with me!"

He snatched his hand from the mouthpiece. "Yes," he said into the receiver. "I do. But I have to stay in." He shot a look at his mother that said she was ruining his life, then said to Rico, "So I can't!"

Elize banged the kettle against the drainer as she filled it.

"Your mom?" asked Rico, lowering his voice.

"Yup."

"Okay, just say yes or no. Do you want us to come over to your place after Parkway? We'll say we just called in on the way home."

"Yes," he said. "That would be cool. I'll see you at school then," he added for his mother's benefit.

"Later, bru," said Rico and hung up. Tristan replaced the receiver.

"Tristan!" hissed Elize. "Why can you never just listen to me? Why do I always have to put up with you arguing?"

"Because sometimes you're not fair!" he snapped.

"Don't you dare judge me," she shouted, snatching up the kettle and pouring hot water into a mug. She turned back to Tristan, pointing the kettle at him. "And unless you want me to really lose my temper, I suggest you go and read those chapters of your set work book which I *know* you haven't done!"

Shocked by the strength of his mother's reaction he retreated to his room. He stretched out on the bed wishing he had told Rico not to come. Opening *Far From The Madding Crowd* he began to read.

It was hot in his room and he wanted some fresh air. He tucked his book under his arm and opened the bedroom door. There was no sign of his mother so he slipped down the passage and listened at the kitchen door. Silence.

Tristan pushed the door open and marched purposefully to the screen door and out into the back garden.

He put his book beside the pool and took a flying leap onto the the inflatable turtle floating on the water. He landed squarely in the centre but still managed to get his shorts wet.

He settled into the turtle and paddled to the side to retrieve his book. His concentration was much sharper out in the mid-autumn sun.

Half an hour later Tristan was bored with Hardy's awkward prose. Piqued by Bathsheba Everdene's over-inflated opinion of herself, he laid the book on his chest and closed his eyes, allowing the turtle to drift gently in the light breeze.

"Tris?"

Startled, he almost lost the book to the depths. "I'm reading it, Ma," he said, waving it at his mother.

"Come over here please," said Elize. She tucked her skirt between her knees and sat on the edge of the pool, letting her legs dangle in the water.

Tristan hesitated then paddled the turtle to the side of the pool.

"Pass me the book please," she said. He handed it to her and she placed it behind her. She took his hand in hers.

"I'm sorry, Tris," she said. "I shouldn't have bitten your head off like I did."

He remained silent. He had been genuinely taken aback by his mother's anger and wasn't quite ready to forgive and forget.

"Won't you come inside?" she asked. "I've made you some lunch."

Still saying nothing he disengaged his hand from his mother's and guided the turtle to the steps. He stepped off the inflatable and out of the pool.

He ran a hand over his backside. The back of his T shirt and shorts were wet. "I'll just get changed," he said stiffly, picking up the book.

"Okay," said Elize. "I'll go and make your shake."

Never one to hold a grudge, Tristan thawed a little. "Thanks, Mom," he said, managing a smile.

Tristan tucked into the tomato sandwiches and then attacked the fresh fruit salad.

Elize smiled, pleased with his healthier appetite even though it was costing a small fortune. But her pleasure was marred by a touch of sadness.

He was no longer her little boy. The hard training had defined his muscles and given him a more grown up, almost sculptured look. She thought he was a little taller too.

Emotionally, the trauma of Andre's accident had left him harder, more serious. He was no longer the carefree child who used to run everywhere barefoot, climb trees and spend hours scooping struggling insects off the surface of the pool; gently lining them up in the sun to dry out before reclaiming their freedom. Tristan was growing up, and it was happening much too fast for Elize.

She found herself staring at her son. He looked up from Jonno's mug, a line of creamy foam along his upper lip.

"What?" he asked, wiping his mouth with the back of his hand.

"Nothing," she said, looking away. "It's just..." she paused. "You're not my baby anymore, Tris," she said. "You're growing up so fast and I'm so afraid of losing you."

Tristan gaped at his mother. "Come on, Ma," he said. "Don't go getting all girly on me. I can't cope."

Elize bit back tears.

Tristan rounded the table and stood behind her. He leaned

down and put his arms around her, resting his chin on her shoulder. "You're not going to lose me, Ma," he said.

She tore a piece of kitchen towel from the roll on the table and dabbed at her eyes then reached up and rested a hand on his cheek.

"I know, my boy," she said. "But please be careful, I don't want you getting hurt."

Sensei Jason didn't want Tristan getting hurt either. As the fight drew closer he watched him like a hawk during training and insisted he wear pads for sparring. He hated it.

"How can I fight well if I'm dressed like a marshmallow?" he moaned.

The tough and highly structured training was beginning to tell on him. Physically he had never been in better shape but emotionally he was feeling the pressure. "I'm suffocating under all this."

"Sempai, you have a week before you step up to some of the hardest fighters you have ever faced. How well do you think you'll fight if you pick up an injury now?"

Tristan sighed and threw his hands in the air. "But what's the point of even training if it doesn't feel the same!" he snapped. "It just slows me down and interferes with my technique."

Tristan and Jason had formed a close friendship during their training sessions together but Jason wasn't about to let it compromise their relationship in the dojo.

"*Sempai!*" he said. "Do not question my judgement! I've been training karateka for tournaments since before you could wipe your own behind. Now get those mitts on and get over here."

"Sorry, Sensei," said Tristan, chastened. He pulled on the gloves and moved to face Jason.

After a light sparring session Jason chased him out of the dojo.

"Go and find your friends and just relax for the rest of the weekend," he said. "You're getting yourself all wound up."

He needed the break and was grateful for his first taste of freedom in weeks. He got home to find no one in. He let himself into the house and read his mother's note.

At Rob and Barbara's for a braai. Come round, or help yourself to lunch at home. See you later.

He couldn't handle sitting in the cloud of pungent smoke that inevitably spewed forth from Rob's barbecuing meat, or Barbara's incessant questioning about his state of *'itemhood'*.

Barbara had been trying to get him and *'our Katie'* partnered up since they were in primary school together.

Tristan didn't have the time or the inclination for itemhood, especially not with Katie Lewis.

He phoned Rico but there was no answer. Andre was out too. He didn't even try Megan's number as he knew she would be at the dojo.

He showered, changed and went out into the garden. Meryl was in the driveway but there was no sign of Jonno. He walked down to the beach hoping to find him there.

"Cheer up," said Jonno as Tristan dropped onto the sand next to him. Jonno was squeezing the water out of his dreadlocks. He flicked the ends spraying Tristan with salty droplets.

He wiped the water off his face and continued to look sulky. "Don't!" he snapped. "I'm not in the mood."

Jonno grinned. "Who's crapped in your salad?" he asked.

Tristan laid back on the sand and threw his arm over his eyes, shielding them from the harsh sun. Although autumn was fast losing ground to winter, the day was pleasant and very bright.

Thanks to the warm ocean current it rarely got too cold along this stretch of coast and the drop in humidity in autumn and winter made it a comfortable time of year.

Jonno rolled onto his stomach and prodded at Tristan's ribs. "You okay?" he asked. "Anything you want to talk about?"

He lifted his wrist and squinted at Jonno from under his arm. "I'm just pissed off," he said curling his toes in the sand.

"Yeah," said Jonno. "I had kind of picked that up. Do you have a reason or is it one of those random teenage mood swing type things?"

He sighed and turned onto his side to face his uncle. "I feel like I haven't had time off for ages. I only ever see the guys at school and the one weekend Sensei gives me some free time no one's around.

"Come on," said Jonno, leaping to his feet. He donned his T shirt and pulled the nose of his surfboard out of the sand. "I'll take you to the Porpoise for a Coke and you can chill with me this arvie."

Tristan rolled onto his back again.

Jonno angled the surfboard to shield his face from the sun. "What now?" he asked, looking down at him.

"I can't drink Coke," said Tristan. "Too much sugar."

"Fine," said Jonno. "But I'm ravenous. You can have a soda water, and I'm sure a veggie burger won't kill you."

He got up and brushed the sand from his clothes and followed Jonno to the Blue Porpoise.

Jonno leaned his surfboard against the edge of one of the outdoor tables and slid onto the bench. Tristan sat opposite him.

"Right," said Jonno, handing him a menu. "What are you having?"

Jonno ordered a beef burger with creamy mushroom sauce, extra chips and a chocolate milkshake while Tristan opted for the French salad and a glass of sparkling water.

"You won't be able to fight your way out of a wet paper bag eating like that," said Jonno pointing the end of his knife at Tristan's plate.

"I eat plenty," he said, fishing out the cucumber wedges with his fingers and lining them up around the edge of his plate. "It's just that there's nothing else on the menu that's not too high in fat, sugar or dead things."

Jonno jabbed the cucumber onto his fork, lifted the lid of his burger and deposited it on top of the mushrooms.

"You're getting obsessed and it's not good for you," he said, waving a chip at Tristan.

"It's just until after the demo." Tristan swiped the chip from Jonno's fork. "Then I'm going to eat an entire packet of doughnuts and drink a whole litre of Fanta Grape."

He ate the chip and took another from the plate.

Jonno grinned. "You want some?" he asked, tilting his plate.

Tristan shook his head, taking another. "No thanks."

After they had eaten they walked back across the road. He made his shake and drank it directly from the blender jug.

"Don't let your mother catch you doing that," said Jonno.

"You've got my mug'"

"Eww! You put that muck in here?"

"Yup," said Tristan. "It's the only one big enough. I'm going for a swim," he added, rinsing the blender. "Are you coming?"

Jonno shook his head. "Uh uh," he swallowed his mouthful of coffee and held up his wrinkled fingers. "I've been in the water all morning. I look like an albino prune."

When Tristan still hadn't emerged half an hour after going to change, Jonno went to look for him. He pushed the door quietly open and peered into the bedroom.

Tristan was curled up on the bed sleeping soundly. He crept in and folded the quilt over him then returned to the kitchen and picked up the phone.

Tristan was confused. It was dark outside but he could hear voices. He sat up and reached for his alarm clock. The luminous green display read 19:47. He flicked the bedside lamp on and blinked in the yellowish light.

He got up and pulled the window onto the catch then closed the curtains. It had turned cool so he swapped his T shirt and shorts for a pair of jeans and a sweatshirt then followed the sound of the voices to the dining room.

"Hello, dozy," said his mother. "Your supper's in the warmer. Are you hungry?"

He blinked. His parents and Jonno were eating salad and fish with heads and tails still on.

He stared at his father's plate for a moment then shook his head. "Not right now, thanks, Ma," he said. "I just woke up. I might eat later."

He pulled out a chair and sat down.

"You look exhausted, Tris," said Brett. "I think your Senseis are working you too hard."

"It's Sensei, Dad," he said resting his elbows on the table and cupping his chin in his hands.

"Which one?" asked Brett. "Jason or Gavin?"

He frowned at his father then smiled in comprehension. "No, I mean there's no s. Sensei is singular and plural."

"Beg your pardon," said Brett. "I stand corrected."

"Tris, take your elbows off the table, please," said Elize. He obeyed immediately, remembering the time on the farm when, without warning, his grandfather had taken hold of his wrist and banged his elbow so hard on the edge of the table that he had struggled to use his knife throughout the rest of the meal.

"You know what I think?" said Jonno.

Tristan looked up at him.

"I think your supper will keep until breakfast and that, right now, you should have a hot bath and get yourself back into bed."

"Jonno," said Elize. "It's spinach lasagne. It would be disgusting for breakfast."

Jonno grinned. "It would be an excellent way to start the day if you ask me," he said. "Anyway, Tris, I'm taking you out tomorrow. Somewhere where you can kick back, relax and forget about everything. By the way, *boet*." He turned to Brett. "May I borrow your car? Tris gets a bit weird about travelling in Meryl."

Brett agreed to his use of the car on one condition, that he brought it, and his son, back in one piece.

Tristan was intrigued. "Where are we going?" he asked.

"You'll have to wait until tomorrow to find out," said Jonno.

Jonno buttered three slices of toast and listened for the humming kettle's change of pitch. He flicked it off at the wall and poured the, almost boiling, water onto the cafetiere. Stirring it with the back of his knife he inhaled the thick dark aroma then put the lid on and waited a while before depressing the plunger.

He ate his breakfast leaning against the counter.

"Morning, J. You're up early," said Brett. He wandered into the kitchen stifling a yawn and pulling his bathrobe tighter against the cool morning air. "Kettle still hot?"

Jonno clicked it back on and let it boil. Brett didn't hold with the theory that boiling the air out of the water changed the taste of the coffee. As long as it was hot and wet it was fine.

"Morning," said Jonno. "Your neighbour's bloody dog kept me up half the night. I'll shoot it if I see it."

Brett grinned. "Welcome to suburbia."

Jonno was staying the weekend because he had finally got round to having his house on the plot fumigated.

When the cockroaches got to be the size of skateboards, not even Jonno could tolerate them as house guests.

The last time he'd had it done he'd stayed at the beach front lock-up where he shaped his surfboards. This time, since Elize no longer viewed him as a moral danger to her son, he had gladly opted for the home comforts of her guest bedroom.

Jonno made the coffee and handed it to Brett.

"Thanks," Brett said. "What time do you want the car?"

"I don't. I only mentioned it because I didn't want Tris lying awake worrying about a trip out in Meryl. He's convinced the passenger seat will go though the floor and he'll end up sitting on the road." Jonno grinned.

"And is that a possibility?"

"A distinct one," he said. "But hardly anyone sits that side anyway."

Brett took his keys off the hook by the door to the garage. "Here," he said. "You're not taking my son in that rust bucket."

Jonno shook his head. "No," he said. "It's sorted. I've got something arranged. I'm going to pick it up when I've finished my coffee."

It was still painfully early but Jonno wanted to leave by six at the latest. Tristan sat at the kitchen table in his pyjamas, sipping his shake. He was tired and feeling more than a little delicate. He hadn't slept well.

With six days to go before the demo, his nerves were beginning to get the better of him, forming noticeable cracks in his thin veneer of confidence.

The microwave pinged and he got up and removed the steaming food. He had allowed it to overheat. The spinach had oozed out and bubbled up the sides of the dish. The lasagne noodle was curled at the edges, the corners like small grey hands reaching for a lifeline in a murky green pond.

When the kettle boiled he made coffee rather than tea, something he did when he was stressed. He set the odd breakfast on the kitchen table and left it to cool while he went to get dressed.

He had no idea where Jonno was taking him so he opted for a tidy pair of khaki cargo pants and a neat white T shirt. He tied a thin jersey around his waist, a sensible precaution for the time of year, even on the coast.

Elize was in the kitchen examining the now cold grey-green goo in Tristan's dish. She looked up as he entered the kitchen, pleased to see him looking presentable for once.

"You can't eat that for breakfast," she said. "It looks horrible. Let me do you some nice oatmeal with apple and cinnamon."

He poked at the rubbery noodle and sucked the sticky spinach off his finger. He remained there, saying nothing, staring blankly at the ruined food.

In that moment he looked so fragile Elize couldn't help herself. She pulled him into her arms and held him close. He had definitely grown taller.

* * *

Tristan didn't resist his mother's embrace. Her warm softness and clean, faintly soapy, smell felt comfortable, safe. He nestled against her neck allowing the tension to drain from his tired mind and body.

Elize released him and smoothed the front of his shirt. "Sit down," she said. "I'll make you some oats."

"Thanks, Ma," he said, subdued.

He was halfway through his breakfast when Jonno burst through the door.

"Come on you lazy toad," he said. "I thought you'd have been waiting on the doorstep by now."

Buoyed by Jonno's enthusiasm, he momentarily forgot the guilt he harboured for neglecting his friends on his one weekend off. He shovelled the last of his oatmeal down and took his bowl and mug to the sink.

"I'll wash those," said Elize. "You get off with Jonno."

"Thanks, Ma." He turned to Jonno. "I'll just get my camera and my sketch pad. Do I need to bring anything else?"

"No," said Jonno, "You won't even need your camera and..."

"I never go anywhere without them," he said.

"Okay," sighed Jonno. "But hurry up, your chariot awaits."

Tristan stopped on the steps, surprised to see a VW minibus with tinted windows parked in the driveway. "Is the president coming too?" he asked. "What's with the windows?"

"No president," said Jonno. "It's all in your honour. The windows are to keep the sun out and it's big so you can move around. We'll be in it for quite a while."

He followed Jonno to the bus. "In it for how long? Where are we going, Cape Town?"

"You'll see," said Jonno, grinning. "Get in."

Tristan hauled himself onto the high seat and almost fell off again as three voices all yelled their greetings at once.

Rico, Andre and Megan were lounging comfortably in the back seats along with an enormous cooler box.

"About time," said Rico. "We've been in here for ages."

"Yes," said Megan. "At this rate we'll be needing a bathroom break before we get through town."

"Woah," said Jonno, his hand on the key in the ignition. He turned to the back. "If any of you want to go before we set off, speak now or forever hold your pee."

None of them did so Jonno fired up the engine and backed out of the drive.

Tristan sat sideways, his feet in the well between the two front seats. The four friends chatted animatedly but no one would give him any clues as to their destination. All he knew was that they were having a picnic for lunch and that there was plenty of what Rico called rabbit food, especially for him.

Tristan didn't mind where they went. As a great lover of nature, he was content to sit back and watch as the lush coastal vegetation gave way to the drier, harsher landscape of the interior.

Jonno stopped outside a run down little tearoom in an equally run down little town.

"Snack time," he said, fishing out his shoes. He always drove barefoot but kept a pair of sandals under his seat in case he was stopped by the police, a strong possibility in the vehicle he was currently driving.

He disappeared into the dark interior of the shop and emerged a few minutes later carrying two plastic packets. Slipping into the driver's seat he kicked his shoes off and rummaged in the bags.

He opened a can of Coke and placed it in the cup holder in his door then passed one of the bags to the back.

"There are all sorts of goodies in there," he said. "But no fighting over the tomato ketchup chips. They only had one bag." He rooted in the other packet and tossed a bag of salted peanuts onto the dash.

"And for you, oh healthy one," he said to Tristan, handing him the packet. "A bottle of sparkling water and a muesli bar, which I dare say will have too much sugar or some no no or other."

Once they were all settled with their snacks and drinks, Jonno set off again.

Tristan felt the tense exhaustion caused by the pressures of the last few weeks ease its grip as the beautiful scenery rolled by, and when they arrived at the gates of the Hluhluwe-Umfolozi Game Reserve he could barely contain his excitement.

Jonno paid the entry fee, drove through the gates and pulled the car over to the side of the dirt road. "Now," he said, pointing behind his seat. Andre reached down and handed him a large package. "You shouldn't really get this until next weekend, it's your birthday present from your mom and dad. But, they thought since you would be getting the crap kicked out of you on your birthday, you might as well have it now." Jonno handed Tristan the package.

"At least that way, if you don't survive, you'll have had a week to enjoy it."

Tristan tore the paper from the box and opened the lid to reveal a single lens reflex camera with two lenses; a wide angle and a telephoto zoom.

Three years ago Jonno had given Tristan his old Kodak point and shoot camera. He had been so impressed with Tristan's creativity and his ability to capture beautiful images with such a simple camera that he had persuaded Brett and Elize that it was time for an upgrade.

"Oh wow," Tristan exclaimed. "This is amazing." He carefully lifted the camera from the box and fitted the zoom lens.

Jonno smiled at his excitement. "I guess you don't need time to go through the instruction manual," he said.

"No," beamed Tristan. "Bring on the animals. Let's go."

By the time Jonno had dropped Rico, Andre and Megan at home and pulled into the driveway it was already dark. Jonno unfastened his safety belt and flicked the handle releasing the door. The courtesy light flashed on, making him blink.

"Wait!" said Tristan. Jonno turned to him, his already radiant face lit further by the orangey glow from above.

"Thank you," he said. "It was a perfect day."

Jonno smiled at him and ruffled his untidy hair. "It was my pleasure, Tris," he said. "You deserved the break."

Jonno headed straight for the bathroom. Tristan bounced into the kitchen and threw his arms around his mother knocking her two steps backwards.

"Thank you, Ma," he said. "It's the best present ever."

Elize closed her arms around him. "I'm pleased you like it," she said.

"I do," he said. "I love it."

"What am I missing?" asked Brett coming in from the back garden. Elize invited him into the embrace.

Brett smelled of chlorine and Tristan inhaled deeply. He liked the smell of chlorine. It was normally his job to do the pool but today Brett had done it for him.

"Thanks, Dad," he said. "The camera is brilliant."

Brett squeezed Tristan's shoulder.

Jonno came into the kitchen, "That's better," he said. "I've been busting for a leak since Ballito. Uh oh." He stopped dead. "Am I interrupting one of those nauseating touchy feely family moments?"

Tristan pulled away from his parents and caught one of Jonno's dreadlocks, playfully winding it round his neck.

"Okay, out of my kitchen you two!" Elize sent them both to shower and told them supper would be ready in half an hour.

Tristan chatted excitedly throughout the meal telling Brett and Elize about all of the animals and birds they had seen.

He even fetched his sketch book to the table, showing them the drawings and notes he had made of the plants and insects that had so captivated him at the view points, hides and picnic area.

A slow eater at the best of times, he was still only half way through his ratatouille by the time the others had finished dessert and started on the after dinner coffee. None of them had the heart to hurry him up and they didn't leave the table until after nine o'clock.

Chapter Twenty One

Sensei Jason had tapered Tristan's training right down in the week leading up to the fight and he had too much time on his hands.

It was only Tuesday and Jason had said he didn't want to see him at the dojo until after school on Thursday. Boredom was already kicking in and he was beginning to struggle with pre-fight nerves.

He went home with Andre after school. Rico and Megan had gone to Parkway to see a movie. Tristan could never sit still long enough to go to the cinema, he preferred videos. Andre's plastered leg made it difficult for him to get into the seats, so they spent the afternoon doing homework and listening to music in Andre's room.

Michelle knocked on the door and brought them each a glass of mango juice. She stared at Tristan and then hopped up onto the bed. Glancing sideways at him, she whispered something in Andre's ear.

"I guess she's still mad with me," said Tristan when Michelle had closed the door. He sighed.

"She's not," said Andre. "She's a bit upset about something. It's not you." Andre seemed agitated himself.

Tristan was lying on his back on the floor with his bare feet up on the bed. He lifted his head and tried to sip the juice, still lying down. He ended up choking, with juice up his nose and running down his neck, soaking into the collar his white school shirt. He put the glass on the floor and rolled onto his side then sat up.

Still spluttering, he cursed his stupidity and wiped his shirt and neck with the tissue Andre had handed to him. His nose and throat burned.

"You okay?" asked Andre, trying desperately not to laugh.

"I'll live," managed Tristan. Talking made him want to cough again.

He turned around and leaned against the bed. He sat with

his legs stretched out in front of him and sipped the juice, letting the cold fluid soothe his throat.

Andre was on his stomach on the bed, his geography book open in front of him. He folded his arms across the book and rested his chin on them. "Tris?" he said, staring at the back of Tristan's head.

"Hmm?" Tristan had a mouthful of fruit juice.

"Can I talk to you about something?"

He swallowed the juice. "Sure."

"It's private," said Andre. "You have to promise not to tell anyone, not even Rico."

"I won't." He didn't turn around, sensing it would be harder for Andre to talk to him face to face. "I promise."

Andre rolled the corner of his geography book cover between his thumb and forefinger. "Remember the time you first came round here?" he asked.

Tristan remembered it well. He still had nightmares about it. Somehow, in his mind, that day and the day of Andre's accident had formed an inseparable association.

He had a frequently recurring dream where he left the house, knowing Andre was still inside. But as soon as he walked out of the gate he saw the car careering towards the grass verge, mounting the kerb and flinging Andre high into the air.

Trapped in the nightmare he tried to scream but no sound would come from his mouth. That was when he always woke up, sweat soaked and sobbing.

He shuddered. "Yes," he said. "I remember."

Andre turned onto his back and stared at the ceiling. "Well, after you left," he said. "My brother..."

"Your brother?" Tristan pulled his legs up and spun round, crossing them in front of him and settling to face Andre. "I thought he was your dad!"

Andre stared at him for a long moment. Then shook his head. "Actually, he's my half brother, Carl," he said. "My dad is 21 years older than my mom and he was married before." Andre cleared his throat and went on. "His first wife died when Carl was fourteen and my dad had to bring him up on his own. He's is only four years younger than my mom. I suppose it must have been a bit weird for him when they got married. I mean, imagine if I ended up with a twenty year old stepmother now."

"Wow," said Tristan. "Really weird. It must have been weird for your mom too."

"I guess," said Andre. "Anyway, apparently, not long after I was born, Carl came out of the army and was completely *bossies,* you know, *really* messed up, and one day he just disappeared."

Tristan was staring at Andre.

"Then a couple of years ago he pitched up out of the blue and asked if he could stay for a while. My dad got really angry. He never forgave him for leaving and not letting him know he was okay. But mom's too soft. She calmed things down and said he could stay." He paused. "It was really cool having him around. He used to take Chelle and me to the beach and help us with our homework, he was great. But he never talked about where he'd been, and sometimes he'd get drunk and fight with dad. One day dad caught him with drugs in the house." Andre sat up and fiddled with his pen, doodling on the back of his exercise book. "It was only a bit of *dagga*," he said. "But he kicked him out of the house."

Tristan plucked at his toenail. He remembered the time Brett had found cannabis in his car.

He had just turned eight, so Jonno would have been eighteen.

It was June 1987, Jonno had recently passed his driving test and wanted a bit of fun before starting his National Service in the July. Brett had lent him the car to go up the coast to surf with some friends. When he brought the car back it was filthy and smelled of vomit. Brett had found the drugs in the ashtray while he was surveying the damage.

Tristan had witnessed the whole sordid affair from behind the net curtain in his bedroom.

"But it's only *dagga*," Jonno had protested. Brett had caught him by the shoulders and rammed him backwards over the bonnet of the car. He said he didn't care if it was fairy dust, it was illegal and he didn't want it in his car.

Brett had given Jonno a choice. He could either call their father and tell him the story, or Brett would handle it his way.

Jonno had been terrified their father would call the police and have him thrown in jail, so Brett had handled it himself. He had punched Jonno in the face, twice.

Brett had hit him so hard that Jonno had fallen to his knees with his head in his hands. Even from behind the net, Tristan could see the blood running down Jonno's arms.

Jonno was still sitting by the car long after darkness had fallen, and Tristan had crept outside. It was cold and he had snuggled up to Jonno for warmth. Jonno had folded him into his arms and buried his face against his head. He had rocked him gently back and forth and sobbed quietly into his hair, pleading with him never to touch drugs.

He never had and couldn't imagine he ever would.

Much as Jonno did Brett, Tristan worshipped Jonno and had felt deeply for him that day. Right now, he found himself feeling more than a little sympathy for Carl.

He couldn't imagine the the horror of losing his mother at fourteen and his dad getting married again, two years later, to a woman only four years his senior.

He stared at a ridge of hard skin on the side of his foot and rubbed his thumb along it. When Andre spoke again it made him jump.

"Just before Christmas," said Andre. "He came back. He said he was in trouble and that he really needed help. Mom and dad argued about it but mom won and said he could stay."

"Was he in trouble with the cops?" asked Tristan.

Andre shook his head. "Nah," he said. "Nothing like that. It was alcohol. Anyway, he managed to stop drinking, got a job and everything was fine until dad had to go to America for six months." Andre fell silent again.

"Then he started stealing money from mom and buying booze. He took the money from their savings account, that's why we can't afford my op. He was a good guy when he was sober but when he was drunk it was awful. He and mom would fight all the time, they even hit each other." Andre was close to tears.

Tristan laid back on the floor, his knees bent and his fingers interlaced behind his head. He felt out of his depth, unsure how to handle Andre's emotion. He stared at the ceiling fan. His reflection in the concave silver blade made him look long and thin and gave him an odd, wavy outline.

"The day you thumped me at school mom totally freaked out when I got home. I think she and Carl had been fighting and she was so mad she took it out on you. That's why she went to the dojo and lost it."

"God," said Tristan. I'm sorry. I had no idea things were so awful for you."

Andre was back in control of his emotions. "When she and Michelle got back Carl was drunk. Mom started yelling at him and he grabbed Michelle and threatened to choke her."

Tristan sat up, horrified.

"I tried to stop him and that's when I got the smack in the face. Mom flew at him too and it was this massive free for all. It was horrible." Andre's voice had tailed off to a whisper. "He calmed down a lot after that but, when I ended up in hospital, mom was too frightened to have him in the house with Michelle so she kicked him out."

Tristan hugged his legs to his chest. He felt hollow and upset. He dropped his head onto his knees. "Oh hell," he moaned. "And I accused your mom of hitting you."

"It's okay, Tris," said Andre. "She understands. You couldn't have known."

Tristan looked up at Andre. "So do you know where he is now? And is your dad still away?"

Andre looked uncomfortable. He couldn't hold his gaze. "My dad's still in the States until next month. Mom never told him anything. Not even about the accident. She was too frightened that he would come home and lose his job."

"And Carl?" asked Tristan.

"He was supposed to be in rehab in Pietermaritzburg," said Andre. "Your dad organised it after mom told him what was happening."

"Supposed to be?" asked Tristan. "Where is he then?"

Andre sighed. He tossed his pen down on the bed and looked up at Tristan. "He's here," he said. "That's what Michelle was telling me when she came in."

Tristan gaped at Andre. "Shouldn't we go and see if your mom and Michelle are okay?"

Andre shook his head. "Michelle will come and get us if there's a problem."

Tristan and Andre worked on their maths in uneasy silence. A moment ago they had heard raised voices from the kitchen. Tristan had wanted to go and see if everything was okay but Andre had said no.

Tristan sat with his legs wide apart and his books spread between them on the floor. He was chewing on the end of his pen while examining a diagram in his text book.

Frowning, he pushed his hair behind his ear and snatched the pen from his mouth in frustration. It rattled against his teeth and spun from his fingers, landing with a thud on the page of his book.

He dropped forward and rested his elbows on the floor, cupping his chin in his hands.

"I hate this stuff," he said. "It just doesn't make sense." He poked the page, running his finger under the question he was struggling with. "A horizontal asymptote may intersect the graph of the function. Is that true or false?"

"True," said Andre.

"But why?" asked Tristan. "I don't get it. I don't even understand what it means!"

Andre patted the bed next to him. "Come," he said. "I'll show you."

Tristan got to his feet and sat on the bed. His attention wandered as soon as Andre began to explain and he knew none of it was going to sink in.

The voices from the kitchen came again. Louder this time, more frantic.

"Stay here," said Andre. "I'll go see if mom and Chelle are okay."

"No way," said Tristan. "If he kicks off you'll need help."

"Tris," said Andre. "He's more likely to kick off if you're there."

Tristan looked at Andre's plastered leg and set his mouth in a determined line.

"All right," said Andre. "But stay in the hall. Don't let him see you and don't come in unless we need you. Okay?"

He nodded.

Andre picked up his crutches and set off down the passage. Tristan followed.

Tristan stood to one side of the kitchen doorway and listened. Kathryn was shouting at Carl, telling him to leave.

He looked up and saw Michelle standing at the opposite end of the hall, wide eyed and afraid. He indicated to her to come to him.

She ran across the hall and tried to enter the kitchen but he caught her arm and pulled her gently to him. Her back was to him and he draped his arms firmly over her shoulders and held her close so she couldn't break free.

"It's okay," he whispered. "Stay here where you're safe. I'll go in if they need help."

It was quiet in the kitchen. Michelle reached for his hand and clumsily took it in hers.

He rested his chin on her head. "Don't worry," he said. "It'll be okay." But he knew, as the words left his mouth, that he had no guarantee.

"I want you to leave, Carl!" Kathryn's voice carried clearly from the kitchen. "You can come back when your father is here and we can discuss it then."

"I don't have a father anymore," yelled Carl. "You poisoned him against me."

"That's not true and it's not fair!" Andre's voice.

Tristan felt Michelle tense in his arms and he squeezed her hand.

"Andre, this has nothing to do with you," hissed Carl. "Now get out of here. Your mother and me are talking."

Your mother and I, thought Tristan, hearing his own mother's exasperated tones in his head. *It's your mother and I!* He marvelled at his mind's bizarre sense of timing. Now was hardly the appropriate moment for an internal grammar lesson.

"Well my mother doesn't want to talk to you," said Andre. "She asked you to leave."

"Andre, it's all right, love. Go back to your room. I can handle this." Kathryn again.

"No," said Carl. "It's not all right. He's an interfering little brat and he had no right to come barging in here like this."

There was a shuffle from inside the kitchen followed by a gasp from Kathryn and a yell of fury from Andre. Tristan heard Andre's crutches clatter to the floor. Michelle began to sob and he eased her aside and burst into the kitchen.

He had the split second it took him to cross the kitchen to evaluate the scene before him. Andre was on the floor to his right and Carl had Kathryn backed up against the counter, his hands around her throat.

Tristan launched himself at Carl, landing hard on his back. He wrapped his legs around his middle and his left arm around his neck. He squeezed Carl's throat with the crook of his elbow and gouged at his face with his free hand.

Carl made an obscene cawing sound and released his grip on Kathryn. Staggering around the kitchen, he tried to free himself of his burden.

Tristan wrapped his other arm around Carl's neck and clung on doggedly. Hardly elegant, but then real fights never are.

Carl clawed at Tristan's arms and thumped his shins. He felt no pain, only a wild rage and a determination to hang on, no matter what.

He heard Kathryn tell Andre to call the police. Carl must have heard her too because he redoubled his efforts to dislodge him.

Swaying furiously from side to side, Carl lumbered round the kitchen like an injured bull buffalo with a lioness clinging to its back. With a final roar of fury, he launched himself to one side, bending his knee as as he twisted his body into a downward arc.

Tristan caught on to his plan an instant too late. He heard the sound of his ribs against the edge of the kitchen table before he felt the blinding agony that shot up his side, claiming his breath and rendering him helpless.

He released his hold on Carl and slipped from his back like a piece of raw liver sliding from a plate. He lay where he landed, his breathing coming in desperate, agonising sobs.

Carl fled the house.

Andre quickly locked all the doors and hobbled back to the kitchen. His heart was jumping wildly in his chest and he was afraid he might be sick.

Tristan was still on the floor. He was curled up with both hands against his side. Kathryn and Michelle were on the floor next to him.

"Andre, sit with Tristan please," Kathryn said. "I'm going to phone his mother." She moved to get up.

Tristan snatched at her hand. "No!" His protest came out as a strangled yelp. He sat up, owl-eyed, staring at Kathryn. The thin ring of honey-gold encircling dilated pupils the only colour in his face. "Please," he said. "Phone Jonno rather. Please don't phone my mom." He gave Kathryn Jonno's number.

Michelle got up as Andre lowered himself to the floor. "Maybe you should lie down," he said.

Tristan shook his head. "I can breathe easier sitting up. I'll be fine in a minute. It's going off a bit now." The fear in his eyes contradicted his words.

"Are you sure," asked Andre, concerned.

He nodded.

Michelle came back with a packet of frozen peas and a tea towel. She carefully wrapped the peas in the towel and eased Tristan's school shirt out of the waistband of his trousers. His ribs were grazed but didn't look too badly injured.

"You once told me to put ice on bumps. Remember? It was that time Paul Hendry kicked me on the shin."

He smiled at Michelle. "Yes," he said. "I remember."

He gasped as she placed the makeshift ice pack against his injured ribs.

"Careful, Chelle," said Andre. "His ribs might be broken." Andre saw the fear again and knew Tristan was thinking about the fundraiser.

Jonno arrived at the same time as the two police officers. Kathryn led them into the kitchen.

"Fat lot of good you lot would have been if the guy had been really dangerous," snorted Jonno. "He could have killed them all and left the country by now."

Tristan cringed hoping Jonno wasn't going to get himself arrested. It wouldn't be the first time.

He was sitting up at the table sipping hot, sweet tea and feeling much better. Although his ribs still hurt the adrenaline had worked its way out of his system and he had stopped shaking and was breathing easier.

Jonno paced around the kitchen while Kathryn, Andre and Tristan each gave a statement to the police. Once they were satisfied, they left with unconvincing assurances that they would do everything in their power to apprehend Carl Turner.

Jonno turned to Kathryn. "I don't want you guys to stay here on your own," he said.

"Thank you, Jonno. But we'll be fine," said Kathryn. "Don't

worry."

He shook his head. "Either you come home with me or I stay here, no arguments," he said. "But first I'd better get Tris to the hospital."

Tristan had put his head down on the table and was taking shallow gasping breaths. He felt like he had toothache in his side. A constant, gnawing, exhausting pain punctuated by sharp bursts of pure agony whenever he inhaled too deeply.

He lifted his head and forced himself to breathe slowly and quietly. "I'm fine now," he said. "I don't need to see a doctor. Michelle's peas worked wonders.

Michelle beamed with pride.

Tristan flashed her a smile. "Thank you," he said. "It really did help."

"Let me see," said Jonno.

"J, I'm fine, really."

"Show me or we go to the hospital, even if I have to drag you there, kicking and screaming!"

The phone rang making Tristan jump. Pain shot across his chest. He sucked in his lower lip and lifted his shirt. Jonno frowned and studied his side carefully.

He prodded gently. "That hurt a lot?"

"No," lied Tristan.

"Well," said Jonno. "I can't feel any unusual movement so maybe it's not too bad. I'm not going to force you, Tris, but I'd rather you saw someone."

Tristan shook his head. "Don't fuss," he said.

Kathryn came back into the kitchen. "Well," she said. "There's no need for you to worry about us anymore, Jonno. That was the police. Carl handed himself in at the station about half an hour ago."

Tristan noticed the undertone of regret in Kathryn's voice. He picked it up because, in some twisted little corner of his own mind, he too, still had some sympathy for Carl.

"Good," said Jonno. "They should have enough to hold him.

At least for a while. But call me if you need anything."

"Thank you," said Kathryn. "But I think it's time I called my husband and let him know what's been going on."

Tristan sat in the back of Meryl. He refused to sit in the passenger seat. "I'm telling you," he said. "The last time I sat there I could feel the whole seat moving. And I can see the road under it from here!"

"Yeah okay, Tris" said Jonno. "Tony Meyer is going to have a look at her next week. If he can't fix her up I'll use her as a bloody chicken coop on the plot and buy another car. Happy?"

"Happi*er*," said Tristan. "J, I just don't want you to kill yourself because your car is a *skedonk*," a wreck, he said. "I worry about it."

"And I worry about your ribs, Tris." said Jonno. "But I'm not going to nag you to death about it if you think you're okay!"

"Sorry," mumbled Tristan, contrite. He gingerly poked at his ribs. He knew he should be checked out but he was too afraid the doctor might stop him from taking part in the fundraiser.

He was afraid the pain might too, but he still had three days to improve.

Chapter Twenty Two

By Thursday afternoon the pain had eased somewhat, but Tristan had a bruise the size of a dinner plate around his ribcage. The graze was itchy and had scabbed over. It took all of his self control not to claw at it constantly.

He taped a piece of gauze over the graze to prevent the heavy fabric of his dogi rubbing against it. He pulled the dogi jacket around him and tied his belt.

He took a couple of deep breaths. *Not too bad*, he thought. He bowed into the dojo, half convinced he could handle whatever Sensei Jason was likely to throw at him.

He tentatively tried a bit of dynamic stretching to warm up while he waited for Jason.

"Sempai."

"Osu!" Tristan jumped and turned to face Sensei Gavin.

"Shihan would like a quick word. Could you come into the office please?"

"Yes, Sensei," he said, his heart rate increasing. His first thought was that Jonno had phoned Shihan and told him about his ribs but Dean's greeting was warm and friendly and Tristan relaxed into the chair.

"Now," said Dean. "I don't know if you remember, but a while ago I said I have a little challenge for you."

He hadn't remembered, but Dean's words jogged the memory loose and the alarm he had felt at the time came flooding back. *Not more public speaking, please!*

Dean grinned. "Relax," he said. "It's not that bad, honestly."

Tristan released the breath he had been holding, feeling it in his side as his ribcage deflated.

"Sanchin kata," said Dean. "I know you love it and I know you perform it well. I would like you to demonstrate it on Saturday. Sensei Gavin will talk the audience through it while Sensei Jason performs the *shime*. Are you up to the challenge, Sempai?" asked Dean.

Tristan was more than up to the challenge. He knew that for Shihan to select him over the higher ranked yudansha was a great honour indeed. But was his ribcage up to it?

"Yes, Shihan," he said. "Thank you. I would love to do it."

"Excellent," said Dean. "We'll use it as a warm up for your fights. Now, off you go. Sensei Jason is going to run though it with you."

Jason pressed his thumb and forefinger against his eyes. They felt gritty and sore. He hadn't been sleeping well and the niggling tension he'd had in his neck since breakfast had moved up into his head.

He pinched the bridge of his nose then rubbed his left temple hoping it wouldn't become a full-blown migraine.

Tristan came out of the office and closed the door quietly. He stood a moment, still facing the door.

Jason watched him. He seemed tense, wary somehow. He knew Tristan would be feeling the pressure of the upcoming fights and that, despite his own agitation, he would have to handle him with care.

"In here," Jason called to him. Tristan turned and bowed into the dojo, crossed the corner and bowed out again to enter the mat room.

Jason smiled at Tristan's conscientiousness. "How are you feeling," he asked.

Tristan hesitated before responding, the pause giving rise to a jolt of mild concern. He frowned.

"I'm fine, thank you, Sensei," said Tristan. "Just a bit nervous."

Jason managed a smile. *That makes two of us*, he thought.

"You'll be fine," he said. "A bit of nervous tension is a good thing."

"I guess," said Tristan.

"Okay, let's get started, shall we?" Jason tried to inject a little enthusiasm into the situation. "Get your jacket off. I want to be able to see your muscle tension the first couple of times we run through."

Tristan crossed his arms in front of him and took a step back.

Jason frowned. "Come on, Sempai," he said. "There's no need to be shy. I've seen it all before."

A hint of pink coloured Tristan's ashen cheeks and Jason remembered how painfully humiliated he had been when his mother made him strip on the doorstep. He wished he had kept his mouth shut.

"Sempai?" his mild concern was fast escalating to the point of major worry. Pale, wide-eyed and close to tears, Tristan looked wretched.

Jason watched as he tugged his dogi jacket out from under his belt. He let it fall open then took the left side in his hand and opened it fully.

Jason's eyes were drawn to the gauze and it took him a full second to register the huge bruise surrounding it. His mouth dropped open but he found himself incapable of speech.

"Sensei, I..."

"No!" Jason found his voice. "Don't!" he snapped. He held up a hand, a strong warning to Tristan to keep his mouth shut. "I don't want to hear it right now, Sempai," he said. "I don't want to know."

He turned and marched across the mats. He yanked the elastic band from his hair and ran a hand through it, causing it to tumble wildly around his face and over his shoulders.

Without bowing he charged through the door to the dojo and literally ran into Dean.

Dean caught him by the shoulders. "Steady, Sensei," he said. "What's wrong."

"Not now! Please." He shrugged Dean's hands away and continued towards the changing rooms.

Dean stood, perplexed, staring after Jason as he strode the length of the dojo and into the changing room. The door swung closed with a loud bang leaving him alone with the echo.

He stepped into the mat room and stopped dead. Tristan was sitting in an untidy heap on the mats. He was cross legged, slumped forward with his forearms resting on the ground, in his hands a small blood spotted scrap of white gauze.

Dean hurried to his side but Tristan was on his feet before he was half way across the mats. He exhaled a long, relieved breath.

The front of Tristan's dogi jacket was hanging open, his shoulders were slumped and his head hung. The picture was one of utter defeat.

"Sempai, what..." his gaze fell to Tristan's left side. He gently moved the flap of the jacket aside. On closer examination it was apparent the injury had not just been inflicted. He felt the blood drain from his head and with it, his self control.

He snatched at the shoulder of Tristan's dogi and dragged him into the office. He shoved him roughly though the door and slammed it hard behind them.

Gavin quickly ended his phone call. Replacing the receiver on the cradle, he came to his feet.

Dean was towering over Tristan, red in the face. The veins on his neck and at his temples were bulging and his fists were balled at his side. "You stupid, irresponsible little brat!" he yelled. "Why the hell didn't you say you were injured? Sensei Jason could have killed you testing Sanchin on broken ribs."

Gavin moved to Tristan's side and placed protective hands on his shoulders. He was tense and shaking.

"What the hell were you thinking? What did you do, for Christ's sake? The demonstration is the day after tomorrow! When did you plan to tell us you can't fight?"

"Dean," said Gavin. "Can we talk outside for a minute please?"

Dean ignored the request. "Do you have any idea how much work went into organising this event? What the hell are we supposed to do now? In case you hadn't noticed you were supposed to play a major role. Who do you think is going to do it now?"

Gavin felt Tristan's knees give way. He caught him and held him upright, guiding him to a chair.

Moving round the chair, he stood between Tristan and Dean. "Come on," he said. He caught Dean's elbow and turned him to the door.

He knew how hard Dean had worked to organise the demo and how anxious he was that it should go off without a hitch. He knew that he was taking a huge risk putting Tristan up against some of his strongest fighters in a public arena. The whole event was monumental leap of faith for everyone involved.

He also knew that Dean still considered Tristan to be emotionally ill equipped for the challenge.

"What happened?" Gavin asked. Closing the door to the office. All of the fight had gone out of Dean.

He looked at Gavin and shook his head. "He's hopeless, Gav," he said. "Absolutely hopeless."

Jason was sitting on the unit beside the washbasin, his elbows on his knees and his head in his hands. He had heard Dean yelling at Tristan and hoped Gavin was somewhere nearby.

He had been on the receiving end of Shihan's temper more than once and had been rendered a quivering wreck every time.

Tristan, sensitive soul that he was, didn't stand a chance of surviving the experience unscathed.

He slid from his perch and turned on the washbasin tap. He splashed his face with cold water and ran his wet hands through his hair.

Smoothing it back he took the band from around his wrist and tied it neatly at the back of his head.

He bowed into the dojo and headed for the office. Dean and Gavin were standing by the door, deep in conversation.

"Excuse me," he said, coming up alongside them. "I need to talk to my kid."

Gavin and Dean stood aside and he went into the office.

* * *

Tristan was slumped in a chair sniffing miserably, his face buried in his dogi jacket. He wasn't the first karateka to be reduced to tears in Shihan Dean's office, and he certainly wouldn't be the last.

Jason crossed the room and took a box of Kleenex from the top of the filing cabinet. He pulled out a wad of tissues and pushed them into Tristan's hand.

Tristan sniffed again and sat up straight. He pressed the tissues to his nose. "Thank you, Sensei," he mumbled.

Jason pulled up a chair and placed it next to Tristan's. "Come on," he said, draping an arm over his shoulders. "We've spent enough time worrying about the problem. Let's see if we can find a solution." Jason gave his shoulder a squeeze.

He felt his eyes well with tears again. He blinked rapidly and bit his lip. Jason had worked so hard to get him ready for the fights. He'd had so much faith in him, never doubted him even when others had, and had stood strong in the face of the criticism levelled at him by some of the other instructors.

Jason had believed in his courage and ability right from the start, and had all but moved mountains to get him to do the same.

And he had succeeded. But now, he had let him down, and he found Jason's calm control so much harder to bear than his anger.

"Do you want to tell me how you did it?" asked Jason.

Tristan shook his head.

"Okay. What did the doctor say?"

He looked away.

Jason caught his chin and forced eye contact. "You have seen a doctor, haven't you?"

Tristan pulled his chin out of Jason's grip.

"Right, and I assume if you haven't seen a doctor, your folks don't know either!"

Tristan couldn't respond. Holding his breath, he kept his eyes fixed on his thumbnail and wished the whole mess would go away.

"Oh come on, Tris," said Jason. "At least tell me when it

happened."

"Tuesday," he said, his voice barely above a whisper.

"Right, come on." Jason got to his feet and held out a hand to him. He took it and Jason hauled him out of the chair.

Not even pausing long enough to bow out of the dojo or pick up their shoes, Jason marched him past Gavin and Dean.

"We'll be back as soon as we can," he called over his shoulder. "And don't try to fix this mess until you've talked to me!"

They crossed the car park and Jason opened the passenger door of his yellow Opal Astra.

Tristan got in. The interior was immaculate and smelled of new leather even though the car was probably older than he was.

The keys were hanging in the ignition. Cars were regularly stolen in the city and Tristan had to bite back the urge to say something.

"I know," said Jason, as if he'd read his thoughts. "I forgot them."

He turned the key. A couple of hiccups later the engine roared to life and he drove to the nearest hospital.

"Well, young man that's quite a knock you've had," said the doctor, pinning Tristan's X-rays up on the light box.

He adjusted his glasses on his nose and tilted his head as he scanned the film. "Fortunately," he said. "There's nothing broken. It was more of a glancing blow than a direct impact so a bit of soft tissue damage, mainly superficial bruising. It looks a lot worse than it is, but I'm afraid it could be rather painful for quite some time."

"No," said Tristan. "It's fine, really."

The doctor's expression said he didn't believe him. "I'll write you up something for pain just in case," he said.

Dr Naiker, Tristan read his name badge, turned and rummaged in a drawer. He came back opening a packet and pulling out a clear plastic tube with what looked like a ping-pong ball inside. He fitted a mouthpiece to it and handed it to him.

"Now, blow," he said. "I want you to get that ball as high up the tube as you can and keep it there for as long as you can."

He took a deeper breath than was comfortable and blew as hard as his ribs would allow. At first the ball just twitched and danced at the bottom of the tube but then it shot about two thirds of the way up.

He did his best to hide the effort it took, but the fine beads of sweat that formed on his forehead told the story better than words ever could.

"Good," said the doctor. "Now, I know it hurts, but you need to do that at least once every hour while you're awake. If you don't breathe deeply you could get pneumonia,."

"What about exercise?" asked Tristan. "Can I still train?"

Dr Naiker's eyes fell to his dogi.

"It'll force me to breathe deeply," he said, hopefully.

"Well, it won't do any harm," said the doctor. "As long as you protect it from impact and listen to your body when it hurts. So don't take the painkillers before you exercise."

"Can I take part in a martial arts demo on Saturday?"

The doctor opened his mouth but Tristan began again before he could speak. "Please don't say no straight away," he begged. "At least not in front of my Sensei."

"What will you be demonstrating?" asked Dr Naiker.

"Kata and kumite," said Tristan.

Dr Naiker frowned and opened his mouth again but Jason came to his rescue. "He was supposed to be taking part in ten fights lasting two minutes each," said Jason.

"But I have a really good left guard and I'll protect my ribs," he pleaded. "We trained so hard for this. Please say yes."

"I'm sorry," said Dr Naiker. "I can't say yes to that."

Tristan felt Jason's hands on his shoulders. "Don't worry, Tris," he said. "There's always another time. And I'll talk to Shihan, he'll come round."

Tristan bit his trembling lower lip and slid off the examination table. "Thank you, Dr Naiker," he said as he pulled his dogi closed and fastened his belt around his waist.

Dr Naiker sighed. "Would it help if I pointed out that I didn't say no?"

Tristan and Jason both looked up at the doctor.

He sighed again. "Look," he said. "I cannot, in all good conscience, say it's okay for you to go out and fight ten fights on Saturday. But honestly? I wouldn't say yes if you were 100% fit. I'm a doctor. It's my job to make people better, not condone them injuring each other in the name of sport."

Dr Naiker paused and looked directly at Tristan. "It's not so much damage I'm concerned about, it's pain. If it hurts you won't breathe properly and that can cause complications."

"I will, I promise," said Tristan. "I'll breathe. I'll blow the ball all the time. But I have to do this. It's really important to me."

Dr Naiker nodded slowly. "I can see it is," he said.

"We won't make any firm decisions until Saturday morning," said Jason. "And I'll pull him out the second he looks like he's struggling."

"Oh, he'll struggle," said Dr Naiker. "He won't make ten fights, I guarantee it."

Tristan narrowed his eyes. "It's at Ridgewood High sports field on Saturday," he said. "You can come and see for yourself if you like."

"Hey," said Jason. "Don't you go getting all bull-headed and stubborn on me. If you're not going to be sensible and work within your limitations I'm not putting you out there. I'll do it myself before I'll put your health at risk!"

"Sensible coach," said Dr Naiker. "I'll trust you to do what you think is best."

"Right," said Jason as they left the consulting room. "We'll go back to the dojo and talk to Dean and then I'm taking you home to tell your folks."

"No way," said Tristan. "Mom will never let me fight."

"Then you won't fight," said Jason. "But I'm telling your

parents."

"But you can't," said Tristan. "Please! At least wait until after the demo."

"Sempai," said Jason, his voice low. "Don't make me pull rank on you."

"Sorry, Sensei," he said. He stepped through the door into the waiting area and froze.

Brett and Elize crossed the room and stood in front of him. Jonno hung back behind them. Tristan glared at him.

"Don't blame Jonno," said Brett. "The hospital called your mother for consent before they could treat you. She squeezed the details out of him on the way here."

"Well," said Tristan. "The doctor said I can do the demo so why don't we just forget about it now so I can go and train?"

Elize folded her arms across her chest.

"Mom, please don't fight with me," he said. "I have to do this."

"What did the doctor say, Tristan?" she asked. "I don't believe for one minute he said you could fight with broken ribs."

Brett rested a hand on her shoulder.

"They're not broken," said Tristan. "He said it looks worse than it is and it's okay to fight."

Elize looked at Jason.

"That's not exactly what he said," said Jason and went on to repeat what Dr Naiker had told them.

Jason continued, "I told Tristan we'll wait and see how he is on Saturday. If he's not fit to fight, I'll do it. If he seems okay he can start but I'll take full responsibility for his well-being and I'll pull him out straight away if he's in trouble."

"No, Sensei," said Tristan. "I'll take responsibility for my well-being. Only I know how I feel and only I know how far I can go."

He turned to face Jason. "Sensei," he said. "We worked too hard for this. We can't just give up now because it got a bit harder."

Jason leaned back against the door and blew out a long breath. "Tris," he said, "This was going to be hard enough without any added extras. But, if your folks agree, and you're sure you want to go ahead, then I'm happy to trust your judgement."

"Thank you, Sensei," said Tristan. He turned to his mother. "Mom? Please?"

Tristan knew Brett would trust his judgement too. But he also knew that he wouldn't override his mother if she said no.

Elize looked at him for a long time. "You know I don't like this, Tristan," she said. "But you're not a child anymore. You have to make your own decision and you have to handle the consequences. But," she added. "Don't you ever keep anything like this from me again. Do you understand?"

"Thank you, Ma," he said. "And I'm sorry I didn't tell you."

Jason knocked on the door and entered at Dean's call.

Tristan remained tight up to his back. He really couldn't face Shihan right now.

Jason reached a hand behind his back and caught him by the wrist pulling him round to the front.

He clutched at his ping-pong ball tube and stepped forward. "The doctor says I'm fine," he said. He stopped fiddling with the tube and looked up at Dean. "I'm sorry, Shihan. I know I can be irresponsible sometimes but..."

"Tristan, Jonno called me and told me the story. Why didn't you just tell me?" asked Dean. "I would never have ripped into you like that if you'd just told me you were hurt and how it had happened."

"I'm sorry, Shihan," said Tristan. "I know I should have. But I didn't want to let you down."

Tristan stretched out on his bed staring at the ceiling. Jason had refused to go through Sanchin with him, insisting that he could do the kata with his eyes closed and that resting his ribs was far more important.

He had done it anyway, in the back garden when he got home. And, as he suspected, the *ibuki*, forced tension breathing, hurt.

He lifted the bottle of painkillers the doctor had prescribed off the bedside table and examined the label. He unscrewed the cap and shook two into his hand. He swallowed them without water.

When his mother called him for supper he was dead to the world. It was almost nine thirty when he finally woke up.

He stumbled drowsily into the TV lounge and sank into a chair.

"Ah, finally decided to grace us with your presence have you?" asked Brett.

"Hmm," grunted Tristan.

Brett and Elize were watching *The Pelican Brief* on video.

"Your supper's in the warmer," said Elize, her eyes fixed on the screen.

"Thanks," he said, but made no move to get it.

Tristan shivered. He pulled the finely woven throw off the back of the chair and wrapped it around his shoulders. He pulled his feet up into the chair and tucked the makeshift blanket around his legs.

"Stop that a minute, will you, love?" Elize said to Brett.

He reached for the remote and paused the film.

"Back just now," she said.

"Is she still mad at me?" asked Tristan as soon as Elize was out of earshot.

"We both are," said Brett.

Tristan sighed.

"Tris, you could have been seriously hurt," said Brett. "You should have told us straight away."

"But I'm fine, Dad," he said. "I wasn't hurt."

"Tris, that's not the point. You should have told us. And Jonno certainly should have known better."

"Don't go off on Jonno about this," said Tristan. "It was my fault. He did his best to persuade me to tell you guys and I knew he would never betray my trust."

"Yes, Tristan," said Brett. "But if anything had happened to you and we weren't aware..."

"Nothing happened!" snapped Tristan. "And it wouldn't have. If you must know, Jonno spent that night sleeping on my bedroom floor so he could be sure I was okay. So don't be mad at him!"

"Great!" said Brett. "I wish he'd told your mother that."

Tristan groaned. "Did she freak out?"

"She certainly did," said Brett.

"Can I phone him?"

"*May* I phone him," sighed Elize from behind his chair. "And no, you may not. I'll phone him. You eat this."

Elize placed a tray with three mugs of tea and a bowl of mushroom and brinjal risotto on the coffee table. She handed a mug to Brett and the bowl to Tristan, setting his tea on the side table by his chair.

"Thanks, Mom," he said. He hadn't realised he was hungry until the food was in front of him and now he was ravenous.

He knew that being allowed to eat his meal in front of the television meant his mother had forgiven him.

Tristan arrived early at the dojo. Jason had told him to be there at seven for the briefing.

There was no training tonight but Dean wanted the yudansha in to go over the last minute details for the demo the next day.

He kicked his takkies off in the mat room and pushed them under the bench. He slipped his thumb into the waistband of his jeans and pulled the button away from his abdomen.

The jeans were too tight. Most of his clothes were too tight but, so far, he had resisted his mother's attempts to drag him to Parkway to buy new ones.

The hard training and carefully balanced diet had added both muscle and height to his once weedy body.

Weeks of pushing, goading, coaxing and the occasional kick in the pants from Jason had turned him into a formidable opponent, and he looked the part. Tristan no longer looked like a wimp.

He bowed into the dojo and went to join Sempai Kathy and Sensei Jim.

As the others began to arrive he wandered off to be alone with his thoughts. He studied the people in the room, trying to assess their strengths and weaknesses, trying to recall previous encounters he had had with them in the dojo.

At seven on the dot, Sensei Jason called the meeting to order.

"Okay," he said. "Just a couple of things. I think you all pretty much know what you're doing tomorrow. There will be a briefing at the venue in the morning but if any of you are unsure, just give one of us a shout." Jason indicated Dean and Gavin, who were standing behind him.

"The other thing, as some of you already know, Sempai Tristan picked up a bit of a rib injury this week," said Jason. "Now, he's been given the all clear to fight but, guys, this is a demo, not a competition. So please, do me a favour and stay away from his ribs. Okay?"

A resounding "Osu!" echoed round the room as the group acknowledged Jason's request.

"Okay," said Jason. "That's it from me. Shihan would like a word."

Jason stepped aside and Dean came forward. "Sempai Tristan, would you come here a minute, please?"

Tristan's heart skipped in panic as he walked round the group of yudansha to stand in front of Dean.

Dean put a hand on his shoulder and turned him to face the group. "I did a rotten thing," he said. "I organised the demonstration for tomorrow knowing full well it was our youngest Sempai's sixteenth birthday."

Dean gave his shoulder a squeeze. "Now," he said. "You have a choice. You can either go easy on him because it's his birthday, or you can kick him from here to Cape Town because he's not a kid anymore. I'll leave that up to you to decide."

"But stay away from his ribs, please," reminded Jason.

The group laughed.

"Anyway," said Dean. "We didn't want the occasion to go unmarked so, Sempai, we have a little something for you."

Gavin came forward and handed him a large, soft package. "I know it's not officially your birthday until tomorrow," he said. "But go ahead and open it."

Tristan carefully unwrapped the gift to reveal two high quality, heavyweight tournament uniforms. He was momentarily rendered speechless. A quality dogi cost over R500 and he had always had the lightweight suits.

He looked up at his instructors. "Thank you," he said. "Thank you so much."

"Well, we couldn't have our star fighter looking like a scruff tomorrow," said Jason. "Now could we?"

"No," said Dean, turning to Tristan. "Now, you wear one for the demo and you keep the other one safe. It's for another purpose. But Sensei Gavin will tell you about that tomorrow."

Chapter Twenty Three

Tristan slid out of the back of the car. The grass was cool and damp under his bare feet. The sun shone brightly, but an early morning chill nipped at his fingers and toes and he was glad of the heavier dogi.

He was expecting to feel nervous but an odd calm had settled over him on the drive to the school. He was alert but relaxed.

"You okay?" asked Brett, coming up beside him.

He was looking out over the sports field. There were stalls and marquees already in place, and others still being erected.

He looked up at his father. "Uh huh," he said. "I think so. I just thought it would be smaller than this. Not so much going on."

"Dean wanted to make sure it attracted a big crowd," said Brett. "More people equals more money."

And more witnesses to my impending humiliation, thought Tristan. He headed off to join what Elize had called the dogi brigade, a group of karateka gathered by the main marquee.

He found Sensei Jason surrounded by excited and babbling young juniors. They were doing a display of the basics later on, and were having difficulty containing their enthusiasm.

Jason saw him and dispatched the youngsters with Sempai Kathy and Sempai Paul for a bathroom break.

"I thought they'd better get a pit stop in early," said Jason. "I don't want anyone needing to go thirty seconds before they're on. At least they'll know where the loos are now." Jason looked at Tristan. "Okay?" he asked. "How are the nerves?"

"As long as I know where the loos are I'll be fine," he said.

Jason grinned. "Ribs?"

He ran a hand down his side. "Not bad," he said. "A bit sensitive, but not really painful."

"Good," said Jason. "Listen, I want you to chill out a bit. Go and find somewhere nice and quiet, get something to eat and drink and just relax for a while."

"Don't you need help with anything?" asked Tristan.

"Not from you, I don't," said Jason. "I want you to relax. If you need something to take your mind off it go and find your friends." Jason pointed towards the grandstand.

Tristan turned to see Andre and Rico sitting on the front row and Megan and a young orange belt trotting towards them. The orange belt was Michelle.

"Osu!" said Michelle as she slid to a halt between him and Jason.

"Sempai," she said. "Mom says I can come back to karate. Can I do the kihon today? Please?" Her round face was flushed with excitement.

"Well," said Tristan. "You'd better ask Sensei."

Michelle glanced shyly at Jason. She had never met him before.

He smiled down at her. "I'm sure that will be fine," he said. "But you really need to ask Sensei Gavin."

Michelle looked around.

"I'll tell you what," said Jason. "I'll ask him for you. Do you remember your kihon?"

"Osu, Sensei," said Megan. "I'll run through it with her."

"Thanks, Megan," said Jason. He turned to Michelle. "It looks like you're on the team."

Jason turned back to Tristan. "Go," he said. "Relax somewhere nice and quiet and meet me back here just before ten."

Megan slipped her arm through Tristan's and led him up to the grandstand.

"Happy birthday," she said. "I hope today won't be too rough on you."

Tristan was feeling overwhelmed. The event had not yet officially opened and he had been surrounded by people clamouring for his attention for the past half hour.

The pile of gifts and cards in the back of Brett's car was getting bigger by the minute. He had no idea that so many people knew, or cared, that it was his birthday.

Jonno caught him by the arm and led him to one side.

"Hey," he said. "Do you want to get out of here for a while?"

He had that same numb feeling that he got when he had a dentist's appointment, resignation, a sense of despair almost.

"Here," said Jonno. "Take my keys and go and sit in Meryl. I'll get Rico and Andre to come and sit with you, okay?"

He nodded and took the keys. "Thanks, J," he said.

He let himself into the driver's seat and climbed over the gear lever to the other side. He sat, staring blankly, watching the parking area begin to fill with cars.

Andre was sitting in the back seat, his plastered leg stretched out almost the full width of Meryl. Tristan sat in the death trap passenger seat and Rico was behind the wheel.

Tristan shifted on the seat and it creaked and moved sideways.

"This car is way cool," said Rico. "I want a Beetle when I pass my test." His hands were on the steering wheel and his feet worked the pedals.

"Don't push the clutch in," said Tristan. "The handbrake's crap."

"It won't roll," said Andre. "There's a big rock wedged under this back wheel."

Rico didn't trust the makeshift wheel chock and quickly abandoned the controls.

"Tris," said Andre. "Have the cops talked to you or your folks yet?"

"Cops?" he asked. "What about?"

"Carl," said Andre.

Tristan glanced over at Rico.

"He told me," said Rico.

"No," said Tristan. "What do they want to talk about?"

"They said if your folks don't want to press charges he can go back to rehab," said Andre. "But if they do he has to go to court."

"Well, I don't," said Tristan. "So they don't. It was me he whacked against the table."

"Cool," said Andre. "Thanks. My mom will be happy now."

Tristan glanced at the clock on the dash for the third time in as many minutes.

"You getting freaked out?" asked Andre.

"A bit," said Tristan. In truth, he was beginning to feel horribly nauseous and he just wanted to get started. The mention of Carl had only made him feel worse.

He looked across to the grandstand and watched Megan going through basics with Michelle and a few of the other juniors.

"Guys, I need to talk to Sensei," he said. He caught the handle of the door and pushed it open.

"Oh shit!" he blurted, as a strip of metal fell to the ground and the window slipped down and out of the bottom of the door.

His hands shook as he picked up the metal bar. He tried to push the window back up inside the door but couldn't get it high enough to reach it at the top. He let it fall down again. There was no way to get the window back in place, or out of the door.

Tristan banged his hand on the side of the car. "Bitch!" he yelled.

Andre and Rico gaped at him.

"I can't do this!" Leaping to his feet, he fled between the cars.

"Stay with the car," said Rico. "I'll get Jonno then try to find Tris."

"Okay," said Andre. He tipped the passenger seat forward and reversed awkwardly out of the car. He lost his balance and ended up on his backside beside the open door. He picked up the metal bar and looked at the window.

By the time Jonno arrived at the car, he had simply used the bar to push the window back to the top and wedged it firmly in place by angling it slightly to one side and resting it on a lip inside the door.

"You're a genius, my man," said Jonno. "I should keep you on retainer. What happened?"

Andre relaid the details of Tristan's crisis of confidence.

"Rico's gone to find him," he said.

"Oh hell," said Jonno. "I hope he's okay."

Rico found Jason briefing a group of green belts about a self defence demo they were going to give.

Jason must have sensed Rico's desperation because he quickly finished up and came to his side.

"Tris has done a runner," said Rico. He leaned forward and rested his hands on his knees. Flushed and panting, he looked up at Jason. "He just freaked out, now I can't find him anywhere."

Jason sucked in his lower lip and quickly scanned the field. He tugged at a cord around his neck and pulled a stopwatch out of his dogi jacket.

"Okay," he said. They both looked up as the loudspeaker system gave a shriek of protest and Shihan Dean began his opening speech. "We've got just over an hour before the kata demo and I still need to calm him down. We need to find him fast."

"Okay," said Rico. "I'll start back at the changing rooms."

"Right," said Jason. "I'll round up some of the guys to give us a hand. If you find him, go to the main marquee and get the guy on the PA to give me a shout. I'll do the same if I find him."

"Will do," said Rico and took off at a run.

Tristan had bolted first to the changing rooms, where he had lost his breakfast to a series of painful, heaving convulsions, and then to the main marquee where he hoped to find Sensei Jason.

He had rinsed his mouth with water but could still taste the sourness of regurgitated banana.

There was no sign of Jason in the tent. He turned and ran outside. Looking frantically around he went to his left and ran headlong into Sensei Gavin.

"Take it easy," said Gavin. "What's so urgent?"

Gavin took one look at Tristan's panic-stricken face and knew they were in trouble. He caught him by the wrist and led him to the car park.

Weaving between the parked cars, he spoke calmly but firmly. "It's okay, Tris," he said. "You'll be fine."

"I'm not fine," said Tristan. "I feel sick."

"Come on," said Gavin, unlocking his car. "Get in."

He put the sun shield in the windscreen to afford them a little more privacy and to block Tristan's view of the rapidly filling sports field. "Talk to me, Tris," he said. "What's the problem? Is it pre fight nerves or stage fright?"

Tristan put a hand to his mouth. "There are so many of them," he said. "I never thought there would be so many."

"Remember how well you did at the school?" said Gavin. "Well, this is the same thing only easier. This time you don't even have to look at the people. Once you get up there all your focus will be on your opponent."

"I know," said Tristan. "But I feel so sick."

"Sick how?"

"Pukey," said Tristan. "I already threw up my breakfast."

"It's just nerves," said Gavin. He leaned in closer to Tristan. "I'll let you into a secret if you promise to keep it."

"What?" asked Tristan.

"Sensei Jason is just as bad. He always spends at least twenty minutes hanging over the toilet bowl before a tournament."

"Really?" asked Tristan. "But he always seems so confident."

"He's learned to hide it well over the years," said Gavin. "But if you ask Shihan Chris Sheldon at the next grading camp he'll tell you a thing or two about Sensei Jason in his tournament days. Tears, tantrums the works," said Gavin.

"Was Shihan Chris Sensei's coach?" Tristan's eyes were wide with awe.

"Yes," said Gavin. "He was. While Sensei Jason was in Cape Town he trained under Shihan Chris. Well, he was Sensei Chris back then."

"Wow," said Tristan. Shihan Chris Sheldon was one of his

biggest heroes.

"Let me tell you something else about Sensei Jason," said Gavin. "He'd never let you see it, but he gets just as jittery when it's one of his fighters stepping onto the mat as he does when he's fighting himself. So I think you'd better go and check in with him before you give him a heart attack."

Dean walked up behind Jason and put a hand on his shoulder. Jason jumped and spun to face him.

His face was pale and strained. A strand of blond hair had escaped his ponytail and was hanging down his face. He seemed oblivious to it.

Dean frowned. It would drive him crazy if it was his hair. It *was* driving him crazy. He wanted to push it away from Jason's face.

Dean turned and looked out over the field. "How's it going?" he asked.

"Good, it's okay," said Jason. "The kids are doing well."

The juniors had taken to the field under Sempai Kathy and were performing their basics with gusto.

"Where's your protégé?" asked Dean. He had spoken to Sensei Mark le Grange who was out looking for Tristan. He knew what had happened and he was seriously concerned.

The only thing keeping him from losing his cool was the knowledge that Jason would step in and take Tristan's place at a moment's notice rather than jeopardise the club's reputation.

Jason began walking back to the main marquee. Dean followed.

"I told him to go and relax somewhere quiet," said Jason.

Dean looked at his watch and arched an eyebrow. "I hope he's keeping an eye on the time," he said. "The kata is up next."

Jason pushed the offending strand of hair behind his ear. *Thank God for that*, thought Dean.

"He will be," said Jason.

"I wish I could say I had that much faith in him," said Dean.

Jason stopped abruptly alongside the marquee. He turned to face Dean. The strand of hair had escaped again. "Well, Shihan," he said, pushing the hair back behind his ear. "Fortunately, I have enough faith in him for both of us, so you don't have to!"

"Thank you, Sensei." Tristan stepped round from the front of the marquee and stood alongside Jason. He held Dean's gaze until he was forced to look away.

If there was one thing Tristan Steyn was disarmingly good at these days, it was making Dean feel bad.

Chapter Twenty Four

The group kata demonstration calmed Tristan's nerves. Just as Gavin had said, once he was focused on his task he was completely unaware of the audience.

For the Sanchin kata demo Jason guided him up onto the raised matted area where the kumite would be performed.

Sensei Gavin explained what was going to happen. "This looks rather brutal," he said, into the microphone. "And if the karateka is not performing the kata correctly it can be quite shocking and painful."

Tristan was performing it correctly and, while he was not oblivious to Jason's blows, he felt no pain.

His focus was such that he was completely unaware of Gavin's commentary and of the audience's gasps of horror at the power behind some of Jason's strikes.

He was aware only of Sensei Jason's movement around him, his own breathing and the sensations of tension and relaxation as he worked through the kata. For Tristan, Sanchin was as calming as meditation.

He came to the end of the kata and became aware of Sensei Gavin speaking.

"It's the ability to tense and relax the muscles that this kata teaches, that assists the karateka to withstand the full contact blows that they receive during sparring," said Gavin.

"And speaking of sparring, Sempai Tristan will be taking part in the sparring demonstration in about fifteen minutes time."

"Sempai Jabulani Mhlophe!" Dean turned a little pale as he read the first name out of the hat. A random member of the audience had just donated R50 for the honour of pulling it out.

Jason pressed the heels of his palms to his eyes then pushed several strands of loose hair back behind his ears. "You'll be fine," he said. "You're ready for this. You've trained hard and you're ready. Even for Sempai Jabu."

"Osu!" said Tristan. "I know. I can do this."

Dean was telling the audience a little about Jabu's tournament pedigree as he made his way to the mat.

"By the way," said Dean. "Someone came up to me earlier and asked why these fights are so short. Well, believe me," he added. "When you're taking the kind of contact these guys will be taking, two minutes can seem like twenty. Not all of the fights will go for the full two minutes. A bout will end earlier if a fighter goes to ground for longer than five seconds, or is rendered incapable of carrying on. The fights you're going to see will be very intense and extremely tiring for both fighters."

He turned to face the audience on the other side of the ring. "Please remember, Sempai Tristan is going to be facing a fresh opponent every two minutes. He's going to get exhausted very quickly and he's going to struggle against some of these guys very early on. All of these fighters are older than him, bigger than him and, in most cases, more experienced than he is."

Tristan bit down hard on his lip and looked across at Sempai Jabu. He looked confident and relaxed. He was sipping water from a bottle and seemed to be looking forward to the upcoming fight.

Tristan unconsciously laid a hand on his ribs. He knew Andre, Rico and Megan, along with hoards of boys from his school, were in the crowd to his left but he didn't dare to look down. He didn't want to make a fool of himself in front of them.

He kept his eyes on Jabu and tried to tune out Dean's voice.

"If any of you doubt how hard these guys actually punch and kick, just go up to any of the black belts and donate R5 and you can hold a kick shield and see for yourself."

"Hey," said Jason, leaning close to Tristan. "Remember, you've got one big advantage over Sempai Jabu. He has no idea how hard you've been training and he's going to underestimate you. Take him hard and take him early because you won't get a second chance."

Hard and early, Tristan repeated to himself.

239

The crowd roared as Dean announced that Sensei Gavin was ready to start the bout.

Tristan stepped forward. His mouth was dry and he wished he'd had some water. He faced Jabu and the two of them bowed.

Sensei Gavin began the bout and Tristan decided to play his advantage to the full. He side stepped Jabu's first attack and backed away. Jabu came in again, and again he avoided the strike and moved out of his range.

On Jabu's third advance, instead of moving back, Tristan moved forward. He lifted his leg and aimed a roundhouse knee strike at Jabu's jaw. Jabu saw it coming and leaned back.

His dark lips curled into a grin as Tristan's knee sailed past its target. What Jabu didn't see was Tristan's knee extend and his foot come straight into the side of his head. He fell to the mat and stayed down.

Tristan had ended the first fight in under ten seconds.

Jason helped Jabu to his feet. Before he left the mat he walked over to Tristan. He took both of his hands in his and looked him directly in the eye. "Osu, Sempai," he said. "I hope I never meet you in a tournament."

"Sempai Helen Johnston," called Dean, as he was handed the second slip of paper.

Sempai Helen had an impressive tournament record and had graded to nidan at the last grading camp. She was extremely flexible and extremely fast and was feared for her high kicks. Sempai Helen's roundhouse to the head had taken out many a more experienced opponent than Tristan.

He knew that Sempai Jabu was the last opponent who would underestimate him. But he also knew he had another ace to play.

He was equally as fast and as flexible as Sempai Helen but he was also shorter, and shorter people needed less room to work.

As soon as the bout began he moved in close. He knew while he stayed there Helen would be unable to use her most feared weapon.

It quickly became clear to Tristan that Sempai Helen hadn't

trained for close combat. He had.

Sensei Jason had drilled him hard for every eventuality and, while Helen's close range punches were weak and ineffectual, his were not. All of his work on the heavy bag paid off as he forced Helen back with a single punch to the sternum.

Helen staggered, off balance and unable to respond. He stepped in close and took her to ground with a well timed·knee to the abdomen. Again, his opponent stayed down.

He was breathing harder now and his ribs were beginning to ache. Sempai Chris Potter was next out of the hat. Tristan felt his gut tighten. Sempai Chris was a scrappy fighter. He was big and strong with a kick like a mule and a reputation for pounding his opponents into submission.

Tristan remembered all too well the shin kick he had taken the last time the two of them had fought. So vivid was the memory that he made his first mistake, he kept his eyes on his opponent's feet.

The error cost him the fight. Sempai Chris' huge fist slammed hard into his belly, doubling him over and causing him to yelp. He staggered back two paces and went to his knees. He couldn't get up even if he had wanted to.

He was supposed to get a two minute break after the first five fights and even though the first three had all ended in under 20 seconds Jason called for a breather.

Tristan shook his head. "I'm fine, Sensei," he said. "I can go on."

Elize couldn't bear to watch but nor could she bear to leave.

Tristan had just been hammered for a full two minute round by Sempai Paul van Rensburg. Both fighters were equally matched. Neither could end the fight decisively but both had taken heavy blows. Tristan was looking untidy and exhausted.

Elize pressed her face against Brett's chest and he hugged her close to him. She felt him press his face into her hair. Perhaps he found it difficult to watch too.

"Oh God," moaned Jonno. Elize looked up, forcing Brett to do the same. Tristan was holding his hands to his face. Blood oozed from between his fingers and ran down his arm.

"No," she said softly and started forward. Brett held her back.

Gavin and Jason were by Tristan's side at once.

Jason had been distracted and hadn't seen the strike, but he was furious at the result. "Sensei, what the hell were you thinking?" he hissed. Tristan's opponent was Sensei Mark le Grange, a third dan and one of the instructors at Dean's Tongaat Dojo. "You know you don't punch to the face!"

Jason glared at Gavin for not calling the foul but Gavin shook his head.

"No," said Tristan. "It was my fault."

He took the tissues Jason offered and pressed them to his bleeding lip. He looked sheepish. "I tried to block Sensei's knee with my elbow and hit myself in the face with my guard," he said.

Jason shook his head. "Sorry, Sensei," he said to Mark. "I hadn't realised I'd coached a halfwit."

Dean came over to survey the damage. "Okay?" he asked.

"Fine thank you, Shihan," said Tristan.

Gavin restarted the bout as soon as Tristan had stemmed the bleeding and cleaned himself up.

Desperate to redeem himself he was determined to win the fight but when he did it was more by good luck than good judgement.

Sensei Mark threw a kick to his head a fraction of a second before Tristan launched his own high flyer. His foot caught Mark just behind the knee of his raised leg and knocked him flat onto his back. Mark hit the ground just as Gavin called the end of the bout.

During the two minute break Jason examined Tristan's split lip.

"I'm sorry, Sensei," he said.

"Just don't do anything else stupid, okay?" said Jason. "Now listen, you're tired so the next five fights are going to be harder

242

than the first, but I want you to get out there and give it everything you've got, okay?"

"Osu! Yes, Sensei," said Tristan.

He turned and looked into the crowd. He had been hoping for some encouragement during the break but Sensei Jason seemed agitated and distant. Several times he had looked over his shoulder rather than at him while he was speaking.

Nettled, Tristan returned to the mat when Gavin called time.

Sensei Paula Scott was his next opponent. He didn't know her at all. Paula fought hard and fast and it was all he could do to stay on his feet.

The fight went the full two minutes and left him gasping for breath and nursing his aching ribs. But he knew he had given as good as he had taken and he hoped Sensei Jason would be pleased.

He glanced at Jason for confirmation but he was looking out into the crowd again. Tristan turned and followed his gaze. He seemed to be looking at three men, smartly dressed in suits and ties. He felt nervous. For some reason he thought they looked like police officers.

"Sensei Andrew Collier," called Dean.

Oh hell, no, he thought. *Not another sandan.*

Sensei Andrew inflicted another heavy beating but Tristan stood his ground. With only seconds left on the clock, he shot in and punched hard to the sternum. He felt, and heard, his knuckles crack against Andrew's breastbone and a bolt of agony shot all the way up to his shoulder. The pain seemed to rattle round his skull and then slide back down his arm and come to rest in his hand again.

Sensei Gavin called the two minutes and Tristan tucked his aching hand into his armpit and staggered over to Jason.

"What's wrong?"

"I think I broke my hand," he said.

"Here," said Jason. "Let me see." Jason took his hand and gently moved his fingers. He felt hot tears spring to his eyes.

"It's fine," said Jason. "If it hurts just use your left."

Stunned, Tristan went back to the mat. *So much for your concern for my well-being, Mr sensible coach*, he thought.

"Sempai Kathy Mason," called Dean.

Tristan was favouring his right hand as well as trying to guard his ribs on the left. He knew he had to finish the next three fights quickly. He caught Sempai Kathy with much the same move he had used on Jabu and the fight was over in seconds.

By now he was in serious pain. Both his hand and his ribs were demanding his attention and he was finding it difficult to focus.

"Sempai Martin Dunn," called Dean. Martin was a nidan. Another opponent Tristan had never met before. He was short and stocky. He was also fast and powerful.

Tristan had absorbed three heavy kicks to his left thigh and was about to take another if he didn't move fast. Martin was exploiting his unwillingness to drop his guard and defend on his left.

He waited for Martin's foot to leave the ground then stepped back quickly. Missing his target Martin's foot sailed on past leaving him hopelessly over balanced.

Tristan aimed a tap just above Martin's supporting ankle. It was enough to put him down but not enough to keep him there and Tristan cursed his soft nature.

Martin was up and fighting again. Tristan landed a couple of good blows with his left but spent most of the remaining time on damage control, constantly on the move trying to avoid taking further punishment.

Dean reached over and took the final slip of paper.

Tristan held his breath hoping for a familiar opponent. Preferably one he knew he was capable of beating. He was tired and hurting and he desperately wanted to win the final fight.

Dean looked over at Jason and then at Tristan. He looked back at the paper and handed it to Sensei Gavin.

"Sensei Jason Swart," he called.

Tristan wanted to cry.

* * *

Jason wanted to cry too. This was the last thing he needed. He glanced nervously at the front row as he stepped up to face Tristan.

He knew Tristan was suffering badly but he also knew he couldn't hold back. If he finished it quickly Tristan would never forgive him but if he didn't, he would take a beating that he could ill afford to take.

Jason was torn and, foolishly, he was the second person that day to underestimate Tristan.

Tristan was angry, and his anger was a stronger painkiller than anything that came out of a bottle.

Throughout their months of training together he had learned that Sensei Jason was not only a strong fighter but an unpredictable one. Jason never telegraphed his moves and he had an excellent arsenal of weapons.

Unlike many fighters, he did not rely on only one or two techniques. He was equally comfortable using hands, feet, elbows and knees and could unleash a vicious attack using whichever weapon was closest to hand.

But during that time, he had also unearthed what appeared to be Sensei Jason's only weakness. It was a weakness Jason knew, and guarded, well. All Tristan needed was a way to exploit it.

Gavin began the bout and he went in hard and fast. He kicked high, catching Jason on the shoulder, trying to force him on the defensive.

Jason stepped away from the force of the blow and responded with a kick of his own. It was low and hard, and Tristan felt his leg go weak and his quadriceps tighten painfully. Refusing to give in to the pain he ploughed in again and again.

Jason had expected Tristan to fight hard. He had expected him to give everything he had left. What he hadn't expected him to do was play dirty.

Tristan had come in hard and then turned, positioning himself in such away that Jason had no choice but to go for his injured ribs or hold back his counter attack.

Almost certain he had done it on purpose, Jason pulled a dirty trick of his own. With only seconds left in the fight, he used his right arm hard against Tristan's left, pushing his guard aside and opening him up. Knowing Tristan couldn't possibly strike, or defend, with his injured right, Jason drew back his left leaving Tristan, and himself, wide open.

Tristan moved like lightning. Throwing the punch from close range, he ploughed his injured hand deep into Jason's abdomen.

Jason gasped at the explosion of pain and, as the little red bag skidded onto the mats to mark the end of the bout, both fighters fell to their knees.

Jason leaned forward clutching his abdomen. No matter how hard he trained and how well conditioned his abs were, a heavy strike to the gut would finish him every time. It was the one pain he simply couldn't bear.

He could hear Tristan whimpering beside him and in that moment he knew he'd been duped. He had just done exactly what Tristan had set him up to do.

Despite the fire in his belly, he got quickly to his feet. He reached down and pulled Tristan up too.

This was a demo and Dean would kill them both if the audience were left feeling they had witnessed anything other than a hard, but controlled, fight.

Dean came over. "Are you two both all right?"

Tristan nodded.

"We'll be fine," said Jason.

"I need a word," said Dean. He inclined his head towards the front row of the audience.

"Yeah, I know," said Jason. "Give me a minute with Tris?"

Tristan was still furious with Jason but he allowed him to drape an arm over his shoulders.

"You did well, Sempai," said Jason, leading him off the mats.

Tristan felt panic rise as they stepped down onto the grass and a mass of people surged towards him. He leaned against Jason's chest as they were both engulfed by a crowd of his schoolmates.

It took them half an hour to extract themselves from the group of chattering boys but Megan, Rico and Andre still wanted his attention.

"Guys," said Jason. "I really need a quiet word with Tris. Give me a few minutes and I'll send him back to you, okay?"

Tristan didn't want to go. He was tired and sore and Jason's clear lack of interest in his fights had left him angry and hurt.

He had worked so hard for this and instead of the expected elation and relief, he felt deflated.

Jason sensed Tristan's reluctance. He knew he was upset and he needed to speak to him before Dean found them again.

"Come on, Tris," he said. "I won't keep you long."

Tristan sighed but didn't make a fuss. He walked in front of Jason towards the main marquee.

Oh hell, thought Jason. *Too late*.

Dean was coming across the field and the three of them were with him. He stepped ahead of Tristan as the men approached.

"Osu!" he said. He bowed and shook hands with each of them in turn.

Tristan had hung back and he put a hand on his shoulder and brought him forward.

"Shihan, Sensei," he said. "This is Sempai Tristan Steyn." He leaned closer to Tristan. "Sempai, this is Shihan Kenneth Barber, Sensei Thabo Silongo and Sensei Dev Naidoo. They're from the National Team selection board.

"That was horrible," said Jason, his head in his hands. "Why didn't you tell me they were coming?"

He was sitting on an upturned milk crate behind the refreshments tent. He was tired and hungry but his belly still hurt and the smell of hotdogs wafting from the tent made him nauseous.

"Because I didn't know," said Dean.

Jason looked up, cupping his chin in one hand and resting the other across his middle. He chewed on his fingernails. "I went to pieces," he said. "As soon as I saw them there my nerves were shot. I wasn't there for Tris and he got mauled."

"Sensei," said Dean. "He hardly got mauled. He did a hell of a lot better than I expected him to. If anybody got mauled, it was you. What the hell happened?"

Jason rubbed his belly. "Let's just say he's a better judge of character than I am," he said. He stood up and straightened his dogi. "I need to talk to him. He's really pissed off with me."

"He's just earned himself a place on the national team thanks to you," said Dean. "I think he might have forgiven you. Seriously, Jase, you're a brilliant coach, you've worked wonders with that boy, but you can't fight their fights for them. You need to let go once they step onto that mat. If you didn't have that emotional attachment you wouldn't have this problem."

"Yeah, I know," said Jason. "But if I didn't have the emotional attachment I wouldn't care enough to get them though the really tough stuff. I need to find Tris."

The field was emptying fast now. The demo was officially over and people had begun to drift away. The air was turning cool and Jason shivered.

Most of the stall holders had packed their wares into their cars and were queueing to leave the grounds. The main marquee was still standing at the far end of the field. Dean had arranged for it to remain up until tomorrow as he had planned a party for the karateka and their families to thank them for their involvement.

Jason found Tristan sitting in the grandstand with his friends. He felt a rush of relief when Tristan beamed widely and came bounding down the steps to meet him. "Tristan, I'm sorry," he said. "I..."

Tristan ignored his apology. "Thank you, Sensei," he said. "For everything. And I'm sorry I was a brat after the fights."

Jason smiled at him. "You had every right to be," he said. "I was a terrible coach while you were on that mat."

Tristan shrugged. "I was a bit upset," he said. "But it's good that you didn't tell me they were coming. Or I would have been a wreck."

"Hmm," said Jason. "I just wish someone had told me they were coming then maybe I wouldn't have been a wreck."

"You didn't know either?"

Jason shook his head. "No," he said. "And neither did Shihan."

"I invited them."

Jason and Tristan turned to find Gavin and Dean standing behind them.

"Sorry, Sensei. I would have told you," said Gavin. "But I asked them if they'd be interested in coming to see his kata. I had no idea they'd want to see the kumite too. I knew you'd freak out as soon as I saw them standing there."

"No harm done," said Jason. "Just a few grey hairs maybe."

Tristan grinned and then bit his lip when Gavin shot him a warning look.

"What?" asked Jason, catching the exchange.

Gavin shrugged. "Nothing," he said.

"You did not!" Jason said. "You did didn't you? Gav! You I told him I freak out before a tourney."

"Oh, come on," said Gavin. "He was in a state. I had to do something."

"Don't worry, Sensei," said Tristan. "Your secret's safe with me." Tristan's eyes fell to Jason's abdomen. "Both of them," he said with a grin.

Jason narrowed his eyes and indicated the end of the grandstand with his thumb. "May I have a word please?" he asked. "In private."

Tristan followed him a little way from the others.

He tapped Tristan's side. "How are the ribs?" he asked.

Tristan's face coloured a little.

"Tell me," said Jason. "Just what would you have done if I hadn't held back?"

"I would have been nursing sore ribs now instead of a sore hand," said Tristan.

Jason shook his head. "I misjudged you," he said. "I didn't think you had it in you."

Chapter Twenty Five

It was warm in the tent and Tristan was feeling pleasantly drowsy. He sat next to his mother on a bench and leaned against her shoulder. He was almost asleep when Dean took to the stage and turned on the microphone. It came to life with a thump.

He blinked and sat upright. He leaned down and picked up the polystyrene cup of water he had placed by his feet.

Dean addressed the crowd. "First of all," he said. "I'd like to thank you all for the hard work you've put in to make this day the success it was. We haven't finished counting the money yet and we still have quite a number of outstanding pledges to collect, but I'm delighted to tell you that we have already passed our target of R35 000."

Tristan was only half listening. He sipped his water. It was warm and tasted earthy but he was thirsty and didn't want to push through the crowd to the drinks table.

"Now," said Dean. "I know it's been a long day and you don't want to hear me droning on and on, but there's one last thing I'd like to do."

Dean lowered the microphone and scanned the room. His eyes stopped on Tristan and he raised the mic to his mouth again. Tristan's heart skipped several beats.

"I know how you hate getting up in front of a crowd," said Dean. "But would you come up here for a minute please, Sempai."

Tristan almost choked on a mouthful of water. He felt a rush of colour to his face and, for a mad instant, considered bolting into the night.

"Go on," said Brett, giving him a shove between the shoulder blades. He moved forward on autopilot.

He wasn't sure how he got there, but he found himself on the stage standing next to Dean. He fixed his gaze on Andre, Rico and Megan who were sitting by the side entrance to the marquee.

Dean put a hand on his shoulder.

"I'd like to congratulate those of you who were called on to take part in the kumite demonstration today. I saw some very impressive fighting from all of you. Well," he said, glancing over at Jason. "Most of you, anyway."

There were a few stifled giggles among the karateka.

"Go ahead," called Jason. "Feel free to laugh at my expense. Just don't forget who'll be cracking the whip in the dojo on Monday."

Dean waited for the laughter to die down.

"I'd also like to thank you all for giving our young Sempai here a hard time because, thanks to the effort he had to put in against you guys today, he has been chosen to join our national team for both the kata and the kumite at the Inter-African championships in Mozambique in November.

When the applause had died down Dean spoke again. "Okay," he said. "Just one more thing then you can all grab something to eat and drink and start to wind down." He stepped back and looked to his left.

Gavin came up the steps to the stage carrying an enormous birthday cake with sixteen candles flickering in the centre. "Happy birthday, Sempai," he said. "Do you think you have enough energy left to blow out sixteen candles?"

As Tristan extinguished the candles the crowd struck up a chorus of Happy Birthday that would have rivalled an entire rugby stadium for noise.

Tristan was feeling overwhelmed and wasn't sure he could trust his voice, but he walked over to Dean and took the microphone from his hand.

He held it clumsily to his mouth. "Thank you," he said. "When I first heard that Shihan had organised this fundraiser for today, I was going to write my birthday off this year. I actually thought I would have a horrible day just being really nervous and getting kicked a lot. Well, I was nervous, and I did get kicked a lot, but today has been a very special day for me."

He looked over at Andre. "I want to thank you all for helping to raise the money for my friend and for helping me to achieve a dream that I thought I'd blown by being really stupid. Thank you."

He turned to Dean and pushed the microphone back into his hand. "Thank you, Shihan," he said and bolted down the steps.

Jonno came up to Tristan and pushed a plastic Spar packet into his hand. "Happy birthday, kiddo," he said. "Your real present is at home but I thought you might need this now."

Tristan peeked into the bag and grinned. "Can I share it?" he asked.

"You can," said Jonno, managing a startlingly accurate impression of Elize. "But you *may* not!"

Tristan swung the bag at Jonno. "Stop it," he said. "That's not funny. She'll kill you."

Jonno waved a finger at him. "You said you were going to eat an entire packet of doughnuts and drink a whole litre of Fanta grape after the demo," he said. "So, if you share that, I'll just have to get you some more tomorrow."

"Tristan?"

He turned and found himself looking directly at a grey and navy tie. He followed it up and stopped at a pair of sharp blue eyes set in a well worn but kindly face.

The man extended his hand. "I'm Michael Turner," he said. "Andre and Michelle's father."

Tristan shook his hand. "Pleased to meet you, Mr Turner," he said.

"The pleasure is all mine," said Michael. "I want to congratulate you on an excellent achievement today but most of all, I want to thank you for everything you've done for Andre and my family while I've been away."

Tristan felt the all too familiar tug of guilt that snagged in his chest every time any of the Turners thanked him for anything.

"Well," he said. "If it hadn't been for my stupidity Andre would never have been hurt in the first place."

"You can't keep blaming yourself, Tristan," said Kathryn. She came up alongside her husband and handed him two mugs of coffee then stepped forward and folded Tristan into a warm embrace.

"You know what Andre said to me this morning?" she said. "He said he's glad the accident happened otherwise he would never have made friends with you."

Tristan couldn't respond.

"Anyway," said Kathryn, releasing him. "They're all waiting for you over by the door. You go and have some fun."

Shihan Dean caught Tristan on his way to the door. "Sempai," he said. "Sensei Gavin wants a little chat with you. Have you got a minute?"

"Sure," he said. He was aching and tired and wanted nothing more than to curl up on the cool grass outside the door with his friends.

He caught Rico's eye as he followed Dean past the open doorway. He held up his bandaged right hand. "Five minutes," he mouthed. Rico nodded and gave a thumbs up.

They found Gavin and Jason chatting to Brett, Elize and Jonno. Gavin stepped towards Tristan as he approached.

"Sempai," he said. "You remember you were told to keep that other dogi for another occasion?"

He nodded.

"Well how do you feel about working with me on Wednesday evenings and Saturday afternoons?" he asked. "I know how much you love kata and I can't think of anyone better to inspire the juniors to practice good form."

"Sensei, I would love to," he said. "Thank you."

"Um," said Dean. "And mind you don't get that dogi too dirty. Because you might want to wear it when you come with me to Japan in July."

Tristan stared at Dean.

"You'd better behave too," he said. "Because I haven't got the letter of permission from your folks yet."

"Japan?" said Tristan, certain he was dreaming.

Every year Dean took a group of his best students to Japan for two weeks of training, sight seeing and an introduction to Japanese culture.

Tristan had dreamed of being one of those students since he was eight years old and Jonno had given him a book about the history of karate in Japan.

"Sempai," said Dean. "I was going to tell you this in my office on Monday." Dean reached down and straightened the front of Tristan's dogi. "But I've put you down often enough in front of these two," he indicated Gavin and Jason. "So it's only right that I say this in front of them too."

He paused and held Tristan's gaze. "Despite the dirty little trick you pulled on Sensei Jason this afternoon," he said.

Tristan blushed and bit his lip. He couldn't believe Shihan had noticed.

Dean went on, "I'm proud of you, Sempai," he said. "You've worked hard and grown up so much in the last few months. I'm sure we'll make a nidan out of you yet."

Tristan lit up brighter than the candles he'd just blown out. Such praise from Shihan Dean meant the world to him.

"Thank you Shihan," he said.

Dean waved a finger in his face. "But that doesn't mean I'll let you grade at eighteen."

Tristan beamed. "That's okay, Shihan," he said. "It'll come to me in time. I'm enjoying the journey too much to go kicking down doors."

4196454

Made in the USA
Lexington, KY
02 January 2010